The novels of
Denise Vitola

Quantum Moon

Ty Merrick is a twenty-first century detective investigating the death of a powerful district councilman. But Ty must deal with an even greater danger, for when the moon is full, she *changes* . . .

"A refreshing change from mysteries where the SF is merely window dressing."
—*Locus*

"Vitola works as hard at creating an engaging mystery as she does at the science fiction. *Quantum Moon* succeeds at both."
—*Time Out Books*

Opalite Moon

Three members of a secret sect—known as the Opalite— have been murdered. Ty must venture into the frozen fringes of a bankrupt society where only a lycanthrope would feel at home . . .

The Winter Man

Nicki Chim is one of the best forensic hematologists her peers have ever seen. Her blood work is fast and flawless . . . almost *too* fast. For Nicki is more than just a scientist. She is a vampire.

Ace Books by Denise Vitola

QUANTUM MOON
OPALITE MOON
MANJINN MOON

MANJINN MOON

DENISE VITOLA

ACE BOOKS, NEW YORK

This book is an Ace original edition
and has never been previously published.

MANJINN MOON

An Ace Book / published by arrangement with
the author

PRINTING HISTORY
Ace edition / April 1998

The Penguin Putnam Inc. World Wide Web site address is
http://www.penguinputnam.com

ISBN: 0-441-00521-7

ACE®
Ace Books are published by The Berkley Publishing Group,
a member of Penguin Putnam Inc.,
200 Madison Avenue, New York, NY 10016.
ACE and the "A" design are trademarks
belonging to Charter Communications, Inc.

PRINTED IN THE UNITED STATES OF AMERICA

10 9 8 7 6 5 4 3 2 1

To Donna McMurry
Sister, friend, and traveling companion
on the road of life.

1

SAMUEL ARKIN STARED out of the bay window of his fashionable loft apartment and searched along the edges of the Black River. The evening had dropped in hazy and humid and the stars were lost behind the gauzy coverlet of summer pollution. In the urban nightmare of District One, there were all those private moments, those times when compassion gave way to violence, and violence to murder. If he wanted to, he could tune in to every act, every defiance, every death. It's what his colleagues and he had been trained for, and now after fifteen years it was finally going to pay off in a big way.

Arkin turned from the fuzzy glow of streetlights to shut off the thermostat controlling the air-conditioning. He had to be careful with the temperature, because his prized Monet painting needed exacting climate control. Too hot and it could affect the beautiful colors, too cold and it would make the canvas brittle.

He glanced at his partners as they sat at his antique mahogany dining table, taking care to set their drinks carefully upon the mother-of-pearl coasters. They knew he couldn't stand seeing water spots—especially on his beautiful table. His colleagues understood what it meant to take care of valuable things.

They'd started ripping people off bit by bit, using the techniques of remote viewing to zoom in for a close look at the skeletons in their closets. They'd done well by it, working during the day for a humanitarian government that didn't trust its citizens and then, in the evening, scalping the information and making it work for their retirement.

"I don't think the courier is coming," Ford said, in a flat voice.

"Give it some time," Arkin answered. "She'll send him."

"This game makes me nervous," he said. "I still don't think we're adequately prepared."

Drake pushed into the conversation. "I talked to Terry about what we're doing. You know we can trust her with our scams, and she says we're safe. There won't be any trouble for us. She couldn't find anything upline that was out of the ordinary."

Arkin chuckled and turned back to the window. He didn't trust Terry's word; he knew better. Remote viewing worked in real time only. There was no peeking into the future, of that he was sure, and that's what made this particular scam so dangerous. Still, the OI insisted on pushing the envelope with paranormal powers. The budget was suspended by efforts that included electronic voice phenomenon, psychokinesis, and the ever-popular spirit healing. It was, for the most part, worthless money spent, but year after year the office continued to add more freaks to the circus show.

Remote viewing had been around for decades, practiced first with great effectiveness in World War II. It had taken Arkin sixteen months to learn the techniques that enabled him to watch a situation unfolding anywhere around the world without cameras or other surveillance devices. All he needed was a notebook, a pen, and a comfy chair. From there, he could take a gay jaunt across the planet using his ESP to show him the way.

Arkin sighed and returned to the window as Ford and Drake talked quietly between themselves. His thoughts turned inward again, as they usually did. It was one of the prices he paid for being able to stretch his mind beyond the limits of its normal tolerance. From the beginning, he was a casualty of the psychic wars, and though he'd earned a reasonably comfortable living, it would never make up for the hallucinations and seizures that disabled him on a regular basis.

A loud knocking made him jump. He crossed the room, stepping carefully around the expensive Chinese rug and making sure he didn't rattle the antique, European porcelain displayed so prettily in the carved, camphor-wood cabinet. The knock came again, this time more insistent. He pulled open the door and smiled to himself.

"Come in," Arkin greeted.

The visitor studied him with a look of one who is displeased at being conned. After a moment of scrutiny, he entered. "Do you have a copy of the pictures?" he demanded.

Arkin nodded. "As agreed. Your benefactor will see that we're not joking."

Drake casually held up the manila folder containing the damning photographs, and the courier walked toward him by taking the direct route across the Chinese rug. Arkin flinched, but didn't say anything. After this deal, he could afford to replace it—times twenty. Still, watching the man leave dusty footprints aggravated him. People had no manners. He snorted softly and took the long way around.

The courier set his tasteful, leather satchel on Arkin's table with a thump and reached for the envelope. Using another moment, he thumbed through the prints and then gave each man a long, dark look.

"Let's not take all night about it," Drake growled.

The courier shrugged, replaced the pictures, and then opened his briefcase. Carefully, with minute flicks of his wrists and hands, he produced three thick sheaves of credit notes. "This is the first installment, gentlemen," he announced. "My benefactor is delaying the next payment until she can be assured of your silence."

"That wasn't the arrangement," Arkin said.

"True. But what choice do you have?"

"Well, we can tune in and see what your benefactor is planning next. She can't hide from us. We could easily go to the marshals."

"True again. But then you would be out the money."

"We know what she's up to. Valquez died and then Emery. Your benefactor was with each just before they went down and I suspect tonight's news will tell us all about the death of Ingrid Calloway. We saw your benefactor making an appointment to visit with her this afternoon. The money better come along quickly if we're to maintain our silence."

The man pulled down a surprised expression. "Maybe, she was just calling Ms. Calloway to invite her for tea and sandwiches."

Ford chuckled and began to untie his stack of bills. The courier touched him on the forearm. "Not yet. I'm required to get your handshakes on this first part of the deal. Will there be one?"

Arkin took a deep breath. He would have liked to get the lump sum up front, but it was what he'd expected. "I suppose it will have to do," he said, extending his hand. "Let me be the first to congratulate your benefactor on her future successes."

The courier nodded again and shook his hand. He had a squeezing grasp that pinched the blood flow up Arkin's arm, and when the man pulled away, his shoulder and neck felt like they were on fire. He tried to ignore this sudden attack of bursitis, watching as his colleagues repeated the ritual. Drake winced from the strength of the man's grip.

Folding up his satchel, the courier bowed slightly and left the flat without a backward glance. Arkin sat down at his beautiful table, scraped his credit stack before him, and attempted to enjoy the moment. Unfortunately, the burn in his neck had wailed quickly into his right temple. Stress. That's what it was; nothing more.

"The guy had a grip like a gorilla," Drake said.

Arkin grunted. "He didn't look that strong, did he? His hand-shake shot pain straight up my arm. It's given me a headache."

"You know, I hurt, too," Ford answered, flexing his fingers. He reached for his glass. "It must be from this red wine. How old is this stuff anyway, Arkin? Four or five hours?"

He couldn't answer, because the pain abruptly tore down the center of his head and then fanned out behind his ears. Drake suddenly moaned. The noise forced Arkin to glance toward his partner, but his vision blurred, and no matter the blinking he did, he couldn't bring him into focus.

Ford pitched forward with a groan and knocked over his wineglass. The liquid spilled everywhere, running off the edges of the table to color the white carpet. Dismay rose in Arkin and he tried to move for a sponge to clean up the mess, but it was a useless attempt, because in the very next second his head exploded.

2

───────■───────

THOUGH THE DAY had barely begun, the heat and pollution made me feel like I stood on a street corner inside the devil's armpit. I paused after surfacing from the subway to take baby breaths and to realize my juicy analogy wasn't far from the truth.

District One steamed and stank, the dirty air holding in the body odor of a million suffering people. Summer isn't a good time to find murder victims, especially when they're a couple of days old and slow-roasted in a closed apartment, but that's exactly what we had. Arriving at the crime scene, I tied a woven handkerchief over my nose and walked into the middle of this latest, sinus-numbing scent.

My partner, Andy LaRue, met me at the door. He wore his own makeshift mask, but I found that he had also tied his waist-length, sepia-colored hair into a neat braid and had wrapped this hirsute cord under his nose and up over his ear, securing it with a clip normally used for a specimen bag. A stranger trailed behind him, dressed in a paper suit. Despite the gag mask this man wore, he looked for all the world like a government employee. I wasn't wrong.

"Casper Conrad, meet Marshal Ty Merrick." Glancing at me, he added: "Casper is the Chief of Public Accountability for the Office of Intelligence."

I shook his hand. "Office of Intelligence, huh? I always thought the OI was redundant in a world government."

"Vigilance keeps our society strong," he answered, harping familiar propaganda. "Dissidents must be dealt with for the good of all."

"And do we have dissidents here?"

LaRue jumped into the conversation and for once I was

grateful to have a partner who didn't know when to shut up. "It's a triple death with an unconfirmed cause."

"Unconfirmed cause?"

"No detectable signs of trauma as far as I can tell. No forced entry, no preliminary signs of trouble. Forensics is coming up with blanks, too. Some smudged prints on the door. That's about it."

I nodded and spun a slow circle around the room. I'd been in a lot of fancy apartments, but this one was masterful in its conspicuous consumption. There were objets d'art that I'd only dreamed of and a bank of bay windows that overlooked the district and the Black River beyond. "Who found them?"

He pointed to an anxious, older woman being questioned by a couple of ward cops. "Cleaning lady."

"I take it the medical examiner isn't here, yet?"

"Coming," LaRue said. "You know how slow Frank moves in the summer."

"And in the winter," I answered, as I edged by him and Conrad to inspect the bodies.

Three men sat around a gorgeous mahogany table. They'd long gone through the physical process of death and the chairs and carpet were stained with it. LaRue was right, there was very little indication of what had killed them aside from runnels of blood coming from their noses and ears.

"What about a colorless, odorless gas, Andy?"

"No. The environmental crew swept this place before we went in. Nothing. It may be a simple case of poisoning. Notice the wineglasses? We won't know for sure until Frank gets his lazy ass in here."

I glanced at Conrad. "Why are you here, may I ask?"

He squinted at me and let his perusal linger longer than it should have. Then, rubbing his bald head, he answered. "Because these men worked on a project for our office. I'm here to cooperate with you on the OI side."

"What did they do on this project?"

He looked their way before replying. "They were remote viewers."

Remote viewing was a legacy from the twentieth century. When our beloved dictator, Vivian Duvalier, drove the UN Peacekeepers into the ocean and took over the planet to form his humanitarian society, he'd decided to keep up this spy network. I had my doubts about the validity of someone being able to see a remote location and then reporting back accurately about the activities there. Still, it was a frightening thought.

"Checking up on the populace, again?" I asked.

"Only those individuals that give us a bit of worry," Conrad answered.

I nodded and let my gaze trace over the dead men and the mounds of paper credits bundled up neatly and separated into three, even piles. "I suppose they were playing the blackmail game?"

"It seems to be a pervasive problem with these kind of people," he said. "Their specific assignment was to remotely view individuals who were possibly members of a terrorist group."

"And you suspect them of playing hardball with these guys? In that case, they deserved to die."

Conrad smiled under his plastic mask. "We can't say for sure it was a scam involving terrorists. I knew Sam Arkin. He wasn't above freelancing, and he was very good at it. You can tell just by looking around you." Pausing, he added: "They could have been ripping anyone off."

I broke away from Conrad without replying, taking a careful swing around the elegant apartment. Technicians dusted for fingerprints along the top of a Chippendale sideboard and photographed dirty footprints on the Asian carpet. One fellow had his nose pressed up against the Plexiglas case holding what appeared to be a painting done by Claude Monet. I stopped to stare at the canvas, momentarily enchanted by its delicate beauty.

So many great masterpieces were lost when Duvalier crushed the resistant governments. The dictator's boot lickers became private collectors, receiving works of art as bonuses for faithfully executing the new standards of the humanitarian revolution. From the looks of this guy's goodies, it appeared the folks at the OI weren't above swabbing spit onto a new generation of bureaucratic leather insoles.

Yanking myself away from the artwork, I continued to make the circuit around the room. The windows were shut tight against the smog, and the place was fastidiously clean.

I turned back to Conrad, only to notice him talking to a pretty, young woman I didn't know. He introduced us.

"This is Kelly Bates," he said. "She works for us as a postmortem photographer."

"We have our own photographers," I answered.

"Not like Ms. Bates." He pointed to her equipment bag. "She takes some really unusual photos."

"What I do is different, but I've had interesting results," she said.

"What is so special about your methods?" I asked.

"About twenty years ago scientists discovered how to use the electromagnetic signature left after a particularly violent death. There's always an abundance of energy remaining behind, you see."

No I didn't see, and I'd been on hundreds of crime scenes. "I suppose you take a picture of this energy."

"It's a unique photographic process that has allowed us to capture these residual images. I was trained by the OI to use my paranormal talents to specifically uncover the visages of the killers involved in murder cases. It sounds strange, I know, but my successes are well documented if you'd like to check."

I stood there staring at her, trying not to let my expression convey my disbelief. Our society, for all its talk of compassion and generosity, is a place of distressing poverty and failing hope. The government feeds empty air to the citizens and in a world of diminishing natural resources, its bland propaganda and breezy promises have made procuring capital the hook and crook of our society. We've become people who sell superstition and magic on the backdoor market, because many times, there's little else to bargain for. Trading potions, charm sacks, and gypsy spells without a properly approved classification designation is illegal. Yet, when the government gets into the act, I start to worry about where my environmental taxes are going.

Still, I had no choice but to cooperate, not because it was a joint investigative effort, but because I'm wedged into one of these supernatural cracks, too. I'm a lycanthrope, and have been ever since a creeping attack of carbon monoxide almost killed me. I'm lucky to be alive, but the gas mucked up my gray matter, so now my days follow a warped circle from full moon to full moon. I don't morph into anything that clearly resembles a wolf, but the combination of symptoms do, indeed, change me.

Conrad filled in the silence between us. "Kelly, why don't you get started snapping pictures of the team?" He shot a quick look our way. "She'll be done in a couple of minutes. It shouldn't impede on your end of the investigation."

"You mentioned team," LaRue said. "These three comprised a unit?"

"Most remote viewing is done in teams, because a single person rarely has the capacity to complete an entire connection. One individual may have a visual sense of the surroundings, another will hear sounds, and a third may actually have a tactile experience. When combined, you have the whole picture."

"Are they linked telepathically?"

"Yes."

I took the opportunity to follow Bates over to the table, letting my gaze trace along the money packs while she set up her camera tripod. It was then that I noticed the ribbons tying up the bundles. They were bright red and delicately made. I always keep an eye out for this kind of stuff because my roommate, Baba, has a weaving loom and uses scraps, rags, cardboard, and even aluminum foil to stretch the available thread.

I flipped over one of the stacks to see how the ribbon was tied up and to check if there were any loose credit notes that might find an easy route into my pocket. The latter was predictable, and using some deft sleight of hand, I managed to secure a decent tip for my time and aggravation. I also came across a buried business card made from shiny green paper. I slipped it free and saw that one side was covered in an intricate pattern of embossed gold leaf. Turning it over, I found one word written there: *Manjinn.*

3

LaRue is one of those rare individuals who think the Soviet Union was the best experiment for social revolution that has ever come along. To this end, he practices Russian cooking and drives an antique East German Trabant, a car so ugly it could have only been designed by unimaginative Bolsheviks. He's also not above a hardy belief in the existence of invisible magic, so when we left the crime scene and rode back to the Marshals Office, he told me how he was being forced to spray for poltergeists.

Apparently, the little beggars were in his belongings, messing up his clothes, and leaving wicked messages on his e-mail.

How it came that he was being haunted was a mystery, and I'll admit, I didn't give it much thought until one of the bastards whacked me to get my attention. LaRue keeps a dashboard doll of Lenin in the back window of his car. It's a piece of pure communist kitsch, because every time you hit a bump, the spring-loaded neck wobbles and it announces itself by squeaking. This day, it flew from its perch and konked me on the head.

"See?" LaRue wailed. "They're everywhere! I can't figure out how I picked them up."

"Maybe they're like the summer flu," I muttered, rubbing the growing knot on my noggin.

"My mom sent me to a kanapper."

"What's a kanapper?"

"A person who specializes in controlling supernatural pests."

"So, poltergeists are like the roaches of the ghost plane?"

"More like flying, stinging, ghost roaches, if you ask me."

"What did this kanapper give you?"

He sighed. "A recipe for making a spray."

Not only does my partner identify with black bread, garlic vodka, and borscht, he also has a healthy fascination for the weird. "How much did that cost you?"

"A week's salary," he muttered.

"And you still have to buy the ingredients?"

"Yeah. This is going to be an expensive problem."

I couldn't help it. I started laughing.

LaRue tossed me his best scowl. "It's not funny, Ty. The little whackers are all over me."

"Andy, this is the craziest thing I've ever heard."

"I know," he answered solemnly. "It's right up there with werewolves."

Touché. His words ticked me off, but I kept my annoyance to myself. "Still, you don't have to spray a lycanthrope down to get rid of one. A polite good-bye is all that's necessary."

"I wish it were so easy with poltergeists." He then turned the corner, smacked into a piece of junk in the street, and once around that, began a lecture on the finer points of stalking invisible entities with his mother's misting bottle.

I let him run out of supernatural steam and idly picked up the Lenin doll from where it had landed between my feet. I wedged it between the front seats, where it bounced along happily in its new place. LaRue was to the part about how poltergeists smell like bat farts, so I decided it was the right time to change the subject from fractious ghosts to the card I'd found at the crime scene. I pulled it from my pocket and studied the intricate design.

"What do you know about remote viewing, Andy?"

He ground gears before changing his dissertation in midstream. "They're the ultimate spies. I've heard that when the government ran the space programs, they used remote viewers to tune in to the activities on the moon."

"Do you think they've got people watching us?"

He glanced at me and frowned, but then we smacked into a chuckhole and it took his attention away. By the time we arrived at the office, I was glad to climb out of the Baltic bitch, because I was sure that my heinie was severely bruised from crossing the macadam obstacle course.

Inside, we found a new disaster brewing. Julie, our ever-

efficient watch commander, grabbed us as we came in the door
to attend an impromptu meeting of the homicide pen.

"It's time for us to assume collateral duties," she announced.
"It looks like we've got a hurricane brewing in the Caribbean
districts, and from the weather models, it appears as though it
will be heading straight for us. The District Council is
mobilizing the Hurricane Management Teams. Are you all
current on your first-aid certifications?"

Every one nodded, accentuating the affirmation with mutters
and throat clearing.

Julie piped above the concerned drone. "All divisions are
being tapped for emergency relief, so in between working your
investigations, you're to begin helping citizens to batten down
their belongings."

It was a monumental job when you considered how many
people lived in cardboard houses and canvas tents. Worse than
that, it wouldn't make tracking a killer any easier, either. Trails
got cold in the time it took for a tropical storm to pass through.

Julie continued. "We've got a sector schedule drawn up, so
make sure you see the squad secretary before the end of the
day." She paused to glare at us. "And be clear on this: If you
conveniently forget to pick up your assignments, I'll put you
on report and you can kiss away any case bonuses you might
earn for the next two months."

That brought more vocal protests, but the growls and barks
did nothing to dissuade her. "Bitch all you want; just do your
jobs."

"When's the hurricane going to get here?" LaRue called out.

"If computer tracking can be trusted, it should arrive in
about a week," she answered. "If it stalls someplace, we might
have a little longer."

Her reply caused my partner to glance at me. The storm
would apparently blow through around the time of the full
moon. I shook my head at him, confirming that I did, indeed,
know how to add the days up. A moment later Julie dismissed
us and we hurried back to our cubicle.

I was worried LaRue would pounce on the subject of my
lycanthropy and I didn't feel like listening to his new theories
on how the violent weather might affect me. Luckily, I was

spared having to come up with excuses not to discuss it, because we found Kelly Bates waiting for us.

Without her protective mask, I could see she was pretty and younger than I'd first thought. This didn't do much to improve my confidence in her supernatural talents, though. My own paranormal problems usually put me in an impatient mood, but I could tell my partner was thoroughly enamored of this woman's figure, so I gave her the benefit of the doubt.

"Did you take a picture of a ghost?" I asked.

She didn't react to the razz. "Something better." She produced an eight-by-ten, black-and-white photo. "Your killer, Marshals."

LaRue took the picture first. Studying it, his face fell into a scowl. My partner is rarely left for words, but this time he handed me the photo without comment.

She'd framed the shot to take in the length of the table. The three men sat where they'd died and the picture was so clear that I could easily see the glasses of wine as well as the pearly luster of the coasters protecting the mahogany. There, standing at the end of the table, was the perfect image of a handsome, bearded, dark-haired man clutching a briefcase.

I yanked my gaze away from the ghostly image to look at LaRue. "Did we have any techs in there that fit this description?"

"No beards," he answered. "Everyone wore masks, too. I was lead on this and I made sure of it."

Kelly Bates interrupted. "I can assure you, Marshal Merrick, this is the genuine article. There was no one present at that table when I took those photos. You were standing next to me." She pointed to the picture. "In fact, I believe that's your hand going through the credit notes."

"How can you tell that's me? It looks like a smear."

"I don't know why you came out so smudgy," she answered. "But that has to be you. No one else was at the table while I snapped these photos."

I gave up the fight before it started and slid heavily into my chair to study the picture once more. "Explain to us in detail what we're looking at."

She nodded and reached into her satchel to show us more

pictures. LaRue drew in close and for some reason we started talking in murmurs and whispers.

"I get different results depending upon the type of film I'm using, the lens, and shutter speed. The first photo I showed you was set in normal lighting at a low aperture. The others are set at various speeds and are taken at different angles. I enlarged several copies. As you can see, the image appears on every picture."

Yes, it did, but of all of them, the blowups were the cleanest. Kelly added more pictures to the pile.

"This last photo was taken with infrared film. It substantiates my claims."

It looked like a blob to me. "How does this show us anything?"

She raised her voice slightly so she could assume the proper tone for a lecture. "You must understand something about how a person is trained to become a remote viewer. The process is taken from the science of remote sensing, an idea that goes back to the early 1800s. There are two types of sensing devices—passive and active. Active forms transmit energy pulses and then detect it as it's reflected back. Passive sensors depend upon the natural reflections of the energy source. A camera is a good example of a passive sensing device." She paused to study me. Then: "I have the ability to absorb reflections of dissipating energy and then channel it through the camera via my brain."

"You're claiming you imprint this energy onto the film," I said.

"Yes. If the energy is old, it doesn't come in as clear. From the photo quality here, I'd say the killer was there less than three days ago. After a week the image gets blurry, and as time passes, it will disappear completely."

I'm never one to go down easy on these paranormal explanations, even though I have to contend with a few of my own. "What about other people who've been in the apartment? Arkin had a cleaning lady. Why doesn't she show up in your pictures? The dead men were alive at one point and in the same room with the killer. I don't see these kinds of images."

She glanced down at her lap and then back up to me. "I don't know why the process works this way. It might have something to do with the intensity of the residual energy."

"Or it might be that it's pure bullshit," I said flatly.

"Ty," LaRue whispered.

Kelly shook her head. "It's all right, Marshal. It's not the first time I've heard these opinions and it won't be the last." She rose and collected her case. "Keep the pictures. You just might be able to use them."

I watched her go, and when she was clear of our cubicle, I turned to LaRue and said, "Andy, it's crap. She doctored these things. Computers are wonderful machines for that."

"It can't hurt holding on to them," he answered. "And who knows? They do a lot of strange experimentation over at the OI, just like the KGB did in the Soviet Union. It was because Russia started working with psychics and telepaths that the United States picked it up. In fact, they used remote viewers in the Kremlin during Khrushchev's time."

The phone rang, interrupting his explanation. I picked up the receiver and heard the characteristic wheeze of Frank Wilson, our medical examiner.

"I've got prelims for you, Merrick."

"I don't think I like the sound of your voice, Frank."

"This isn't going to be an easy one."

"Why?"

"My handy-dandy scanner tells me that all three of the men died of cerebral hemorrhages."

"They had strokes?" I asked.

"That's right. The affected areas were the same on all victims as well — the region of the brain known as the occipital lobe. The times of death were close, too. Within the same hour is my guess."

"Any ideas what caused three men to have strokes at the same time?"

"Maybe they stuck their fingers into an electrical socket," he muttered.

"What is that supposed to mean?"

"I can't explain it. Their central nervous systems were fried. The cellular damage in this region is consistent with what we find in electrocutions."

"But?" I asked.

"But when a strong electrical current passes through the body, it destroys internal organs, because our craws are filled with moist, gooey, salty things that conduct the juice. Your freakie boys showed only signs of tissue damage in the brain. Every other part of them look normal."

"Maybe it was a mild electrocution," I said.

"There is no such thing as a mild electrocution. It takes less than a tenth of an amp of electricity through the heart to cause a fatal arrhythmia." He stopped speaking, and I knew he was unwrapping one of his wife's famous pickle sandwiches. I heard the satisfying crunch as he worked into the food. After a moment he threw in the rest of his thought. "Despite the woeful lack of evidence and the strange nature of the deaths, my guess is someone used a cattle prod on them, but how it could trash only specific locations in the bodies is something that defies logic."

4

THE UNPREDICTABLE NATURE of my lycanthropy has gotten me into enormous trouble in the past. Because of these problems, I'm trapped by the same government that spawned those three dead ESP freaks. My days are monitored by Dr. Lane Gibson, a neurologist whose custody I was placed in when I made a teensy, professional mistake and tried to cut off a perp's leg. If I want to keep my classification designation and my job as a marshal, I have to listen to Gibson and participate in a variety of experiments intended to foster a cure or help control my lycanthropy.

The good doctor uses my supernatural illness as a stepping-stone toward a career in a research institute and he doesn't deny it. His prospective future is a sore subject, and because of it, Gibson and I are like soap bubbles: We emerge from the bottle separately, the air blows us together until we stick, and then we commence to push at each other until one of us pops.

He's a ruggedly handsome fellow with long, sandy-blond hair he pulls into a tight ponytail. His most expressive feature is a wild-eyed squint, and when I see it pasted together with a jacked-up jaw, I know I'm in for an ass chewing. Gibson entered our cubicle carrying both.

"Where were you yesterday afternoon?" he demanded.

I was supposed to meet him at the Planetary Health Organization for a lecture he was giving on my lycanthropy. In fact, I was supposed to be the stage specimen and answer the personal questions the doctors would ask me. I ignored him until I finished my conversation with Wilson. Dragging out the moment by leaning back in my chair, I said in a quiet voice: "Where was I? I was right here working."

He ruffled like a rooster ready for a cockfight, his voice gruff with restrained fury. "You left me in an embarrassing and humiliating situation. How dare you?"

I stood slowly, giving my anger a minute to fester, and then expertly let it ooze into my tone. "How dare I? You don't know what embarrassment and humiliation is, you bastard. Try having total strangers ask you if your shit smells different on a full moon." It was then that I realized my temper had stoked my response and I'd barked it loud enough for the folks in the homicide pen to look up and pay attention. I cut a glare around the room and heads ducked and swiveled. Turning back to Gibson, I let rage muster into my expression. "I told you I wasn't going. I have no intention of being some sideshow freak just so you can win the door prize at the next neurologists' convention."

"You knew these meetings were going to be part of our arrangement," he growled.

"And you knew from the beginning that no amount of coercion was going to get me to attend. Give it up, Gibson. I won't do it. You're taking the circus too far."

He glued on an ugly look. "You told me you would be there. You promised."

I probably should have felt guilty for lying to him, but I was already pussed up with indignation and so the shame could do nothing more than leave a greasy slick on my thoughts. Still, it made me add vinegar to my next statements. "I promised to be at that lecture to get you off my back. You're like a fucking bulldog sometimes. Why can't you take no for an answer?"

LaRue grunted, but swung toward his desk and pretended to ignore the argument by studying a file.

"After all I've done to help you, Merrick," Gibson said, "it was the least you could do for me."

"You forget," I answered. "I never asked for your help in the first place."

"But it's been there, nonetheless, and believe it or not, I've worked in your behalf."

There was some truth to that statement. For months Gibson had taught me the nuances of hypnosis and biofeedback. I can consciously control my temperature and heart rate and even initiate a stretch upon command, but I still can't stop a seizure from happening or direct the course of my transformation.

Having taken that particular application to its bitter end, he'd switched his focus to mapping my brain's frequency harmonics and measuring my neurochemicals. It was a lot of talk, complete with incomprehensible analysis, but no new discoveries.

Regardless of his efforts, genuine or not, our relationship bends to the dissension between us, and I wasn't about to simmer down on the issue so he could again twiddle with my ego. "We can go on for years studying my lycanthropy and never come up with a solid, workable solution for it. The way I figure it, as soon as your research grant comes through, you'll immediately dissolve our convenient arrangement. Hell, I'll bet the moment it happens, you won't be able to remember my name."

His fury evaporated with my last remark, and so, apparently, did his steam for the conversation. He stared at me for a minute, turned on his heel, and stalked from the cubicle.

5

BEFORE LARUE COULD start on me about being nasty to Gibson, Julie interrupted us with word of another murder involving an employee of the Office of Intelligence. It was the break I needed to escape the whispered opinions of my nosy coworkers, too. The fight had soured my enthusiasm in the day and even my partner's running commentary about the effects of temperature inversions on the local pigeon population did nothing to renew my interest.

The car's interior had sucked up the morning's heat, preventing LaRue from grasping the steering wheel. A few seconds ensued where he cursed St. Ophelia before finally finding a dirty rag to protect his hands. Muttering, he fondled the Trabi's choke and gingerly palmed the metal knob of the stick shift. With all this commotion, I almost believed I was going to be spared his unsolicited suggestions regarding my personal relationships, but LaRue is one of those who tries to fix the world with positive thinking and a variety of harmony potions.

"You need a chicha vial," he explained.

"Well, that's a new one," I said. "What's in this elixir?"

"As far as I can tell, it's a dram of homemade beer fermented with spit."

"That takes the concept of the microbrewery to a new level, wouldn't you say?"

He chuckled, but let the discussion drop in favor of working the clutch and the gas pedal at the same time. I was left with my silent considerations as to how to quell the aggressive energy between Gibson and me.

At the corner of Third and Alameda, our steady forty-mile-an-hour speed was drastically curtailed when we pulled behind a lumbering public announcement truck. The driver used his loudspeaker like a gaffer at a carnival, spreading word of the hurricane while reminding the citizens of their responsibilities toward our great, humanitarian society. His audience hung from windows and porch stoops, but turned dead-eyed to the message of the impending high winds, too stinking hot to care if District One was blown completely off the map.

Thirty minutes later we arrived at the Office of Intelligence. LaRue parked his precious Trabi partially on the curb and climbed out slowly, stopping for a moment to admire the daunting multistoried, gray monolith.

After surviving one misdirection by the OI security guard, we finally found the crime scene in a third-floor office in the building's west wing. Casper Conrad had beat us there, and entering, I saw him standing before the expansive oak desk, studying the victim as though his unquenchable gaze could raise her from the dead. When we approached, he flipped a sad expression our way.

"This was Ingrid Calloway," he said simply.

The woman was a white-haired grandma type, dressed in a conservative black business suit. Her postmortem symptoms mimicked those of the three dead men—runnels of dried blood flowed from her ears and nose. Lividity had not yet colored her skin purple and there was only a hint of rigor mortis. This was a fresh kill, if it was indeed a kill.

"Ingrid was in charge of project funding," Conrad announced.

"Bean counters make people nervous," I said. "Did she have enemies that you know of?"

He grunted. "Of course she had enemies. She approved the research budget and a lot more people have heard the word *no* from her than they have *yes*."

I stepped away to take a swing around the large office. It was tastefully done in hunter green and shades of yellow. The walls boasted artwork by Erté, Picasso, and de Kooning, and the canvases were arranged according to color, not painter. So rich were the furnishings I tripped over the edge of a thick Oriental carpet when my eye caught the turn of a Duncan Phyfe chair.

"Ingrid sat on the OI Review Board and sent funding

recommendations to the minister," Conrad continued. "She was very careful with how the taxpayers' money was spent."

From the looks of this office, it appeared she was careful to the point of using the funds for herself.

LaRue pushed the interview forward. "Who found the body?"

"I did," he answered. "We had a meeting scheduled this afternoon."

"To discuss what?"

"We were going to talk about funding issues for a public-works project."

Public works translated into a program of public conscription. More and more, the district tapped the citizens to serve as the low-waged labor in its more questionable endeavors. This embezzlement of people, their intelligence, their energy, and their resiliency had turned flagrant over the years. No excuses, monetary bonuses, or governmental favors were offered to the family units who came up with missing members.

"Was Ms. Calloway in her office all day?" I asked.

"Her staff assistant thinks she went out to lunch."

"Thinks?" I said. "This is ESP Central and you're trying to tell me her people don't know where she was during the day?"

"Ty," LaRue murmured.

"Ty nothing," I growled, laying a hard look onto Conrad. "Let me be completely clear about this, Casper. We don't play games. We're here because there's a threat to the community. We are not here to stretch our innate precognitive abilities."

He dropped his tone an octave. "I'm not trying to give you the runaround."

I snorted. "Each time we get mixed up with the government, we get the runaround."

"Ingrid's appointment secretary has the week off. We're purging the computer for the day's schedule now and I'll get it to you as soon as I can, but don't expect much. Ingrid wasn't in the habit of writing anything down." He paused to insert a baleful sigh and smoothed the lapels of his cheap suit. Then, speaking quietly, he said: "Two other people from the OI have recently been listed as deceased."

"Who else?" LaRue demanded.

"Amarilo Valquez and Dixon Emery. They were technical

specialists on a project the OI was doing in conjunction with the Planetary Health Organization."

My partner kept up his bullying. "Did they die at the same time?"

"A couple of days apart, if I remember correctly," he said. "I do know they were found dead in their offices."

"Why wasn't it reported?"

He shrugged. "I don't know. Maybe because it was just coincidence."

"What PHO project were they working on?" LaRue asked.

"A study involving paranormal healing of diseased or injured body tissue."

Upon hearing his words, the wolf in me came alert. My lycanthropic nature rests on part in my body's ability to heal its wounds. This enhanced stamina rides within the agony of every stretch, getting stronger by delicate strokes until it peaks on the full moon.

I shivered and tossed my thoughts away like wet cigarette butts. Words had failed me for the moment, but my partner warmed to the subject.

"You're talking about spirit healing, aren't you, Casper?" LaRue said.

"We prefer to think of it as micro-PK phenomenon," he answered. "It's in the same category with teleportation and poltergeists."

LaRue's mouth fell open, but no sound came out, so I found my voice and spoke for him. "Strange you should mention ghoulies. My partner appears to have a poltergeist problem."

Conrad wigged his eyebrows, an action that rippled the skin across the front of his bald head.

"What does PK mean?" I asked.

"PK stands for psychokinesis, or perhaps, easier to understand, the concept of mind over matter."

Yet again, I had a hard time swallowing the tangy sauce of supernatural explanations. "You're saying poltergeists have something to do with extrasensory perception?"

"Not exactly," he said. "You have two types of psychokinesis issues: macro-PK and micro-PK. Macros are those effects you can see: levitation, metal bending, things like that. Micro-PK takes place at the microscopic level, or in the case of poltergeists—the subatomic level. We believe all these occurrences are mutually exclusive—one can't work without the other. Kelly Bates is a good example of someone who can consciously utilize both macro- and micro-talents."

"How?" LaRue croaked.

"Take the photo of your killer, for instance. On a subatomic, micro-PK level, she can sense strong energy vibrations left in the ether. She then converts the energy by making an impression on film, a process considered to be done in a macro-state." His answer worked down into silence as he turned to stare at the body. When Frank Wilson stomped by to take over the show, he cranked his neck toward us again and resumed his lecture. "Poltergeist activity was once considered to be caused by strong thought patterns which disrupted normal, observable frequency bands. Hence the presence of flying objects or the sound of footsteps. We have revised that theory, though. We now think it's a perceptual disturbance and nothing more."

My impatience slid out on molecules of spit. "So, what is a poltergeist?"

He shrugged. "As far as we know, it's some kind of goblin."

6

WE RETURNED TO the office, only to be dragged into another meeting with Julie. Yet, this time, it was private.

Our watch commander is a stern, old broad with twenty years' experience working the homicide beat. She keeps her own caseload as well as supervising the usual screwups happening in the pen. When she brings you into her office, she's either taken a special interest in your investigation or she's about to give you bad news. With us, it was both.

She silently pointed to the seats positioned before her desk. We obeyed the order and waited patiently until she sat down and pulled a bottle of vodka from her top drawer. Glancing at LaRue, she said: "I like the garlic-and-onion chaser you added to this batch. Makes the liquor smooth."

"Not to mention what it does for your breath," I answered.

"I like what it does for my breath, Merrick. It keeps disagreeable people at arm's length."

"It keeps away the agreeable ones, too."

Shaking her head, she poured a jigger into her coffee cup. "There *are* no agreeable people. That's why you're sitting here now." She slugged the drink, following her swallow with a wince as the liquor branded the back of her throat. Then: "I've received new orders from upstairs. You're not to include the circumstances of Ingrid Calloway's death in your investigation. You're not to interview anyone concerning her death, and you are not to mention it in your weekly reports or daily logs."

There was an invisible spoon stirring the stew already. "That didn't take long."

"No, it didn't," she answered crisply. "There's more. I have information on two other questionable deaths in which you're

25

not to proceed." Scraping through the papers before her, she cursed when she couldn't find the note she needed.

LaRue interrupted this time. "Two men," he said. "Valquez and Emery. We just found out about them ourselves."

"Well, they're off-limits as of now." She sighed, but the sound held more disgust than weariness. "I suppose I don't need to tell you we're dealing with a deep, dark conspiracy, and being the OI, I'm sure it will turn out to be murkier than even we can imagine."

We stared at her, waiting for her to finish her thought. She dragged it out by pouring another drink. "Watch out for Casper Conrad."

"Why?" I asked.

"He deals in lies and false leads. Every person over there has some psychic trick up his sleeve. Don't forget it."

"Don't they have any of your normal, scum-sucking, run-of-the-mill bureaucrats?"

"No, they don't. Listen to me on this. Believe only half of what you hear and that half you scrutinize until you think your scrutinizer will fall off."

"Have you had dealings with these people before?" I asked.

She leaned forward and popped in an ominous tone for effect. "Let's just say I drag around some of their junk, and leave it at that." Sitting back, she rifled the drawer for a jar of olives and threw two of the wrinkled fruits into her drink. She then took a slow moment to knock off her makeshift martini in a mug.

I tried to glance at LaRue to see his take on her claims, but Julie caught my look before I could gauge his expression.

"Don't be too sure I can't read minds, Merrick. It's none of your business what my junk is. Clear?"

"Clear as crystal," I murmured.

"I need your stubborn skepticism, Marshal. That's why you were specifically chosen for this case." Glancing at LaRue, she said: "As for you, try not to let your imagination run away with you."

LaRue grinned, but didn't reply.

She considered him with that steely expression before continuing quietly. "Between the three of us, this is the way the investigation will work: I'll cut you slack on interviews with people who knew Arkin and his team, as well as Calloway and the others. But remember, you're there to interrogate only on the murders of the remote viewers. If you ask delicate questions that could come back on me, I will split your gizzards. Got me?"

We nodded. It was the same old ring around the roses.

Julie scribbled a note and handed it to LaRue. "When you get a chance, stop in and have a conversation with this gentleman. He can be very enlightening. If he gives you any trouble, you tell him I'm calling in a marker."

7

THE MOST VALUABLE and sought-after coupons in the locality are known as red sevens. Bureaucrats and favored citizens who, according to the government, have exemplified the humanitarian standard of our great society are rewarded for their unselfish efforts with these little gems. One RS voucher will buy enough food to feed a family of three for a year, provided that is, there's food in the district-run stores to buy.

To this end, folks will go to great lengths to trade for red sevens, often paying far more in time and trouble than what they're worth. People like Stanley Briller boondoggle the system by using their extensive skills to counterfeit these coupons, turning a tidy profit with them on the backdoor market. Stanley is an expert in ink and cardboard and usually copies whatever he get his hands on. If anyone could tell us about the strange card found at the crime scene, he could.

Vice keeps Briller on a short leash and busts his butt once every fiscal quarter to make the logs look good. It was about time for a roundup, so they shoved ahead the appointment schedule to the next morning, allowing LaRue and me to tag along in hopes of getting the info we needed.

The counterfeiter lived and worked out of an old warehouse where the district once stored drums of ammonia to use as refrigerants on the big buildings. According to the records, they moved the barrels out six years before I was born, but each time I walk inside, my nostrils pucker from the caustic stink still permeating the place.

Gibson attributes my bloodhound sniffer to a lycanthropic increase in the number of olfactory bulbs, those tiny, budlike organs at the top of the nose that turn odors into signals the brain can read as scents. Whatever the reason, I'm the only one who gets a whiff of the stink in this warehouse, and this day, the ungodly heat made things worse. It was all I could do not to gag when we stormed the building.

Weapons drawn, the four of us quietly climbed the metal steps leading to Briller's coupon factory. Once through the front door, we fanned out into two units and wove our way through the dimly lit storage area, moving past industrial-sized shelving units.

The vice boys chattered to each other over our com-link. They were more concerned about the alchemy necessary to turn a pressed meat sandwich into something edible than they were about the three thugs Briller employed. Their noise finally became so annoying, I deleted them by yanking the pickup from my ear. It was fortunate I did, because I heard the scrape of a footstep just around the next bend. I signaled to LaRue, who worked his way to my left with his sidearm leading.

The thing about using street muscle for protection is this: You will not find a person of intelligence and finesse. Since most of these yahoos are as dumb as a liver spot, all you have to do is put out your foot and trip them. And that's exactly what I did.

Briller's bruiser launched over my leg and belly-flopped right in front of us. His gun discharged when his elbow hit the deck, the bullet whizzing dangerously close to LaRue's head. It was enough to piss off my partner and he stomped on the idiot's hand, grinding the pistol loose while he laid a barrel to the bodyguard's fat head.

I slipped around him to gather up the gun and cuff the guy to a shelving unit. By that time we received word from the vice cops that the place had been secured on their end. Five minutes later we were admiring the view through the sooty windows in Briller's office.

Briller is a grizzled old man, who could easily be mistaken for one of those harmless geezers consigning themselves to benches in Washing Machine Park. His clothes are tattered, his teeth are missing, his breath is raw from thirty years of smoking illegal cigarettes. Yet, somewhere, this con artist has a credit stash to rival the richest of the dictator's bureaucratic bootlickers.

So often had Briller done this dance with the Marshals Office that when we pounded into his inner sanctum, he remained calm and greeted us pleasantly. He pointed to a large gray cabinet at the other end of the warehouse, mechanically sending our colleagues in that direction. He waved us to a couple of flimsy chairs.

"Looks like it's time for my free meal and shower courtesy of the authorities," he said. "I suppose I'm going to have to hire new bodyguards, too. It's getting a little difficult to find good men, because I'm pulling down a reputation for trouble. No one wants to work for me anymore. At least, not at a decent, fair price."

"Maybe you should think about going straight," LaRue said.

"My talents prevent me from considering it. I suppose you understand that. Poverty is not my cup of tea." Before we could answer, he continued. "It seems it's a little early for your visit, though. I do recall being in the tank just a month or so ago."

"If you help us, Stanley," I explained, "you won't need to go in for processing this week."

"What, and miss a safe place to stay during the hurricane?" He snorted and smoothed his scraggly white beard. "I guess you two are the reason the roundup is early."

I fished into my pocket for the card we'd found at the crime scene. "Can you tell us what this is?"

He took it by the edges as if touching it would release some spell packed into the cardboard. "My, my, my. Isn't that the most beautiful thing? Real gold leaf. Expensive stuff and hard to work with." He turned it over, and when he read the word, he scowled, but didn't comment on it.

I pushed him. "What do you know about this thing, Stanley?"

He continued to study it, obviously memorizing the swirling design for later forging. Stalling, he barked at one of the marshals to take care while rifling his cabinet.

"Is it a fortune-telling card?" LaRue asked.

Another minute passed before Briller replied. "It looks like an antique, but that's a common forging technique that won't fool a trained eye such as mine. I'd say it was recently painted. Still, it's probably worth a few hundred credits. Do you want to sell it? I might have a collector, if you're interested."

"It's evidence," LaRue said. "We need to find a killer, and this is the only physical clue we have."

"Well, then, I'd say you don't have any clues at all."

"Why?"

"This thing is called a tulpa card. I've created a few of these gems in my time. Nothing as fancy or expensive as this, mind you." He paused again to let the impact of his statement hit us, but when we didn't react, he continued. "A tulpa is a thought form brought to life. The Buddhist priests in ancient Tibet were the first ones to demonstrate the power to create these phantasms and set them off on their personal business. If the creator brings one of these demons into manifestation with motives of greed or disharmony, the tulpa can break away. To keep it from happening, most of your practicing sorcerers use these cards. It's said to contain the life force of the phantom."

"You're talking about creating ghosts?" I asked.

He shook his head. "A tulpa can be anything, Marshal, from zombie to vampire to werewolf."

He threw my train of thought right off its tracks. "Werewolves?" I whispered.

"Yeah. I've heard that those tulpas are the most vicious kind there are."

LaRue escorted me over the subject. "I take it you speak the word *Manjinn* and it releases the tulpa."

Briller acted like he'd just been stabbed. "Shhh! Don't ever say that name out loud. At least not here. I don't need any bloodthirsty critters loosed on me." He thrust his chin toward the two cops rummaging through his things. "I've got enough already."

"Do you have any idea who may have designed this card?" LaRue asked.

"No."

"What about the name of your collector?"

"I can't just give that information out, you know," he answered.

LaRue stiffened and his words turned cold. "Briller, if you think we're going to trade for the name, you're out of luck. Not this time."

"Well, I guess I can't help you, then."

My partner hammered him with the truth. "If you don't talk,

you'll find yourself going to prison for fraud and impeding a murder investigation. Not quite the same as a few days spent on the office tab."

"You wouldn't do that to me."

"Don't try us."

He let his gaze linger over LaRue before he opened a parlay, anyway. "You tell those couple of donkeys to leave my shit alone and I'll give you the answer you want."

"Name, first."

Briller huffed and puffed, but finally came up with the appropriate response. "See a fellow called Raymond Vinson. Rumor has it that not only does he collect these things, he's been known to send phantasms out like party favors."

8

THE MOMENT WE stepped onto the cracked sidewalk in front of Briller's warehouse, I experienced an explosion in my solar plexus, the burn of which traveled up my esophagus like a flamethrower until the force behind it finally launched me into a lycanthropic stretch. I fell where I stood, howling in pain. The dry heaves came on to silence my groans and herald my transformation, and if Briller could be believed, my tulpa escaped me.

Gibson thinks stress as well as environmental factors determine how my illness will manifest each month. He theorizes that at one time, these seizures might have been nothing more than an inconvenience caused by the resplicing of my damaged neuron pathways, but since I've lived with it all these years, he now believes I've turned the wolf into a willing and necessary compatriot. I unconsciously gauge my needs as far as strength and endurance are concerned and that's what determines the severity and frequency of these convulsions.

LaRue has been with me many times when I've gone down and he automatically helps me fight for control, but this time the pain was so intense, I lunged from his grasp to roll into the gutter. The smell of urine and blistering tar, combined with oppressively humid air forced my gagging into choking.

Several minutes later the agony faded and LaRue helped me to a seat on the curb. He jogged over to the Trabi, wrestled the trunk open, and returned with a bottle of water. I splashed more on my face than I drank. LaRue sat down beside me, mercifully silent for the moment.

The lunar cycle had been an easy one in that I'd had only two seizures. Those had stretched my bones by an inch, heightened my visual and aural sensitivity, and popped my muscles, making my uniforms strain over my upper arms and thighs. As I slowly recovered from this latest onslaught I checked the catalog of my body parts to discover how the wolf had materialized this time.

There was an old saying about how a lycanthrope wears his fur on the inside of his skin. Sitting here in the harsh afternoon light and stinking air, I felt like my body had been packed with cotton batting and pulled snugly over my skeleton. I glanced at LaRue, sure he would tell me if I'd turned into a stuffed sausage with hands and a head. He smiled comfortingly, but didn't say anything, instead following me without comment when I labored to a stand and took several jerky steps toward the car. We rode back to the office in blessed quiet as I forced myself to settle into my latest supernatural disposition.

The moment we walked into the homicide pen, the squad secretary informed us the labor files on the three remote viewers had been sent over from the OI and that the air-conditioning was on the fritz. Large fans stirred the heat around, doing nothing to cool off the cubicles or the hot tempers flickering to life. We slid into our chairs, but before a minute passed, LaRue started digging into his desk drawer. He came up with a bag of thick, pink paste. Squeezing it onto his fingers, he spread it carefully across the tops of our computer monitors.

"What is that stuff?" I asked.

"White glue, ground rose petals, a touch of red wine, a sprinkle of thyme, and a spiffy spell intended to keep the poltergeist out of the electronics. At least temporarily. My aunt Jen assures me this trick will work until I can collect all the stuff for my spray."

I tossed him a critical look, but kept quiet. It's useless to point out the ingredients of old wives' tales so I gave him a quick nod and turned to the file on Samuel Arkin. I had just flipped the folder open when a chill rolled through me, causing my inside-out fur to ruffle. A second later LaRue slammed his fist against his desk and cursed like a blue-nosed sailor.

"What's wrong?" I demanded.

"The goblin got through," he snapped, swinging his computer screen toward me. "This bastard is watching us, Ty."

If I'd believed in the existence of these fretful demons, I

would have had to agree, for there, typed in capital letters was the sentence: TELL AUNT JEN SHE FORGOT TO ADD LARD TO THE RECIPE.

LaRue's clever little poltergeist startled me, but also left me with some sudden questions about our remote viewers. While he bitterly complained of ghosts and ghoulies, I gave Conrad a call.

The man's tone of voice sounded like he was half-dead himself. His words barely punctured a sigh. "Hello, Marshal. What can I do for you?"

"You said poltergeists are a perceptual disturbance on the subatomic level," I said. "What is a perceptual disturbance?"

A pause inserted itself in his answer. Then: "What does this have to do with the murders?"

"Just tell me, Casper."

Another silence followed before he explained. "Humans naturally perceive their world from several different planes of reality. You might say our bodies are like a self-contained communication array. We gather information from our senses, but we also receive it from sub- and super-normal ranges. Poltergeists mess with the electromagnetic fields in the sub ranges that humans can detect. That's why you'll get different things—rappings, objects being disturbed, teleportation, and precipitation of matter."

"Precipitation of matter?"

"That's when solids pass through solids. Scientists early this century theorized that before such a thing is possible, the components of the atomic structure must be rearranged."

"You're suggesting poltergeist activity is caused by a third party, something or someone who can manipulate the building blocks of materiality."

"Yes."

"Can you train someone to do this?"

Another pregnant pause. "Well, it sounds a little ridiculous, doesn't it?"

I nodded as though he could see me. "Yes, it does, but alas, it's my job to ask the ridiculous questions. Your job, of course, is to answer me honestly."

His reply plodded in, drained of life. "I really doubt it, Marshal."

"Could remote viewers at least tamper with electronics? Perhaps send messages to computers using PK techniques?"

"Thought transmissions? You bet. They can fiddle with electromagnetic connections."

"Can they cause perceptual disturbances that might be defined by an average person as the maliciousness of a poltergeist?"

For some reason, he grunted. "Sure, especially if you believe in them in the first place."

"Has the OI ever used remote viewers' to manipulate a person's environment in an effort to secure a confession?"

"That's unethical. It violates Duvalier's Privacy Act."

"But has it been done?"

He paused; then: "Probably."

"And could Arkin and his buddies play these little games?"

Again, his answer came slowly. "Yes, and they would have been good at it."

"It's logical to assume, then, that remote viewers employ these techniques for their own gain."

"Yes," he said. "Does this give you some ideas?"

"Yeah. Thanks, Casper." I hung up and, sucking a deep breath, glanced at LaRue, who returned my gaze intently. "Andy," I murmured, "I think we might be on the receiving end of an unpleasant scam."

9

MARSHALS MAKE A lot of enemies, so if LaRue's name was on a short list kept by someone with extrasensory nuisance abilities, then mine probably was, too. Considering the possibilities, I think I liked the poltergeist theory better, although I didn't admit it. I explained my idea to LaRue, and he conceded that we might be under paranormal attack, but decided to cover all the metaphysical bases by continuing his search for the ingredients for his goblin spray.

While he did that I finally managed to push my attention toward Samuel Arkin's file and began reading about a man who had the talent to coerce unsuspecting people into doing the OI's bidding. His main focus had been on affecting the lifestyles of various ex-cons. What he did, or how, remained a mystery, because many of the paragraphs explaining his actions had been inked through. One report was completely gutted. About the only thing legible was the OI letterhead it was written on. Despite the missing portions, I started to get the idea that Samuel Arkin and his team were responsible for a variety of covert activities. Still, my skepticism remained in place. Until I had a firm handle on their method of operation, it would remain a stone in the road.

A short medical history was included in Arkin's folder and this is where I found out about a man suffering from a variety of illness. He was diagnosed with acute adult onset diabetes, which required an insulin regime to control it. Six years after he came under medical care, he suffered an episode of diabetic shock that almost killed him, and was forced to take a leave of absence for nine months to recover. Apparently, thereafter, he experienced migraines so incapacitating, he worked only a

limited schedule. Two years into this new program, he under-
went treatment for temporal-lobe epilepsy.

I stopped to stare at this section, as though I would find more
words. Gibson's stroll through my brain had produced evidence of something similar. This version of epilepsy left the
victim to deal with hallucinations, paranoia, and bouts of
confusion. I'd had my share, and each full moon brought
newer, hardier symptoms.

Not long after I grew bored reading this fact file, Frank
Wilson showed up. He slid heavily into the chair in our cubicle
and paused to work me over with a bleary-eyed appraisal.
Then, in a whisper, he said: "Julie asked me to go mole for you
guys on this OI investigation."

LaRue grinned. "Bless those mean old watch commanders,
everywhere."

Wilson shrugged. "Yeah, whatever. I just got off the phone
with an honest fellow over at the District Census Division.
Your cause of deaths for Amarilo Valquez and Dixon Emery
were officially listed as heart attacks."

"Not strokes?" I asked.

He sucked on his teeth before answering. "As I said:
officially, no."

"But your honest fellow happens to know an honest fellow
over at the PHO."

"Remarkable, isn't it?"

"For that place, it is. What do we have on the catalog, then?"

"Brain hemorrhages. The PHO informant claims it was the
most complete devastation of organs he's ever seen."

"Why?"

"Strokes are usually localized. They're often caused when a
blood vessel in the brain erupts. Think of it like an exploding
volcano. The blood floods the area and the parts caught
downwind from the rupture have their oxygen supply cut off.
That's what determines the extent of the brain damage. With
these two victims, the explosions chewed up most of their
brains. At one point the autopsy doctor surmised that they may
have each suffered multiple strokes in different regions of their
gray matter."

"Why were they registered as heart attacks?" I demanded.

"Why else?" he answered. "Someone got to the medical

examiner. My buddy didn't know who or why." Wilson leaned toward me. "After my contact gave me the yoo-hoo on this one, he disappeared down his rabbit hole again. He's a closed door, so don't bother to ring the bell."

"What did you come up with on Ingrid Calloway?" I demanded.

"Zip. That one is definitely off-limits. I'll keep asking around, but don't expect too much."

"You got a good look at her," I said. "What do you think could have happened?"

He shook his head. "I don't know. I wasn't allowed to do any kind of scan on the body."

10

————◆————

JUST ABOUT DINNERTIME, Casper Conrad sent an interviewee into our midst. His name was David Bacon, and according to the information given us by our watch commander, he was Sam Arkin's control.

I detected a wave of arrogance wafting from him the moment we met in the interrogation room. He was a big guy with short-cropped brown hair that accentuated the bullet shape of his head. Dabbing at the sweat on his face with a soiled, yellow handkerchief, he grunted when we asked him to tell us exactly what a control was.

"A control is a remote viewer's baby-sitter," he said simply.

When nothing else followed his one-sentence explanation, I immediately got a case of the ass. "Mr. Bacon, we're not playing games here. Several people have died under mysterious circumstances at the OI. If you don't want to be put on the implication list, you better start talking. Now, what was your relationship to Samuel Arkin and his team?"

"I told you. I'm a baby-sitter. I make sure the remote viewers are mentally healthy and in control."

"Then, you're a psychologist?"

"I have a university certificate as a therapist."

"Did Arkin and his cronies have problems with their mental health?"

"Nothing out of the ordinary, as far as I could tell."

"Is mental degeneration a serious problem among remote viewers?"

"Yes."

"Why?"

"Remote viewing produces a great deal of stress upon an

40

individual. They occasionally suffer from depression. A control takes care of them. I was there if they needed to talk."

I slipped off the chair and took a swing around the room, stopping before the slowly chugging fan. Standing in the sluggish breeze, I unzipped my cammies down to the waist and let the air rush at my sweat-soaked T-shirt. LaRue continued to stare at the man and was rewarded for his effort when Bacon fidgeted.

After I blew my stink off, I turned back to him. "Here's what I think is going on: Samuel Arkin left his entire brass band at a truck stop somewhere along the road of life. He was wired to the max, wasn't he?"

"Who told you that? Casper?"

I frowned, but didn't respond to his question. Instead, I kept hammering him about Arkin. "He had temporal-lobe epilepsy, which means he suffered from a variety of hallucinations. You were there to maintain control over his daily activities, weren't you?"

He blinked at me and swatted at the sweat beads on his cheek. "It comes to that point, eventually."

I climbed into the chair pony-style and used the back to prop up my elbows. "Why does it come to that?"

"As you are apparently aware, the continued experience of remote viewing affects brain function. The team members begin to suffer periods of paranoia and insecurity, as well as a host of other psychological problems. They're unpredictable, but predictable within the context of the unit."

"Why does this occur?"

He sighed. "I'm not supposed to reveal that information."

"You don't have a choice," I snapped, irritated that he'd stop explaining. "The civil matter takes precedence here."

"Civil matter. What does the government care about civilians?"

"Well, technically, we're on the bureaucratic payroll, but we care."

He snorted. "I doubt it."

"Mr. Bacon," LaRue said, "you don't have a choice about telling us. If you're not going to cooperate, we may be forced to detain you, especially if we feel you may know something pertinent about these murders."

He studied us, shook his head, and answered in a whisper. "The OI has ears and eyes everywhere. You know the old saying: the only good society is a controlled society."

LaRue backed off, shoved his hands into his uniform pockets, and took a stroll around the room while I continued with the interview.

"You still haven't explained why it's necessary to monitor the daily performance of the remote viewers."

He hesitated for a minute before laying it on the line. "It was discovered way back in the 1960s that behavior and complex thought patterns could be transferred from individual to individual at a chemical level. They first tried it with an experiment involving rats, successfully transmitting a phobic fear of the dark from one control group to another."

"How can that be done?" I asked.

"It involves neurotransmitters, which are compounds secreted by nerve cells. They, in effect, allow us to think, to make connections in the brain. Surprisingly, these compounds are nothing more than molecules made up of very simple amino acids. In the beginning, the scientists extracted a person's aminos and injected them into a host. They found they could rebuild the host's thought patterns to match that of the donor—everything from intelligence to conceptual thinking, psi-talents, attitudes, and emotions. The researchers learned to synthesize the individual brain chemicals, but the results were apparently not worth the expense. There's not much information from the early days, but suffice it to say, the levels of technology and science made the process possible. It just didn't make it cheap. There was the moral dilemma proposed by the study as well. It made funding almost impossible to obtain. I suppose money was tight, even then."

"But now the technology is in place," LaRue said. "And the money has mysteriously appeared."

"Yes," he murmured. "Unfortunately, the science still isn't there yet, but the lack of knowledge has never stopped the government."

"What does that mean?" I asked.

"It means you can't just collect an amino acid like you would siphon gasoline from water. Neurotransmitters have different functions and different molecular structures, so you introduce new behavior bit by bit until the host's perception begins to change. They call the process amino dubbing. A series of injections as well as a variety of psychiatric techniques actually rebuild a person. The whole program can take several years. If the donor suffers from mental instability, then these problems will eventually be conveyed to the receiver."

This confession was enough to make a sane person pee himself. "Are you saying Arkin was dubbed?"

Bacon nodded. "Arkin's thought processes were refined and rebuilt and his team members were then dubbed from him."

11

DAVID BACON SWORE upon his mother's breast that he didn't know anything about Sam Arkin's paranormal scams. He also declared his ignorance about the man in Kelly Bates's photograph and so we had no choice but send him back to his ESP buddies.

His confessions of the government's latest scientific manipulation left us a little short of breath. LaRue and I remained in the interrogation room after releasing Bacon, but instead of discussing the implications of what we'd just learned, we stared off into space. By the time we returned to our cubicle, we had not broached the subject, and as if to drag out the moments of reflection, my partner rummaged inside a tattered wicker basket he keeps under his desk. He produced two jars of saffron tea, one of which he tossed to me. The liquid was steamy hot, and I found myself wishing for ice cubes even as I guzzled it. LaRue sucked at his drink before finally speaking.

"Can you imagine actually volunteering to be dubbed?"

I shook my head. "Don't fool yourself, Andy. People don't volunteer. You'll remember, I had no choice in joining Gibson's campaign. When the government wants something, it will get it. Maybe the remote viewers don't know what's being done to them until it's too late."

He shivered and made a face, covering it slightly by tilting the jar to his lips. "It's a horrible thought," he said, after sipping his tea.

That it was. I kept wondering about my own brain chemistry and how effectively the carbon monoxide had mucked it up. Gibson had long maintained that part of my problem stemmed from changes in the firing sequences within the neurotransmitters. Weighed against the information delivered by David

Bacon, my imagination treaded over my logic. I kept thinking
that my lycanthropy could have been caused by factors
established as a child. I grew up in an orphanage. Helpless
children always make the best fodder for amoral experiments.

LaRue's statement proved that paranoia is the standard of
our society. Did Bacon's admission actually suggest unautho-
rized intrusion into our minds by a government bent on
complete and utter control or had we just been in the business
of uncovering nasty secrets for far too long?

Before I could do more than chew on the possibilities,
Conrad sent over another interviewee by the name of Teresa
Yarnell. The homicide secretary installed her in our slimy
interrogation room, where we found her twitching and wring-
ing her hands.

We pulled chairs up to the table and introduced ourselves.
LaRue studied her openly, letting his gaze pass slowly over the
dainty lines of her face. When he spoke, he used what I call his
"Zen" voice: that serious, husky tone delivered in such a way
as to encourage relaxation and inspire confidence.

"It's Mrs. Yarnell, correct?"

She nodded. "I'm married and have two children."

"Good for you," he answered. "Does your husband work at
the Office of Intelligence, too?"

"No. He's a fireman at the coking plant. Class-C designation."

"Class C? He doesn't earn much, then. I suppose he doesn't
receive any kind of hazard bonus, does he?"

She mouthed a no and touched her wheat-colored hair,
fluffing her bangs so they wouldn't stick to the smear of sweat
on her forehead.

LaRue remarked upon it immediately. "There's no need to
be nervous, Mrs. Yarnell."

"I'm not nervous," she squeaked. "It's hot in here."

"Like an oven," he said. Leaning in, he added a layer of
cream to his next comment. "You were good friends with a
man named John Drake."

"Yes."

"And you were the personal assistant to Ingrid Calloway."

Her answer came weakly as she tipped her chin slightly and
sighted along her clasping, white-knuckled hands. "Yes."

"And now both are dead."

This time she responded with defiance, snapping her head back and scowling. "I thought you weren't supposed to ask me about Ingrid?"

LaRue glanced at me and then focused a hard stare onto Yarnell. "Who told you that?"

Her lips moved, but her words took a moment to follow. "Casper Conrad."

"Did Conrad decide that we shouldn't talk about Ingrid?"

She shrugged. "I don't know."

"Still, we have several folks who won't be able to attend the Annual Black River Fish Fry. What do you say about that?"

"I had nothing to do with any of these deaths and you better not be implying that I did."

LaRue remained monotone. "We're not implying anything. We're just trying to find a place to start. So, would you mind telling us how you couldn't be involved in these deaths?"

"Well, for one thing, I was on leave all week. I didn't even know Ingrid was back in the district. She had meetings in other localities and I hadn't seen her in at least ten days. As for John, we were just friends. I hadn't talked to him in a couple of weeks, either."

"You don't seem very upset about your superior's death."

"What's to be upset about?"

"Didn't you like her?"

"Sure," she answered flatly.

LaRue nodded and tacked a different direction. "Is it true your first few years spent at the OI were as a remote clairvoyant and clairaudient?"

"Yes, so? I haven't worked in a parapsychology unit for six months."

"Why?"

"It caused me too much stress. I couldn't handle it."

"Looking into the future takes a strong personality able to withstand the rigors of stress?"

She studied her fingers again. "Yes."

"Why?"

"Because sometimes you see things you wish you hadn't."

"Did you see the impending deaths of Samuel Arkin, Kenneth Ford, and John Drake?"

She kept her attention firmly fixed upon her hands as she answered. "No."

"What about Ingrid Calloway's death?"

"No. I told you I don't practice remote clairvoyance anymore."

"Then why did you take off these last few days?"

She sighed in exasperation and fluffed her bangs some more. "My child is sick with the summer flu. I took her to the free clinic in my neighborhood. You can check there for the records. I've been home with her, too. My landlady stopped in several times."

"Someone with preknowledge could have engineered that excuse within the appropriate time frame."

"Well, I didn't!" she snarled.

LaRue sat back and tossed a look my way. I picked up the interview, showing her the photo Kelly Bates had taken at the crime scene. "Do you know this man?"

Mrs. Yarnell stared at the picture, puckered her lips, and shook her head no. "He doesn't look familiar."

I felt my inside-out fur ripple. Glancing down, I noticed goose bumps on my arm. "Are you sure? Take a good look."

She didn't bother. "I told you I don't know him."

I nodded, but studying this woman, I came to a singular conclusion: I may not have ESP, but I can tell when someone's lying.

12

———■———

WE LET TERESA Yarnell leave after telling her to make herself available for further interviews. She practically ran from the interrogation room, but before she did, she shook her head and tossed me a squinty look as though she'd peeked into my future and found it to be a dismal place. I certainly didn't need a prognosticator to tell me that.

LaRue decided to check out a lead on an ingredient for his poltergeist spray, so I called it a day. I walked home, stopping along the way to urge the folks in my ward to take the threat of the storm seriously.

The evening sweltered and the pollution from the smelting plants hung heavy and thick at ground level. I swung down by the Black River to talk to people who lived in sagging canvas tents and fished in the sludgy water. The Marshals Office demands that each investigator pull a foot beat a couple of times a month and these folks were on my regular route. Despite their poverty, they appreciated my halfhearted effort at protecting them and sent me away with tokens of gratitude: a catfish with an extra fin, a shaker of salt professed to have healing properties, and a bunch of computer disks woven on a string. This last item was supposed to influence the flow of the hurricanes' magnetic qualities. It didn't take me long to turn this generosity into three brittle pieces of plywood, fourteen used nails, and a ripped shower curtain. Like everybody else, I had to do my best to shore up the windows in my flat.

In a humanitarian society, the amount of privacy you have is based upon the number of people who share your toilet. I was luckier than most, because I had a fifth-floor apartment and only one roommate. When I reached home, I found her

48

industriously preparing our ramshackle dwelling for the up-coming hurricane.

Upon her retirement from the sanitation plant, Baba had taken up weaving as her main livelihood, turning out trash blankets, charm bags, and anything else she could think of to trade on the backdoor market. She once convinced a neighbor that she could relieve him of nightmares by making him a special cushion that would strain off the dark energy as he slept. He bargained a red seven for this scam and she happily presented him with a pillow made from bits of aluminum foil and packing tape. The fellow tried it, announced it to be a miracle, and brought her four other customers willing to trade their firstborn for a good night's rest.

Baba not only took up weaving, but she also took up drinking, and when I entered the flat, I almost barfed at the strong smell of an opened bottle of LaRue's homemade hooch. Half-tooted and standing atop a rickety chair, she busily decorated the front window with several strands of small, burned-out fluorescent tubes while singing a bawdy rendition of "St. Ophelia's Anthem." A sticky breeze blew in to tinkle the little lights, and as I wrestled my plywood piece through the narrow door, I asked her what the hell the makeshift wind chimes were for.

She didn't answer me until she'd finished the final verse of the song and then said matter-of-factly: "They're air fresheners."

I dropped my junk on the floor, placed my hands on my hips, and stared at the back of her head. "Baba, step off that chair before you fall out into space and I'm forced to find an even more disagreeable roommate."

"I suspect you'll find plenty of those," she answered, hanging another string of tinklers. "Like attracts like." Climbing from her perch, she paused to grunt when her bones cracked loudly. "We can't even turn on the frigging fan to spin the air around. The district rotated the electricity at noon. I supposed they figured we're going to lose power when the storm comes through anyway, so why waste it on us until then?"

I sighed, removed my shoulder holster, and stripped down to my sweat-soaked underwear. My black T-shirt looked like it had been tie-dyed from the salty crust of dried perspiration. Flopping onto our ragged couch, I watched Baba string another bundle of bulbs.

Air fresheners are a popular item on the backdoor market. They're found in every conceivable form and do everything from clearing a room of evil demons to actually leaving an agreeable fragrance behind.

"Who bit into your pension check this time, Baba? Selma Teague?"

"It's not a joke, Ty."

"Sure it is," I muttered. Then, louder: "What are these fresheners supposed to do?"

"Drastic changes in the barometric pressure disturbs the energy of matter," she answered. "When that happens, demons can come through to settle into the molecules of this plane. They like furniture, you know."

I laughed. "Sprout like mushrooms on the arm of the couch, do they?"

She eyed me like a drunken pirate, finally saying: "If the energy of your favorite chair changes and develops a demon, you'll find spikes in your seat."

"What's that supposed to mean?"

"They can affect your health. You rub against them and they can give you sore muscles, bad sinuses, iron-poor blood, and hemorrhoids."

I stared at her for a minute, deciding she was serious. Puss demons. My mood flexed, expanding from weariness to that point where I just don't give a shit. Baba must have noticed something in my expression, because she changed the subject.

"I did trade for some canned goods today. The supply won't hold out through the worst of the problems, though." She wobbled to a broken cardboard box sitting on the kitchen table and rifled the contents. Turning, she tossed me a tin. "Look at that—real tuna fish."

I read the can. "Baba, this is cat food."

"I know, my dear. Do you think I'm blind or something?"

I didn't reply, because I was wondering if it was time to cut my throat and be done with it all. Had we really been reduced to scrounging for this junk? I glanced around the flat, momentarily overwhelmed by our poverty. Even with Baba's pension and my paycheck, we lived barely better than those forced into the streets.

The only thing of value in the whole apartment was Baba's loom. The thing took six strong men to move, but the violent winds of a killer hurricane would have no trouble heaving it into the next district.

Baba must have read my mind. "You can't change fate, Ty."

I thought of Teresa Yarnell. "Even if you know your cards before they're dealt?"

She nodded. "Even then."

13

THE NEXT MORNING LaRue picked me up, but rather than driving to the office, he had a line on another spray ingredient, so I was forced to tag along while he stopped in at an illegal hurricane rummage sale.

People gathered in a large alley in a neighborhood known as the Whiskey Bottle, because it was long associated with moonshining and drunks. LaRue bought many of the supplies for his family's still from a rumpot named Juicer, and my partner was sure this nefarious character was to be found at this gathering of unlicensed merchants.

It took a while to scrounge up this guy, and as we wove our way deeper into the crowd, LaRue stopped twice—once to buy metal filings and the other to purchase frog hairs. This last purchase cost ten credits and a bag of potato chips. When the old woman handed over the fluff of magic, I could tell instantly LaRue had bought a gallon-sized baggie filled with the delicate threads of rice noodles. Packaged under the Truth in Selling Law, the stash would have been worth no more than a Duvalier dime.

Juicer had a seller's stall in this makeshift market, and while pushing his booze, he tried to move copper line, brass fittings, and shoe polish. According to LaRue, this last product was occasionally necessary to give whiskey just the right flavor. In fact, his grandmother had used it frequently when she made up her special blend, and as far as his family was concerned, her death from stomach cancer had nothing to do with years of drinking brown dye in her hooch.

When we finally stumbled over him, Juicer greeted LaRue with gushing joviality, but upon seeing me, his extravagant attitude disintegrated into suspicion.

"Who's this?" he demanded.

"My partner, Ty Merrick."

Juicer nodded curtly, but still regarded me with a sideways look. "You're agreeable to our little outdoor shopping mall, ain't you?"

"Of course," I answered, pointing to the bag of frog hairs. "We're here to buy, after all."

"Now, that's what I like to hear," he said. "What can I do ya for?"

LaRue spoke up. "I need a half-pint of hundred-fifty-proof alcohol."

Juicer squeezed a frown. "You're in luck, Andy, my boy. I have just about that much left. People have been buying it right regular since I got here at the crack of dawn. There's gonna be some kind of hurricane party. If the storm don't kill folks, then their alcohol levels will."

"I'm not going to drink it," LaRue assured him. "I'm making a poltergeist spray and that's one of the ingredients."

"Oh. Sounds like you've got Anna Sorrell's recipe."

"That's the one. Ever try it before?"

"Yeah. As a matter of fact, it was before a big old hurricane just like the ragger coming in now." Juicer pushed a finger into his mouth to readjust a wad of chewing tobacco. "Goblins lurk in these pockets of intense energy. I've had two or three people just in the last week who bought for the same reason. I'm going to have to put the cooker back into action to make up for the turnover, but I don't figure it will be that easy."

"Worried about the revenuers?" I asked.

He eyeballed me again. "No. All this commotion in the weather. Don't make for fine brewing. Seems to upset the fermentation. These danged hurricanes and typhoons are caused by sunspots, you know. Until things settle down, hundred-fifty-proof is going to cost an arm and a leg."

I'd almost been interested until he loaded bullshit into the opening price of the parlay.

"That's right," he said, not waiting for a comment. "When the old sun starts spouting flares, it comes all the way to earth, where it affects the electromagnetic energy."

"So how do these occurrences promote goblins?" I asked.

He stared at me, and from his look, I realized he didn't understand the meaning of the word *promote*.

"What causes goblins to appear?" I said. "The gooing up of electromagnetic energy?"

He shook his head. "No, the gooing up of your brain cells."

"Excuse me?"

"Electromagnetic waves affect the way you think. You get enough of these waves going through your gray matter and it makes you see things that ain't always there. But once you notice them, they can cause a sorrowful bit of mischief."

"You're saying poltergeists are a figment of the imagination?"

"No, I didn't, Marshal. I'm saying if you realize they're there, you give life to the little bastards."

I stared at the filthy man. Gibson and my shrink had been trying to fill me with this same kind of bunk where my lycanthropy was concerned. It's unsettling when science and invisible magic come together. "Exactly why is my partner paying you for a jar of one-fifty, then?"

"Because it's in the recipe," he answered.

"But if what you're saying is true, then a spray won't take care of the poltergeists."

He paused to spit tobacco juice and wipe his mouth with the back of his hand, leaving a black stain as he did. "Don't know why the spray works. There's lots of scientific reasons, I suspect."

Or none at all. I dropped the conversation and waited for LaRue to dicker on the price. The bargain was just done when the storm clouds mixed with the pollution to produce a sudden downpour. We grabbed the jar and headed toward the Trabi. Just our luck, we didn't make it.

Screams erupted in the crowded market, and as blackhearted human nature dictates, instead of going to someone's assistance, everybody scattered. There was a stampede and a couple of kids were trampled before we shoved our way back into the alley, where we discovered a man beating a pregnant woman with a whip made from a frayed electrical cord. She rolled on the greasy pavement, and while several greedy merchants worked to collapse their flimsy stalls, not one moved to help her.

The perp saw us heading his direction and turned the whip on gawking bystanders. They rushed out of his path, but like a boat cutting through water, the people formed a wake and slid back on us.

My lycanthropy charges my stamina in ways that defy reasonable explanation and one of the things it does is give me incredible speed. I can haul ass faster than a greyhound chasing a mechanical rabbit around the racetrack, so while LaRue stopped to help the woman, I turned on the afterburners and began pursuit.

The wind drove the rain into stinging squalls that pelted me as I pushed behind the man. He was a block ahead of me, weaving in and out, finally ducking behind a parade of people carrying black tattered umbrellas against the sudden storm.

Thunder rumbled, echoing down the street between the crumbling high-rises, and when it did, I felt a tingling sensation conduct through my inside-out fur. The surge made my skin crawl, and it kept on crawling as my lycanthropic hearing was beaten by the Doppler effect of the sound vibrations. At one point I stopped running, momentarily confused by this intense rippling. This odd feeling passed with the thunder and I was once more off after this newest lunatic.

Citizens, enlivened by a chase in lousy weather, snitched on the guy by silently pointing after him. Before long I had him cornered in an abandoned brickyard.

I pulled my service revolver and slipped through a tear in the chain-link fence. A valence of concertina wire had come unraveled and it clutched for my uniform, but I managed to slide past the barbs. Inside, I found stacks of cinder blocks, twenty feet high and fifty feet long. They formed a dangerous maze, a situation further complicated by the mud and the rain.

LaRue's voice slammed across my com-node, the noise being so sharp, I almost lost my balance. I yanked the mike from under my T-shirt, growled my location, and flipped the nuisance over my shoulder to get it out of the way.

The rain continued to drench the world, like God Himself had decided it was finally time to hose down District One. I listened for the perp, but the force of water droplets hitting the ground set up a static noise that drowned out the background arias of my lycanthropic hearing. Flexing my finger against the gun trigger, I had to rely on intuition to tell me where the bastard was hiding.

I hugged the cinderblock stacks, tossing my sixth sense out in front of me. A moment later I found him.

It could have been a classic scene from an old police vid: I came to the end of the stack and knew the man balanced on top of this man-made concrete mesa. A second was all I needed to take a deep breath, spin, and have him in my gun sights. With a burst of lycanthropic strength, I started into my acrobatics, only to be stopped in mid-turn by the brilliance of a lightning bolt and an earsplitting thunderclap.

The noise forced me to my knees and I dropped the gun. A cold sweat mingled with the rain battering my face. The storm remained unrelenting.

I stiffened with sudden, unexplainable fear. As the sound grew louder and the flashing electricity closer, I suffered more and more with a trapped feeling, one that triggered my survival mechanism. I stirred long enough to grope for my weapon, but the rain and my terror prevented me from finding it. The perp slipped off the wall, stared at me as I squeezed my knees to my nose, and tried to make myself a mere bump on the landscape. I suppose he decided it might be the only time to get even with a cop and so he kicked me in the side and then ran away.

LaRue found me a few minutes later cowering in the mud. I ached from the surprise attack, but truth to tell, I was more banged up in my psyche than my body.

My partner squatted beside me and placed his hands on my shaking shoulders. "What's wrong, Ty?" he asked urgently.

I blinked, trying to think around my stunning fear. It was a moment more before I could coax my throat muscles into moving.

His tone turned demanding. "Are you hurt?"

"No," I grunted.

"Did you have a stretch?"

"No." Try as I might, I couldn't summon the consonants and vowels that would give me more words.

Thankfully, he left it at that. The storm slackened overhead, and the downpour transformed into a gentle shower backlit by a stream of sunlight lancing through the clouds. My lycanthropic vision revealed the beautiful, prismatic colors in the water, but my human frailties kept me from enjoying them.

LaRue squeezed my arm reassuringly. I closed my eyes, fighting this new agony by mentally pushing it away. It fled, but instead of being left with curious disquiet, my crippled mind explored the concept of embarrassment. I shook off LaRue and stood up, barely able to look him in the face.

14

────── ■ ──────

We returned to the office and scraped off the mud before going out again. This time we ignored the bounty of crime going on around us and headed for Angela Whitehead's basement hideaway.

I was in a shitty mood after the events of the morning and ready to chew someone up. Unfortunately, Angela was one of Baba's dearest friends, so I was forced to squeeze civility out between my clenched teeth.

Angela had worked for many years as a housemaid for some of the more affluent individuals in our society, but her class designation left her at the bottom of the heap financially. She never married, never worked harder than she needed, and never managed to petition for a change in her class designation; yet Angela's life was filled with abundance. Her source of success was simple: she ran a haunted-house scam that paid her dividends that I could only imagine.

When the old woman invited us inside, her prosperity was announced in the fine furnishings, thick carpet, and handmade lace curtains. The electricity was off the grid for everyone except the government offices and essential services, but she'd gotten around the problem by using a high-voltage battery pack to drive her small refrigerator and fan. Her tiny apartment felt cool and inviting, which, in my current frustration, was a welcomed relief.

She offered us glasses of fresh lemonade, but instead of home-baked cookies, she asked us if we wanted to share the contents of her can of snuff.

"We'll pass, Angela," LaRue said with a smile. "We're not allowed to indulge on duty."

She fluffed her neat array of powder-blue curls and nodded.

"Such a shame. Calms the nerves like nothing else." To prove it, she pinched a bit from the can and sniffed it delicately before placing the wad against her gums. A moment later she sneezed like a longshoreman. This whole thing was followed by a minute of fumbling for a dainty linen hanky. "I haven't seen you in a while, Ty. Each time I visit Baba, you're not at home. Do you still have the moon madness?"

"Yes, ma'am," I answered.

She shook her head sadly. "Despite all the love and care that nice Dr. Gibson gives you?"

I frowned at LaRue, who grinned, but remained silent. It was already time to change the subject. "Angela, we need your help with an investigation."

"My help? Whatever could I tell you about murder?"

"Perhaps quite a lot."

"What, then? I'll answer if I can."

"We were wondering about your haunted-house scam."

She smiled and sat straighter. "Is someone working that old con? My word. Some things just never go out of style."

"How do you run the hustle?"

"Well, that's easy. First, you have to decide what you want and who has it. Take this chair of mine. Pretty, isn't it? You can't find this quality of chintz material anywhere on the backdoor market. This stuff is reserved for folks who have an extra red seven or two."

"So where did that come from?" I asked.

"A bureaucrat who worked for Solid Waste Management Agency. I cleaned his house for a year after his regular maid passed away. He'd just rented this place—a real swanky deal in Ward Eight. Well, I almost fell over the first time I walked in and saw all the furniture dusting I was going to have to do. This chair, here, sat at the head of a huge dining-room table. When I laid eyes on it, I knew I had to have it."

"What did you do to get it?"

"I got to know that fellow real well and found out he'd had an affair with the maid who died. She had complications of childbirth—the child being his."

"He was feeling terribly guilty," I said.

"Oh, more than you can imagine," she said. "So much so, I

convinced him that the chair was possessed by this woman's angry spirit."

"How did you do that?"

"Little things. Stuff that's easy to rig. When he would sit in the blasted chair, the leg would fall off and dump him on his ass. He must have fixed it forty times and forty times I sawed through it just enough to make it crack again."

LaRue chuckled. "What else did you do?"

She leaned toward him and spoke in conspiratorial tone. "Psychological stuff. The person has got to believe he's in a haunted house and under supernatural attack from a vengeful ghost. I kept working on him." Pausing, she repeated her snuff sneeze and daintily wiped her nose. "I talked about poltergeists and demons, rigged a few things to fly across the room when he walked in, even got my nephew to record some strange noises onto an audiotape. I hid the recorder in the air-conditioning duct, set on an automatic timer. The sounds would start up at two in the morning. You can do all kinds of things: rotten food in the fridge, moving objects around. I even got hold of some of this woman's clothing by going to her mother. I put those in his closet. That was enough to undo the fellow."

"What happened next?" I asked.

"He called in a snaker to get rid of the ghosts. Of course, the vipers didn't work. I don't know where people get these thoughts, do you? How can a rattlesnake chase off a ghost? It doesn't make a bit of sense to me."

"People will believe anything," I said. "What happened after the snaker came through?"

"Well, I convinced this man it was the chair that was haunted. I told him to take it to the dump and be done with it. He'd had about all the aggravation he could stand and did what I told him. I had a friend waiting right there to put it in the back of her old pickup truck." She patted the chair arm. "And here you are. Couldn't be more simple, or more fun."

"Do you know many people who pull off these scams?" I said.

"I did once, but since retirement I've lost contact with most of them. Of course, if I did know anyone it wouldn't be right to mention names, you know."

"We've got a case involving employees of the OI. Six people

have died under suspicious circumstances. Three of them were remote viewers."

Her expression flattened. "Dangerous folks, those remote viewers. Murder befits them."

"Why?"

"Because they're dishonorable thieves. They don't just take someone's possessions, they often take their sanity. Like that's necessary."

"How, exactly, do they do that?"

"Telepathy. They work on your head by putting the thoughts there. They don't have to rig anything. It's scary to know someone can just peek into your privacy and take your life away without ever setting foot near you."

15

DUVALIER'S INTEREST IN the occult set the governmental policy as far as investigative work is concerned. To this end, the Marshals Office employs a variety of people who are psionically talented, but truth to tell, most come to us because they can't cut the psychic butter at the OI. As far as I'm concerned, it's a serious waste of district funding, but I go along with the program like a good little grunt, even though I make sure to get my barbs in about their paranormal accuracy.

I will admit that once in a while their supernatural crap has juggled up the answers by pointing me in a whole new direction. We needed to jump-start this probe and the guy who could help was Ethan Fraley.

Fraley claims not to have a bit of psychic power on his own. His specialty is channeling a discarnate entity he calls Hakeem Manu. I always have to hide my laughter when he goes into his act, because Hakeem Manu is supposed to be an ancient Egyptian sage. The spirit speaks the Barrier language with a strange accent and will refuse to give up any information unless Fraley is consuming a jelly doughnut while fingering the evidence. A ghost with a sweet tooth.

LaRue sprang for the baked goods, and before we knew it, our cubicle had become a crossroads where everyone helped themselves to the goodies after leaving a chunk of silver for their share. It wasn't long before Fraley found us.

"We didn't even get a chance to call you," I said, watching him immediately dip for a doughnut. "Is this the result of precognition?"

He laughed. "I didn't conjure up a vision of your arrival, if that's what you mean."

"How did you know we had the doughnuts?"

"Well, for cripe's sake, Merrick, I'm just down the hall. I could smell the goddamned things as your hairy partner here carried them in." He cocked a frown my way. "Don't tell me you suddenly believe in psi-shit."

It was my turn to chuckle. "I try not to leave myself open for convincing. Still, our latest case seems to push the supernatural envelope just a wee bit."

"The deaths at the OI. I heard Julie talking about it to my watch commander. Sounds like you pulled the big winner this go-round."

Before I could reply, Mr. Barkley stopped in to rifle through our doughnut cache. He nodded to Fraley, who gave him a genuinely pleasant smile, but the moment he left, Fraley turned off the expression and said: "He's cheating on his wife."

"Are you tuning in to the ether for that one?"

"No," he answered. "It's my tender nose again. The bastard reeks with Debbie Sutton's perfume. That janitor's closet down the hall doesn't smell too good, either." He changed the subject. "So, what do you want me to read?"

I handed him the card found at the crime scene. "Do me a doobie on this."

He took it the same time he bit into the doughnut. I didn't expect him to nearly choke on the cake, though. Fraley sputtered filling and sugar all over the card.

"What is it?" LaRue demanded, slapping him on the back.

A moment passed before Fraley could inhale enough to speak a sentence. During that time his rubbery features seemed to lengthen. He squinted at us, waved LaRue off, and started speaking in his discarnate voice. "The entity known as Ethan Fraley has just experienced a rather painful tingling in his hindquarters."

I hid a snort behind my doughnut. "The seat on that chair is broken."

Fraley shook his head. "Do not let your skepticism make you stupid to the truth."

Chastised, I thoughtfully chewed my sweet and demanded his take on the whole thing.

"You have death and danger here," he prophesied. "Be wary. The demons associated with this card are real. One of them killed the Pharaoh Ankanomen, you know."

"No, I didn't," I answered, glancing at LaRue. "Who the hell is Pharaoh Ankanomen?"

"Only the greatest king the Upper Valley has ever known," Fraley stormed. Taking another bite, he added: "Do not discount the power of the supernatural. The Lord Osiris saw that the Underworld was balanced with these avenging forces. They come into the material realm to keep the energy moving." Fraley polished off the doughnut and rifled the bag again. "Speaking of energy: this connection is weak because of the coming hurricane. I require more sustenance to continue." Stuffing a blueberry cream into his mouth, he added: "Show me the photograph."

I will admit to being surprised sometimes, and this statement stunned me down to my shorts. I fished out the picture and handed it to him.

There was a moment when it appeared Fraley was having a private conversation with Manu. His lips moved, his head jerked, and his eyes rolled back. Then, recovering, he boldly used the tip of his tongue to lick the filling from the pastry. "This man is a demon," he said. "He is also an assassin, whose compensation comes from emotional satisfaction."

"You mean he likes to kill?" LaRue asked.

"No. I mean he receives emotional satisfaction from another party for a job well done." Fraley fidgeted and said, "That is all I can tell you about him."

"Why?" I demanded, feeling shortchanged for my doughnuts.

"There is nothing else. This demon has no soul. Without a soul, I, Hakeem Manu, cannot read him clearly."

I wasn't about to stop there. Forensics hadn't managed to get any clear fingerprints, but they had pulled personal effects from Arkin's corpse and passed them on to us. I stuck my hand in the evidence bag and came up with the dead man's black horn-rim glasses. Pushing them over to Fraley, I said: "See what kind of vibes you get off these, you hustling, camel-shit cleaner."

Fraley's eyes went wide. "There is no need to be rude. I was not a camel-shit cleaner, as you say. I was a royal scribe."

"Well, royal scribe, what about the specs?"

"Odd contraptions, aren't they?" he commented, slipping them over his nose. A moment followed where he blinked and talked to himself. After going for another doughnut, he finally spoke. "I shall make a believer of you, Marshal Merrick. The man who owned these lenses was methodical to the point of ludicrousness. He would make the pharaoh's chief accountant look like a slacker. This gentleman kept records for everything. You will find an entire locker full of paper files, but you'll have to hurry, because someone wants them more than you do."

"Would that someone be the guy in the photo?"

"I told you I cannot see more of him, so desist in your efforts to weasel an answer from me." He glanced at LaRue. "You will find what you need at the Sixth Street subway station."

16

JULIE APPROVED OUR request for a couple of ward cops to check out the subway station based on Fraley's psychic interpretation. I chucked the afternoon by managing to squeeze in an appointment with my shrink.

Myra Fontaine is a beautiful woman and a knowledgeable psychiatrist. She also has a high-pitched, nasally voice, which she uses with laserlike precision to drill her opinions into my psyche. I've never called to schedule a session; in fact, I usually try to escape these meetings before they're over. Yet this time I came to her troubled by the unreasonable fear I'd felt that morning and geared myself to sweat out the screech to learn if I'd gone around the lycanthropic bend.

I got to the point as I slipped onto the couch. "I'm becoming unreliable to my partner, Myra. I'm afraid I'm not going to be there when he needs me."

"Has he confessed this concern to you?" she asked, settling in behind her notepad.

"No. Andy trusts me."

"But you don't trust yourself."

I glanced at her, abruptly irritated that she'd used her shrink sight to zoom in on my problem. "Before you and Gibson came into my life, I could count on regular lunar cycles. The same things occurred each month, but since you two have been dinking in my noodle, I'm not sure of a goddamned thing anymore."

She watched me silently. I knew from her squint, she was waiting for me to stop dancing around the maypole.

"No, I don't trust myself anymore." A sigh got by me and gave away my frustration.

"What happened?" she asked.

"I can't keep doing this to Andy. He's becoming more like a nursemaid than a partner."

Her tone turned squeaky and demanding. "What happened?"

Why was it so difficult to let go of this? When I didn't answer, she started talking about brain chemicals and the harmonics of the subtle mind, but after her first sentence, I lost her lecture. Instead, I focused upon the shrill quality she exuded. The moment my eyes started watering from the sounds, I stopped her by blurting: "I experienced a sudden, uncontrollable fear today while I was pursuing someone."

She didn't miss a beat, turning immediately with the stream. "Did you have a seizure?"

"No."

"Have you experienced a seizure lately?"

"Yes."

"What changes did you have during this episode?"

"The usual. Hearing, vision, changes in my skeletal structure and musculature."

"And what else?"

I studied her for a moment. "You should have been a marshal. You really know how to press down on a point."

She smiled, but ignored my attempt at veering off the subject. "What else did you experience in this last stretch?"

"Tactile changes," I answered finally. "Lots of static electricity. I can't seem to touch anything without getting zapped."

"With this weather front coming in, everybody is experiencing that. What else?"

"It feels like I'm wearing fur on the underside of my skin."

Her face took on that crusty look shrinks give you when they think they have a new symptom to play with. "Have you talked to Lane about this?"

"Gibson and I have been holding a yelling match for the last three days. And no, I haven't discussed it with him."

"What does this fur feel like?"

I shrugged. "Kind of itchy."

"Did this itchiness get worse with this dramatic increase of fear?"

"I didn't notice."

"What does it feel like now?"

"Like I'm wearing a scratchy wool sweater." I was tempted

to let my impatience rocket into the room, but I managed to keep myself from growling. "I'm not worried about the inside-out fur. It's this fear I felt. I froze. Paralyzed. Stiff as a stiff; and I'm lucky not to be a stiff."

"Why?"

"Because I had my weapon drawn. The perp could have used it on me." I slid from the couch to take a stroll around her well-appointed office. Pausing before a shelf decorated with pre-Columbian art, I made a show of studying a small sculpture. This feigned interest didn't fool her.

"What else did you feel besides fear?" she asked.

"I had that shakiness you get when you think you're trapped," I answered, without turning.

"You don't like that feeling. We both know that."

She had a blitzkrieg bedside manner. "Yes. You're right." I spun on my heel and settled onto the couch again before throwing in a logical reason my ego could live with. "The trapped feeling could have come from the fact that I'd lost my sidearm and had an unpredictable perp on my hands."

"I agree," she said. "What else did you experience?"

I thought about keeping this insane part to myself, but found to my chagrin that my willpower was laced with a need to know. "I felt as though something terrible might happen. You know, Myra, I've faced down killers and not had that sensation. I don't like it."

She nodded and studied me silently.

"What do you think happened to me?" I asked tentatively.

"Without further tests, I can't be sure, but from your brief description, it sounds like you had a phobic panic attack."

That didn't sound good. "What causes it?"

"Well, we believe the brain has a hiccup, of sorts. The normal flow of neurotransmitters abruptly reconfigures and sends in conflicting signals. It's a disorder that can affect people at different times of their lives and many more women experience it than men." She stopped speaking to gauge the impact of her words. I must have been a blank slate, because she continued with her lecture. "The thunder and lightning could be the cause of the phobic panic. It might also be the sudden downpour. One thing we do know, though—the anticipation is worse than the actual situation. Our imaginations really do make mountains out of molehills."

I sat there nodding as I gnawed around a burning question. Finally, I shoved it through my lips. "Tell me something, Myra. Is it possible I could be experiencing stretches on some new level, one that doesn't involve the pain I've come to associate with these transformations, but instead reacts within a zone of panic attacks?"

She frowned and, for once, could not give me the whining answer I'd hoped to hear.

17

WHEN I RETURNED to the Office, I found out Casper Conrad had sent over another OI freakie for interviewing. There was a note from LaRue as well, informing me he was off to purchase the next ingredient on his poltergeist spray list—powdered zebra hoof. Apparently, Frank Wilson had told him he had a friend with a stash sure to rearrange the metaphysical molecules of an errant goblin for the nominal return of cold, hard credits.

I snorted at my partner's interest in this latest paranormal ploy, picked up the background folder, and stepped into the interrogation room to meet Andrea Pio.

She was an attractive woman, who came in sporting a beehive of jet-black hair and wearing a crisp pink business suit. In spite of the heat, she wasn't perspiring and her dramatic makeup was as sharp as the lines of her double-breasted jacket. She accented her look by brazenly showing off a pound of jewelry, including a large, gold-edged cameo brooch.

As I approached I smelled the odor of spray lacquer and felt a momentary gush of satisfaction. Her tresses obviously couldn't stand the humidity any better than mine.

I kicked back a chair and slid heavily into it, taking a moment to scan the info provided by the OI. She didn't speak until I popped the first question. "How long have you worked for the Office of Intelligence, Ms. Pio?"

"I thought I was here to discuss Sam Arkin and his team?" she said.

I had another nudge of pleasure when I heard the tension rise in her voice. "We'll get to good old Sam in a moment, but right now I want to know about you."

The pancake on her face cracked ever so slightly as she scowled. "I've been at the OI for almost a year."

"You're the head of the Remote Viewing Unit. Correct?"

"Yes."

"How does someone get a job like that?"

"I beg your pardon?"

"Is it a political appointment or are you a regular civil-service entrant with paranormal abilities?"

She laughed, but it sounded forced. "You must be joking. I'm an administrator. Not everyone who works for the OI is telepathic. You need a few normal people to run the place."

"Who brought you on board?"

"Casper Conrad."

I nodded and provided some silence by writing a note in the file. It was enough to get her to continue without a further prod.

"My job is to make recommendations for action on projects being worked by the remote viewers."

"Who did you report to?"

"Ingrid Calloway."

"Ingrid decided which of your recommendations she liked and which ones she thought were noise. Is that right?"

"Yes."

"You invented projects by having your remote viewers tap in on unknowing parties?"

"We do some scans, but mostly they filter through Casper. The ones that pan out go to Ingrid for consideration and approval."

"But she juggled the needs of a lot of other sections, too, didn't she?"

"Yes." Frowning, she added a question. "I understood we wouldn't be speaking about Mrs. Calloway."

"We're not," I answered. "We're only establishing background. Now tell me, did she ever pull your people for other projects, despite your recommendations?"

She remained as cool as one of LaRue's garlic-vodka smoothies. "Yes."

"Was that what happened with Teresa Yarnell?"

Her composure waffled, but she fixed it before she answered. "I thought we were going to discuss Sam Arkin," she said again.

"As far as I'm concerned, we are," I growled. "Did Ingrid Calloway request Mrs. Yarnell to be her personal secretary?"

"No," she said. "No, I recommended she be reassigned."

"Why?"

"Because she was incompetent as a remote clairvoyant. They made a mistake with her. She had negligible abilities. Her reasoning broke down when she needed to submit her reports. She may have gotten images and sounds, but she didn't know what she was looking at or when it was to take place."

"So she made a better secretary than a psychic."

"Typing doesn't take any great skill."

"If you can't do it, it does."

She shrugged. "Whatever."

"What project was Arkin's team involved in at the time of their murders?"

"Their major focus was uncovering psychic terrorism."

"And what? Replace it with the OI psychic terrorism?"

Again, she shrugged. "Policy maintains that we defend the citizens against insurgency. What is done to meet out justice changes daily."

"Who specifically was Arkin looking in on?"

"I can't tell you that."

"Why not?"

"Because it's classified. Need to know and all that."

"Well, I need to know."

"I can't tell you."

The fabric of my patience suddenly wore thin. "Who can?" I barked.

She flinched, and for a moment I thought her makeup threatened to jump off her face. "Why don't you ask Casper Conrad?" she said.

18

I MISSED CONRAD at his office, but reached him just as he came into the front door of his home.

"You are most persistent, Merrick," he greeted. "What unusual theory do you have for me this time?"

"Actually, I have more than one," I answered. "But my latest question is this: Why did you hire Andrea Pio?"

"Why did I hire her? What does that have to do with anything?"

I sighed. "What is it with you people? Every time I ask for info, I get the same runaround. Don't worry about what it has to do with anything. Just please answer the question."

"I hired her because I thought she was right for the job."

"That's the standard response I expected. What's the real reason?"

"The truth is, I had a billet to fill," he said. "We're currently looking for a permanent administrator for Ms. Pio's position. She understood it was to be a temporary assignment."

"Her file says she came from the Ministry of Humanitarian Prudence. What did she do over there?"

"She was a juror who listened to appeals for civil hearings in cases of humanitarian rights violations."

"I'll bet she heard a lot of them."

"Yes, I'm sure she did."

"I'll bet a lot of the ones she heard had to do with the sneaky shit the OI is up to."

He snorted. "Our society is in the bottom of the toilet and people are paranoid. If you ask anyone on the street, they'll tell you they think they're being watched. Truth is, we only tap in to those special cases. Why would we waste our time with the little Joes?"

"Who was important enough for Sam Arkin and his crowd to be remote viewing?"

"I told you it was a terrorist group."

"Yes, but what kind?"

He paused. I waited for an excuse and was surprised when he came up with an answer. "Psychic terrorism."

"That's a pretty broad definition, I'd say."

"All right," he answered, with a heavy breath. "Arkin kept surveillance on a psychic healer named Clement Noone."

It was just ridiculous enough to be the truth. "Psychic healing is psychic terrorism?"

"We believe he's the head of a network using the guise of the traditional healing arts to telepathically convince his patients that rebelling against the government is proper and justified."

"That sounds absurd," I said.

I heard impatience steam through his response. "Really? The government doesn't feel it's an absurd possibility, and it's the OI's mission to be on top of these things."

"It doesn't just sound absurd, it sounds like you're coddling bureaucrats suffering from runaway paranoia rooted in invisible magic."

"I'm sure there's a lot of that, too," he said. "What do you want from me? I do my job. That's it." He paused. Then: "Tell me, do you believe in the backdoor magic you see everywhere?"

"No."

"I'm surprised. Most people do."

"Well, I don't."

"Come on, Marshal. You can't tell me you aren't a little intrigued by the potential of things like love potions or good-luck charms."

"No. Every bit of it is bogus."

"I can't believe you don't have a sneaking suspicion certain supernatural things exist. What about vampires and zombies? What about werewolves?"

If I didn't know better, I would have said the guy was trying to push my buttons, but after a moment I let go of the intensity I'd wrapped into his last remark. "There is always rational, scientific theory to befoul these claims."

I could almost see him nodding as he said: "And there's always some science behind the magic, no matter how outlandish."

19

AFTER MY CALL to Conrad, I decided to get my aggravation's worth by going over to Gibson's flat to see if I could weasel some information out of him.

The good doctor's apartment always looks like it's just hosted a medical-supplies convention. He uses the main room as a storage suite and the bedroom as a makeshift lab, complete with refurbished monitors and computers, pickling jars filled with strange chemicals, and several how-to manuals on brain surgery.

As I let myself inside he was sitting on the floor picking through a new box of surgical clamps. He glanced up, but didn't offer a smile or a word of greeting, which instantly annoyed me.

"If I'm not welcome, just tell me," I snapped.

"You're welcome," he answered huskily. "You're always welcome. You know that. Is there a problem?"

"There's always a problem. It's just different week by week." I studied him before asking the favor. "I need some medical information."

"About your lycanthropy?"

"About a case."

"Oh." He picked up a foam cup and slurped from it. "You've got some gall, Merrick."

It's true—I'm made from the stuff. "I didn't come to apologize, Gibson. I still don't want to parade my lycanthropy in front of a bunch of old men who want to come up on stage and fondle me in the name of science."

"You want my cooperation," he said, tossing a package back into the box, "but don't want to give in return. It seems we've been down this street before."

"You should have accepted my feelings on this. I don't want the whole world to know."

He unfolded into a stand and eyed me with one of his squinty expressions. "You're a fucking biological wonder. The whole world should know."

"That's bullshit. From the people I've come across in the last few days, it's clear I'm no biological wonder. I'm a freak of nature, just like they are. We're scientific oddities and I'm beginning to think it's hard to build a case for a research grant when you're working with someone who should be pulling in crowds at the circus arena."

It must have been my tone of voice, because he mellowed immediately. "Who have you come across?" he asked quietly.

I sighed and stomped over to the couch. Parking my butt, I said: "We've been unlocking the secrets of the OI, and let me tell you, I don't like what I'm seeing."

He joined me on the sofa, but instead of answering, he simply frowned out into space, so I plied him for his opinion. "Do you believe in poltergeists?"

His face registered surprise and he swiveled his attention onto me. "Poltergeists? You mean goblins?"

"Well, actually, I was thinking more about the occurrence of psychokinesis."

"I have an open mind on the subject," he said. "Are you plagued by poltergeists?"

"Andy is. He's busy collecting the ingredients for a spray that's sure to kill the beggars. That is if the ingredients don't kill Andy first. One of the things he's supposed to find is mercury. He's tempted to break open a thermometer to do it."

He snorted. "Tell him not to. It's very messy and very poisonous."

"Have you ever worked with anyone who could make objects fly around rooms or appear out of thin air?"

"No, I haven't. Has this happened with LaRue?"

"He's been getting a lot of odd messages on his computer and finding his personal items ransacked. Things like that. I have a feeling we're the victims of a psionic scam."

"Now, that's interesting. You think you've angered an OI employee?"

"Could be. Is psychokinesis a functional possibility?"

"Yes," he answered. "Every person out there retains some psychokinetic ability. Still, there are very few people who can affect objects with a thought. At least, by themselves."

"What do you mean—by themselves?"

He held up his finger as a signal to pause, and then slid to a stand. Retrieving his foam cup, he rifled through the box, producing a packet of replacement needles for hypodermics. "Come here," he ordered, stepping to the kitchen table.

I did as he asked and took a seat in the chair. Gibson uncorked a plastic jug to add a little tepid water to his drink. He then floated a needle in the liquid.

"This is supposed to prove something?" I asked.

"Yes. Hold your hands, palms out, about ten inches from the cup."

I obliged.

"Now concentrate on spinning the needle."

It sounded like the good doctor was using the drugs he dispensed. "You're kidding. Right?"

He smiled. "You've spent months learning to control your lycanthropy through biofeedback. You can even initiate a stretch upon command. What makes you think you can't influence an object with thought alone?"

"I've never done it before."

"Try it now."

I shrugged and gave it a whack by imagining waves of energy coming from the center of my palms to slowly push the needle. In fact, I worked on the visualization for five minutes. The needle bobbled once, but didn't turn a circle.

Gibson came around behind me, placing his hands gently upon my shoulders. "Now, I'll transfer my psychokinetic power into you and together, we'll see what we get."

It sounded ridiculous, but I have to admit, I found his touch comforting and I didn't want him to let go, so I complied and focused on the object. No more than a minute passed before it began to spin slowly. When he moved away, the needle stopped. I glanced at him. "Why can two do it?"

"We're not sure. It may simply be a combination of magnetic forces. I haven't read about any neurological breakthroughs in psychokinesis."

It seemed I'd stumbled upon another reason for remote-viewing teams.

Gibson did an about-face on me by changing the subject. "I heard from Myra a short while ago."

"What did she say?"

"She said you finally opened up a little bit. She said it surprised her."

"It surprised me, too."

"She mentioned you may have had a phobic episode. Is that true?"

"A phobic episode?" I chuckled, but the sound slid out more darkly than I'd intended. "Is that what you call it? She referred to it as a panic attack."

"You've never experienced anything like it before?"

"No. I would have told you if I had."

"You mean the same way you told me about having stretches accompanied by an overall tingling? What did you call it? Inside-out fur?"

I shrugged, but didn't reply, basically because I didn't have any excuse ready.

He fished the needle from the cup and slid it into the plastic packet. "This time, though, symptoms occurred that surprised you, but more than that, made you worry about leaving LaRue behind on the line. Has it ever occurred to you that you place everyone else's needs above your own? That is, everyone's but mine."

"I didn't come here for a lecture, Gibson."

"It wouldn't do any good anyway." He tossed the needles back into the box. "So, what frightened you?"

"Thunder and lightning, I guess."

"Was it the noise or the electricity?"

"I'm not sure. All I know is that I couldn't move, because I was terrified."

"We discovered a few years back that phobias often arise when the brain's neurons misfire while sending an impulse along nerve axons."

"You've lost me already," I said.

"Neurons are nerve cells and axons are the neurons' conducting fiber. Think of it as an electrical cord. The analogy fits, because the nerve cells produce electrical impulses. When the jolt reaches the axon terminal it releases the chemical combination for the neurotransmitter. Depending on the stimuli, there are various chemicals involved."

"And these substances are made of amino acids," I said.

He frowned. "Yes. Amino acids form peptides, which are protein fragments found in the nerve cells. How did you know this?"

"The case we're dealing with right now may have something to do with amino dubbing."

His expression slid into a scowl, but he didn't comment on it. "There are different kinds of nerve cells, and the ones we think are involved in phobias have to do with sensory receptors. These receptors are found all over the body and are attuned to the external environment."

"What you're saying is that a problem exists somewhere between the receptors and the neurons and either the noise or the light of the storm prompted my brain to release inappropriate chemicals."

"It may not be a problem, Merrick. It may simply be a change that comes with your lycanthropy."

"How do I control it?"

"Mind over matter. Mental paradigms can be programmed into your physiology. Your thoughts actually control which brain chemicals are stimulated." He raised his hand.

"Before you ask—we don't know how or why it happens. Psychiatric techniques are the best thing to combat a phobic panic attack."

"Back to Myra, huh?"

"While I'm paying for it you might as well take advantage of the help."

I rose, definitely ready to go home and hide from the world for eight hours. "I'll see you, Gibson," I said, my hand contacting the doorknob.

"Yes, you will," he answered. "Tomorrow, in fact. I made an appointment for you to undergo a neural scan at the hospital tomorrow at eight A.M. Don't be late."

20

THE HOMICIDE SECRETARY on the night shift had been his ever-efficient self and had completed the rundown on Clement Noone. LaRue picked me up from the hospital with the interviewee's address in hand and a car that smelled like it had been dowsed in kerosene. In fact, it had.

I glanced toward the rear dashboard and saw his Lenin doll bobbing peacefully in its place. "I take it the stink in here is the result of an interim poltergeist fix?"

LaRue grinned, ground the gears, and headed for the chuckholes. "I think it's working."

"It smells bad enough to keep anything away," I answered. "In this heat, Andy, it's going to really hurt to draw a deep breath."

"We'll leave the windows open."

I know when I'm up against a metaphysical principle I can't lick, so to combat it, I sowed the seed of doubt in LaRue's mind by telling him about the experiment of the evening before, ending with: "Gibson thinks goblins are crap."

My partner threw me a quick glance. "I just don't like to consider the possibility that we're under psionic attack. It goes against all my sensibilities." He took the corner too sharply and scraped a tire against the curb. Another thirty seconds passed while he fought to keep control as the Trabi bucked over a bump on its way back to hug the double yellow line.

I tried a little logic on him. "He told me this morning that scientists aren't even close to understanding the biological structures necessary for psi-talent. They haven't identified a particular place in the brain where these abilities originate, but they have measured chemical changes within neuron activity."

LaRue grunted. "Like I said, it makes my crotch itch just to think about it."

My partner always works from the "better safe than sorry" theory. I would be made to sniff noxious fumes until we found out for sure what caused our haunting.

I let the subject drop and listened to his theories on goblins, ghosts, and residual energy. He then moved into quantum theory busted up with occult hypotheses, and reflected upon the possibility that the absurd daytime temperatures were causing fractures in our space-time reality and that's why we were experiencing poltergeist activity. By the time we arrived at Clement Noone's apartment building, I was ready to jump into one of those dimensional fissures just to escape the one-sided discussion.

The high-rise was dingy and run-down. Because nonessential buildings were deleted from the energy grid, the elevator was out of order and we were forced to climb eleven floors up a grimy stairwell. People crammed the landings, pushed from their makeshift hovels on the street by the Hurricane Management Team. They were the poorest of the poor, beggars who rallied around guilt, the touchstone of our humanitarian society.

LaRue tossed out a bag of stale cookies and I handed over a broken watch Baba had found in the garbage dumpster by our walk-up. The odors of urine and sweating bodies threatened to undo me, but I made it to Noone's front door without gagging. He answered immediately, and to my surprise, I saw that he only had one leg.

"We'd like to speak to you about a murder investigation," LaRue announced in a low, serious tone.

Noone scraped his dirty hand through his thin, greasy, brown hair and reversed direction on his crutch to let us enter.

I expected a dismal atmosphere, but again, found my amaze-o-meter on tilt. The apartment was large, airy, and filled with plush needlepoint pillows, bright rag rugs, and hand-knitted afghans and blankets. Noone hobbled to a couple of canvas beanbag chairs and watched us flop onto the cushions and skootch our butts around in search of comfort and balance. It was hard to look menacing when it was possible to tip over backward at any time.

He offered us some tea and then sat down in a heavy mahogany rocker. "I'm a healer," he said quietly. "I don't know anything about murder."

"You're not under suspicion, Mr. Noone," I said. "At least, not from us. Would you be so kind as to tell us what kind of healing you do?"

"I work with people's L-fields."

"And that is?"

"Scientists have discovered that every living thing produces a weak, though measurable, electric field. It's believed this field contains the blueprints of the organism and shapes it according to transient fluctuations. In fact, it's well known that each cell in the body possesses an electric field of its own. By taking readings with a digital millivolt meter, I can determine various changes in a person's physiology."

His explanation made me think of Baba and her odic tinklers, and so to avoid saying something smart-ass, I drank my tea, letting LaRue engage in the philosophy of spirit healing.

"I take it diseases cause various pulsations within a stable L-field," he said.

Noone smiled. He was missing one of his front teeth. "That's right. You understand this science, I see."

"Some of it," LaRue answered. "Once you find a problem, how do you cure it?"

"We know that the L-field contains and controls the organism's basic patterns. I have the ability to intervene in the patient's electric flow, and like a catalyst, I can assist the cells in re-forming and restructuring."

"How do you do that?"

"The energy is carried as impulses through the nerve endings in my hands."

Upon hearing the words *nerve endings,* I jumped into the conversation. "Do you touch the person?"

"No, I don't," he said. "I don't have to."

"Have you had any verifiable medical successes?"

"Healing is my purpose in life," he answered simply.

"Do you keep the names and addresses of your healing miracles?" I snapped.

"Yes."

"We want your list, please."

He shrugged. "I suppose I couldn't stop you from taking it anyway. I'll get it for you before you leave."

"How much do you charge, Mr. Noone?"

"Nothing."

We both stared at him, and he laughed. "Is that so hard to believe?"

"Yes," I answered.

"A cure is free."

A one-legged man, who gave out freebies, didn't sound like a terrorist, psychic or otherwise. It was time to cut the calf from the thigh. "Mr. Noone, do you realize that you've been under OI investigation?"

"It comes as no surprise."

"They believe you're engaged in subversive activities."

He took a swig from his drink and paused to set it on the small table flanking his chair. "Tell me, Marshal, how am I supposed to be doing this?"

"Telepathic brainwashing was how it was related to me."

He laughed again. "I'm not a telepath. The people over there are hallucinating, as usual."

"You deny there is a psychic network?"

"There might be, but I have nothing to do with it."

"Have you ever heard the term *Manjinn*?" I asked.

He frowned. "It doesn't sound familiar."

LaRue switched gears. "You used to work for the OI, didn't you?"

"Yes, I did. It was a long time ago and then, not for very long."

"Why?"

"Because they didn't consider me talented enough for their needs."

"But now they think you're dangerous."

He shrugged. "I help people. That makes me dangerous, I suppose."

I tried to lean forward in the squishy chair, but couldn't. "Do you work with other spiritual healers?"

"Well, we don't hold conventions, if that's what you mean. I do keep in touch with friends who have the power to change lives."

"Do you know if any of them have been dismissed from OI service?" I asked.

"It's possible. You'll have to ask them." He paused to pick up his drink and sip it.

LaRue jumped into the lull. "Have you ever promised to heal someone and then found you were unable to do it?"

"I make no guarantees," he said, smacking his lips. "I'm sure there are people I've tried to help who were lost causes. It's not just the initial healing, you understand. The patient must then take responsibility for his own life after that. If a person thinks his days are filled with pain and suffering, then his days are piled high with it. You can't cure the body without working on the mind."

"To your knowledge, have you been on the receiving end of an OI paranormal scam?"

"I don't have anything anybody would want," he said simply.

I pulled Kelly Bates's photo from my pocket and showed it to him. "Do you recognize this man?"

He hid any expression with his tea glass. "I don't recall ever seeing him before." Lowering his tea glass, he asked: "Is this your killer?"

"According to the person who took the picture," I said.

Noone dropped the subject abruptly by standing up and balancing on one leg. "If you'll wait a moment, I'll bring you my files." As he hobbled off toward the other room he paused to stare directly at me and said: "Tell me, if the psychics and telepaths over at the OI are so good, why can't they track down the murderer themselves?"

21

As WE WERE leaving Clement Noone's apartment, dispatch called to inform us that Samuel Arkin's mother waited to speak to us. We hurried back to the office, pushing through streets crowded with folks who had been dismissed early when the factories closed in preparation for the hurricane.

I listened to the reports coming over the array while LaRue did his best not to run anyone over. The communications were dismal, to say the least. Two districts to the south had been completely annihilated. The management teams had already transferred thousands of refugees into safer districts; yet it remained a tragic situation with a large loss of life. The information focused on the expanding humanitarian relief effort, but instead of sympathizing with beleaguered family units, I grew more and more worried about the toll it would take on my pocketbook. I could almost count the increase in my environmental taxes.

When we arrived, we found Mrs. Arkin waiting patiently in the interrogation room for our return. Sam's mama sported long red tresses teased into a springy bouffant. Her turquoise eye shadow and ruby lipstick clashed with her atomic-pink blouse, green striped pedal pushers, and yellow plastic sandals. She sucked on a warm can of soda and boldly toked on an illegal cigarette, flicking the ashes into the air with a flourish.

"I've been in such a state over Sammy's death," she wailed. "The doctor recommended nicotine to calm my nerves. If I don't get some information soon, I'm going to be addicted to ciggies again." She paused to push a stare our way. "Those bastards at the OI wouldn't tell me a damned thing, so I came here."

85

"We can't tell you much either, Mrs. Arkin," I answered, sliding a chair up to the table. "Maybe you can help us."

"Anything, anything. My Sammy didn't deserve to die like that, even if he was a shithead."

"Pardon me?" I said.

"He was a son-of-a-bitch, Marshal. Those are the only kind of people the OI hires. And you can be sure, he didn't get that act from me. I'm the kindest soul the Creator ever put on earth, even if I've got to make the claim myself."

"We don't have much personal information on your son."

"Well, let me be the first to bring this glaring fact to your attention. He was greedy, arrogant, and obsessive."

LaRue sank his teeth into the subject. "Obsessive?"

"Yes. St. Ophelia knows he wasn't that way before going to the OI. I taught him to be a humanitarian. He even got some awards for service to his fellow man. But that was a long time ago. After he signed on to be a remote viewer, he changed. Six months of working for them and I didn't recognize my baby boy anymore."

"What was he obsessive about?" LaRue asked.

"Well, being clean, for one thing. He would drive me nuts with his picky crap." She leaned forward and spoke in a conspiratorial tone. "I don't keep a nice house. Never have. I've always been more interested in my career. I was a caseworker for the Office of Humanitarian Welfare." She paused to puff and then said: "Anyway, helping folks has always been more important than chasing dust bunnies around the bedroom floor."

"But after Sam started at the OI, he no longer agreed."

She flicked her ashes, watching a moment as they floated down to the table. "That's right. I knew there was something different about him when one day we had a fight over a stain on the living-room rug. That stain had been there for twenty years. In fact, it was Sam who made it. He spilled raspberry juice. Well, one day he decided he would scrub that spot until it came out. He spent hours hunched over it and wore the rug down. I could see the floor beneath it! That's when I got mad and told him to stop."

"What happened then?"

"He threw the sponge and the bucket at me and stomped out. So, there I was, left with a bigger mess."

"Did he demonstrate any other mental problems?" I asked.

"As far as I'm concerned, he did. He had a crazy thing about being afraid to go out of his apartment. After a while he stopped visiting me altogether. When his father died, he didn't even go to the burial." She halted to drop her cigarette butt into the soda can. I heard the hiss as the liquid extinguished the ember. "It was a nice service, too. We donated the body to science. At least his father didn't become furnace fuel at some factory."

My thoughts steered toward my own panic attacks, but wound back around to Arkin. "Can you tell us if your son suffered from phobias?"

"Well, I don't know that you would call them phobias, exactly. Sammy said he would die if he went outside. I just think he was scared of someone hurting him."

"Did he have a lot of enemies?"

She pulled another smoke from her purse and made a production of lighting it before she answered. "My son didn't have one enemy when he was living at home with me. Everybody loved Sammy."

"Did your son ever tell you about how his team would run scams on people by using their remote-viewing talents?"

"I don't know about that. He had some nice things, though, and I'm sure his paycheck didn't cover the cost of some of them. By the way, I'm laying claim to his stuff. There wasn't a will, you know; least none was filed in the district court. I checked. Since I'm his only living relative, those things are mine. When do you think your folks will be done with his apartment? I'd like to see what I inherited."

"We don't have a time frame at this moment, Mrs. Arkin," LaRue said. "Getting back to your son. What else can you tell us about his mental stability?"

She sighed dramatically. "He imagined things."

"What kind of things?"

"Once, he thought I was a hooker. Do you believe that? Me, a prosti?"

I kept my opinion down a rabbit hole. "What did he do?"

"What?" She placed the cigarette firmly between her lips,

stood up, and lifted the back of her blouse slightly, exposing a jagged scar. Speaking around the cancer stick, she explained. "This is what he did. Pretty, ain't it? Took my boyfriend and three others to get him off me. I was in the hospital for days. Almost didn't make it."

"Why did he believe you were a prostitute?"

"Who knows? Personally, I think it was because he was working on something over at the OI involving ladies of the evening."

"Do you know any of the particulars of this case?"

"Only that the hookers weren't the kind of sluts who walk the streets. These were the telepathic kind. The guy running the ring billed it as a psychic peep show. It was real popular on the back-door market a few years ago. You can't imagine the number of folks who get off on some bitch telling them particulars about their private lives while doing their private parts." She chuckled and lowered her shirt.

LaRue glanced at me. "We never get the really juicy assignments."

I grinned, but directed my question to Mrs. Arkin. "So, he confused his own reality with the one he picked up telepathically?"

She sat back down, drew another smoky breath, and spoke while she exhaled. "That's what the doctor said. He told me it happens a lot. When the hallucinations get bad, they're supposed to retire them."

"You're speaking about remote viewers. Is that correct?"

"Yeah. I don't know how they treat other folks at the OI."

"But the OI let your son keep working."

She looked at me like my nose had grown into a wolf's snout. "Who told you that? Sammy left the OI a couple of years ago. His buddies, Ford and Drake, did, too."

"He retired?" I said.

"No, they were forced out. All three of them."

"Why?"

"Because the OI didn't want to give them the pension they deserved. Simple as that."

22

AFTER OUR CHAT with Samuel Arkin's mother, we decided it was time to check out some names on Clement Noone's list, but the only one who answered our call was a psychic healer called Parnell Bowen. We tracked down his address to a place in Ward 65, a neighborhood known as the Great Sleazy Cheesy Way. The carnal pleasures of this strip worked in conveyor-belt fashion: a person could get screwed, stewed, and tattooed, and be on his way by hour's end, armed with a hefty pepperoni-and-anchovy pizza for the wife and kids. It was the last place you would expect to see people spray-painting their doorways with mystical signs, yet the shacks and walk-ups looked like they were decorated for Halloween.

Bowen lived in an apartment over a bar-and-grill. As we walked up the narrow steps I caught the fragrance of greasy french fries mixing with musky perfume. The floor of his flat was no barrier against this rise of smells, and once inside, I almost fainted when I breathed in the heavy essence of sandalwood.

My lycanthropy comes with a variety of confusing sensations. Its onset will occasionally leave me with a condition known as synesthesia or blended senses. If, for instance, a strong smell overwhelms me, the odor will register as a blast of colors on my optic nerve. In this case, I saw splotches of olive green and yellow. Gibson has yet to tell me why I desensitize after a couple of minutes and the colors fade, but true to form, I started to regain my eyesight within moments.

Bowen greeted us wearing a sweaty, blue spandex body suit that did nothing to enhance his slight build. He had wispy blond hair and a warm smile and he talked about the weather as he led us through a front room decorated with floor pillows and strange sculptures made of brass hangers and fluorescent bulbs. I thought about Baba's tinklers and was grateful she didn't create charm magic on a large scale.

"You're just in time to see a healing," Bowen said. "That is, if you can stand it."

"Why?" I asked. "Is it going to be bloody?"

"Oh, yes. As is per the usual."

I stopped walking. "I thought spirit healing was a no-fuss, no-pus, no-blood occupation."

Bowen opened the door to the back room before answering. "Well, it is difficult to extract teeth without getting a little red on you."

"You're a dentist?" I asked, unable to hide my surprise.

"Yes. Didn't Clement tell you?"

"No. He gave us a list of people he'd helped and your name was on it."

He nodded. "Clement is the reason I'm in business today." His explanation drifted into an introduction with his client. She sat in a worn-out examining chair, wearing a paper bib and a swollen jaw.

"Miss St. Clair has an impacted wisdom tooth," he explained. "Her PHO dental insurance ran out and she needs to have this thing pulled."

"An impacted tooth?" LaRue said.

"That's right. It's under the skin and growing sideways along the jawbone."

He went to a chest of drawers and removed a pair of rubber gloves. As he slipped them on he announced that his medical knowledge was gained by conventional means. "Her X rays are on the counter, if you'd like to check."

LaRue did just that while I continued to hammer Bowen. "You mentioned it was because of Noone, you're a healer. What did he do?"

"He healed me of spinal cancer."

"Excuse me for asking, but are you sure you had it?"

"It's well documented through the PHO. I had three months to live, maybe less. When I finally found Noone, I was close to death and praying it would come sooner than later."

"So, in a blinding explosion of white light, you were all better?"

"The first time I met with him, I couldn't move. The cancer had caused paralysis and I was in constant agony."

I winced, despite myself.

He saw my expression and nodded. "I'm telling you the sad truth. Since I was so far gone, Noone had to bring me back by stages. He did a series of intercessionary healings."

"Which are?" LaRue asked as he squinted at the tiny X ray.

"He changed my healing frequency with thought."

My partner lowered the picture to stare at Bowen. "How did he do that?"

"Well, it's an old concept. Back in the mid-twentieth century, there was an experiment where researchers paired prayer and petri dishes. The experiment was to see if they could change a collection of diseased cells into healthy cells just through the power of directed thought."

"Did they?"

"Yes. That's what Clement does. His central nervous system sends out some sort of impulse and he heals the tears in the L-field."

"You said his thoughts heal," I interrupted. "You're talking about an energy source contained within his nerves."

"That's right. You have to remember that thinking is involved on two levels. The invisible manifestation of the subtle mind and the electrochemical process of the brain, that which comprises the central nervous system."

"So, this intercessionary healing is just temporary," LaRue said.

"That's right. A complete recovery depends upon how successfully the person can change their thoughts at both levels."

I began to smell a scam floating through the sandalwood. "Let me guess?" I said. "Noone invited you back repeatedly to teach you how to do this."

Bowen looked surprised. "Yes. He holds meditation sessions almost nightly."

"How much does he charge per session?"

"People donate as much as they like." He turned back to his patient. "Open wide, please." As she did he pushed his fingers into her mouth and then angled his attention toward us. "Clement Noone is an upstanding individual. He taught me

how to cycle my L-field so I could pass my fingers through
flesh without harming the person."

LaRue and I didn't reply because we were busy watching
him grope his way down the woman's throat. She appeared to
be in no pain from his probing.

"Have you ever worked for the Office of Intelligence?" I
asked.

"No." With that, he muttered, "I've found the root." He
placed his free hand against the woman's shoulder and yanked.
Blood spurted around his fingers and dripped onto the bib.
When he disconnected, I saw that he did, indeed, hold a tooth.
Unfortunately, I couldn't tell whether it was the actual thing or
a deft sleight-of-hand trick.

"What did you do before becoming a spiritual dentist?" I
asked.

He smiled and tossed the tooth into a metal bowl. "I was a
plumber."

23

WHEN WE RETURNED to the Trabi, LaRue characteristically glanced in the rearview mirror, but rather than turning his attention to the dashboard choke, he paused to curse at his reflection.

"What's wrong, Andy?" I asked, sliding in beside him.

He didn't respond. Instead, he knocked the mirror my direction. There, printed in small red letters was the message: DO YOU KNOW HOW ENTANGLED YOU ARE?

Fascinating. I rubbed at the words with my fingernail, but they wouldn't scrape off. Squinting didn't make them change or disappear.

LaRue smoothed his hand down his braid, clipped on a baleful expression, and sighed.

I pushed the mirror his direction again. "Andy, someone is tugging on our shorts."

"But who?"

"The more people we interview, the more I suspect everyone."

He didn't add any more to the current conversation; instead, he shoved the clutch into first gear and headed back to the office. I expected some comments about spiritual dentistry, but his attention was fixed soundly upon the street and the growing confusion of the citizens. He carefully wove his way around a district dump truck reassigned to collect and transport refugees from neighborhoods where the houses were made of corrugated aluminum and sticks. At one point we were halted by a cordon of ward cops, who tried to contain an outbreak of looting. We narrowly escaped being squeezed into service when the sergeant begging for our help paused to chase a guy who ran down the street carrying a pawnshop vid machine.

When we heard gunfire, we knew we had better things to do and hurried away.

While we were at the office Julie called another quick staff meeting to add more urgency to our day. All nonessential government agencies had closed down for business until the storm had passed through. Electricity was scheduled to be rotated off the grid at six P.M., except at the Marshals Office, the hospital, and the fire departments. According to the official reports, the hurricane had reached number five on the Saphir-Simpson Scale with sustained winds clocked at 175 miles per hour. Emergency shelters had been organized, but with a tempest like that, many of the buildings wouldn't be there by the time it was over. One thing was certain: This storm was going to blow us up the butthole of the universe.

We tried not to worry about the inevitable and sent a couple of idle cops to invite Mrs. Hibiscus Greeley in for a conversation. Greeley was Sam Arkin's maid and the poor lady who'd found the team after their mysterious demise. She responded to our request within the hour, bringing an offering of homemade mint cookies with her.

"I had some extras," she said, unloading a wicker hamper onto the greasy table in the interrogation room. "I thought it would be prudent to do as much cooking as I could before the district turned off the power."

LaRue gobbled up two of the patties before he'd even swung into the chair. "Thanks for the kindness," he said, but then launched immediately into his questions. "Mrs. Greeley, how long did you work for Samuel Arkin?"

"Just a little over a year," she answered.

"Did he introduce you to any of his team members?"

"Well, I knew Mr. Drake and Mr. Ford. I never got acquainted with the others."

"Others?"

"Yes. There were always five or six people working when I would come to clean."

"What kind of work were they doing?" I asked.

She shrugged with her hands. "They would sit around with paper and pencil, stare off into the distance, and then quick— write down stuff. I thought they were writing reports or something when I first started, but then I found out what they really did."

"Which was?"

"Spying on people," she whispered.

"Do you know which people?"

"No. I'm not sure about any of that and I tried to steer clear of involvement. You don't want the OI on your back. I've heard the horror stories."

"That's odd," I said. "I'm not aware of these stories."

"Oh, I've heard them for years. Awful stuff. Such things as only can be done in fairy tales." She leaned forward. "I've heard they have successfully given a dog a human brain."

I almost laughed, but then realized she was being genuine. "We're more interested in what they do to human brains inside human bodies."

"Oh. I don't know much about those things. I suspect I wouldn't like it if I found out."

"Did you ever see Samuel Arkin lose his temper?" LaRue asked, reaching for another cookie.

"Once. He slammed his fist through the wall. He was mad about something. I never did know the what-fors, though."

"Did he ever harm you?"

"No. Mr. Arkin was always polite."

"Did he ever give you trouble about the way you cleaned his house?"

"Not that I recall. He did ask me not to touch his expensive Monet painting. I suppose he had a special way of cleaning that."

"What about going out? Did he ever leave the house while you were there?"

"He was always home when I worked. I can't tell you about his social life, because I just don't know anything."

"Are you aware of anyone ever coming to his apartment to threaten him?"

"Not while I was there."

"Do you recall anything unusual on the day of the murders?" I asked.

She thought a moment. "He asked me to come early that day. He said he, Mr. Ford, and Mr. Drake had a business meeting that evening and he wanted everything to be sparkling."

"Were you there when the meeting began?"

"No. I left right after finishing my chores." Then, frowning slightly, she added: "I did have to come back, though, because I forgot my house slippers. Bunions, you know. The big toe on my right foot gives me a fit sometimes."

I suddenly felt hopeful. The maid's bad feet might give us the break we needed. "Did you walk in on the meeting?"

"No. It was over. I found them dead." Her tiny hands flickered over the hamper.

"Is there something else?" I asked.

"I don't know how much help it will be."

"Anything, Mrs. Greeley, could help."

"I'd just stepped off the elevator when I noticed a man come out of the apartment."

My spit traveled down my windpipe and I hacked a question as I cleared my throat. "You didn't mention it in your report."

She winced. "I know. I didn't think about it. I was pretty shaky, as you might guess."

I pulled the photo from my pocket and, in my impatience, tore the corner. "Is this the man you saw?"

Studying the picture, she nodded. "That's him. He was very kind. I dropped my tote bag and spilled a bag of beans on the carpet right there in the hallway. This gentleman stopped and helped me scoop them up. We had a pleasant conversation for about fifteen minutes."

"What did you talk about?" LaRue asked.

"Bean recipes."

"Is that all?"

"Just beans. He seemed very knowledgeable."

"Did he introduce himself?"

"No, not that I remember. He did make sure to shake my hand, though."

24

IT WAS TIME to see our tulpa-card collector, a man by the name of Raymond Vinson. From what we found, it appeared dealing in demons was a lucrative enterprise. Vinson owned a mansion, the grounds of which were protected by a twenty-foot stone wall, and once through the double cast-iron gate, we had to follow a long, winding driveway to the front door.

This decadent fantasy came complete with a butler to lead us through rooms molded in money, and entering by a set of French doors, we found ourselves standing in the middle of a lush, cool arboretum. He had wealth and air-conditioning, two facts that irritated me to no end. My annoyance tripled when Vinson stepped from a steaming hot tub wearing a nasty attitude and nothing else.

"Your visit places me at an inconvenience," he snapped. "You could have at least had the courtesy to call for an appointment. I'm preparing for a gathering tonight and this puts me behind schedule." He then ignored us as his butler dried him down with a thick white towel and covered him with a red terry robe. Sliding into a lounge chair, he took another moment to order a cigar from the servant.

LaRue started the inquiries in a serious tone. "Mr. Vinson, we're here concerning a triple murder."

He shrugged. "I'm sure there are triple murders every day. Why should this one concern me?"

I slammed into the conversation. "As it stands, you may well be an accessory to this crime."

"Oh, come now," he answered languidly.

It was all I could do not to launch myself toward his throat, so LaRue came to the rescue by holding his hand out for the photo. I slapped it into his palm and decided it might be better if I made an inspection tour of the arboretum while my partner worked the interview.

LaRue walked to the table and presented Vinson with the picture. "Do you know this man?"

I didn't have to turn around to hear uncertainty bite into his voice. "Is this your killer?"

"Perhaps. Again, I ask: Do you know him?"

Vinson hedged the answer by relighting his cigar, and when an answer didn't arrive in a punctual manner, LaRue was forced to grab the man by his lapels and haul him to a stand. He went nose to nose with the guy, which must have caused Vinson considerable displeasure. My partner had eaten a raw onion sandwich for lunch.

"Your labor designation hasn't been activated since you moved to this district," he said. "For a man who doesn't work, I'd say you have a nice house. I'm inclined to think you're doing something illegal to pay the mortgage."

Vinson was as young and as muscular as LaRue, but was powerless against my partner's grip. If he was going to free himself, he would have to tear the fabric. "I inherited my wealth," he whined. "My family were Duvalier supporters. My money is legitimate."

"We don't know all your money is legitimate, now, do we? As marshals, it's our right to question inconsistencies, and since we have some doubt about your claim, I guess we'll have to turn our suspicions over to the Office of Environmental Taxes."

LaRue had tapped just the right button, because Vinson scowled, but nodded. "I'll tell you what I can."

With that, my partner released him. "Now, I will ask one more time. Do you know the man in the photo?"

Vinson reseated himself. "Yes. His name is Jerome Taggart."

"How do you know him?"

"He wrote me a letter."

"Why?"

"He said he was a student of Tibetan art and he wanted to talk to me about my tulpa-card collection."

"Did you invite him over?"

"Not at first. I didn't have a background on this man. I wasn't sure who he was."

"What changed your mind?"

Vinson glanced at the floor. "You know, it goes against everything I usually do, but I reconsidered. I don't know why. The district is full of hooligans and I try to avoid these unsolicited entanglements."

I shot a look toward LaRue. His face was hidden to me, but his body had stiffened upon hearing this confession. I'll admit, I experienced a moment of rigidity as I considered the possibilities of remote mind control, but then discarded them as theories of a runaway imagination. Considering that wealth always fosters big egos, it seemed logical that Vinson had merely reviewed and reevaluated the request.

"What happened next?" LaRue demanded.

"I invited him to dinner so we could discuss the collection."

"Did anyone come with him?"

"His sister."

"What was her name?"

Vinson opened his mouth to speak, but then shook his head. "It's the strangest thing. I can't seem to recall." He picked up a small bell from the table and rang it. Several seconds later the butler returned. "Charles, do you remember the name of the young woman who came with Mr. Taggart the evening we dined together?"

The servant grunted. "No, sir. She did not introduce herself to me."

Vinson shrugged and glanced at the both of us. "Sorry. It's rude to ask someone their name a second time and I have such a short attention span when it comes to minutiae."

"But you do recall discussing the tulpa card collection?" I asked.

Vinson waved away the butler. After he was gone, he said: "Mr. Taggart was quite knowledgeable about Tibetan mythology."

"Did he mention something called a Manjinn?"

"Yes."

"Tell us what a Manjinn is, then."

"The ancient Tibetans relied on the existence of demons to explain the hardships of everyday life. One story refers to a powerful priest who wanted to bestow a special gift to the people of the local village for their service to the Buddhist temple, so he created the Manjinn. This demon is considered to have two faces—one of a man and the other of a djinn—a magical creature capable of granting everlasting life."

LaRue sprinted past Vinson. "So, the Manjinn was squeezed together from beings that already existed."

"A tulpa is a thought form. It can be made from anything the creator desires."

"What did this demon do?"

"This tulpa was responsible for healing disease in the village."

"But it got away from the priest."

"Yes. In turn, it started dealing out disease."

"Why did Taggart want to know about the Manjinn?"

"I don't know his motivation. He didn't tell me."

"Did you show him your collection?"

"Yes. He was appropriately awed."

"I take it you own a Manjinn card?"

"As a matter of fact, I don't. I have texts that show pictures of it, but not the real thing."

I whipped out the card I carried and flashed it at him. "Would this be the one?"

Vinson's whole body seemed to collapse under his fluffy robe. "My God, yes, that's it. Where did you get it?"

"At the crime scene."

"May I see it?"

I flicked it to LaRue, who passed it on. Vinson studied the card, shaking his head. "It's beautiful, but not genuine, of course. A real one is worth several thousand credits."

"Did the sister say anything during this time?"

He shook his head and handed the card back to LaRue. "I really don't think she said much of anything. If I remember, she wasn't very interested in the whole proceeding. She didn't even seem interested in the prime rib."

"Did Taggart offer to buy any of your cards?"

"No. Besides, they're not for sale." He thought a moment. "It seems the whole conversation wove around how to identify a tulpa."

"How do you?"

"By what it can do to you."

"Do you believe in the existence of phantasms, Mr. Vinson?" LaRue demanded.

He hedged. "Science has proved there is no such thing."

I thought about my own lycanthropic disposition and suddenly wasn't so sure. "Do you believe Taggart defined himself by the tulpa?"

He shrugged. "I don't know. That subject never came up. His question to me was basically this: He wanted to know if a tulpa could be self-aware."

"Can it?" I asked.

"Only when it breaks the hold of its creator," he said.

25

As we drove back to the office I let my thoughts blind me to the commotion going on in the district. I didn't even register LaRue's opinions on Russian psychics of the twentieth century or his ideas about psychokinesis. Instead, I kept hearing lycanthropic theories harped on by Gibson and Fontaine, and melding them with what we learned about tulpas from Vinson, I was getting an unsettling metaphysical picture.

If a werewolf could be a tulpa and a tulpa was created from raw thought, then this occult idea suggested I was responsible for my own illness. Yet when the wolf manifests, I'm unable to control my thoughts. Gibson had worked with me for months, running biofeedback experiments during full moons in the hope that I could change the emotional content and the hallucinations that accompany the end of my lunar cycle. I'd gained a little leverage, but for the most part, when the seizures occur, my neurons bounce off into incomprehension.

Fontaine has maintained from the beginning that my problem stems from the assertion of a functional entity, a being that cannot exist until I call it into form. So, giving my lycanthropy a tulpa twist, I wondered if this thought form escaped my normalizing influence each time I had a full moon stretch.

I usually don't deal in occult concepts, but after working with my lycanthropy from such a close angle, I did realize the power of a crippled psyche. If Taggart was, indeed, our killer, then it was possible he used his own strange powers to define himself in the midst of a malignant world.

As if to test the soundness of my hypotheses, I had a stretch soon after we returned to the office. Luckily, I had just walked into the ladies' john, so at least my bolting brain waited until I had some privacy.

The convulsion's intensity drove me into the space between the broken toilet and the rusty vanity. I used this divot of cracked linoleum to help squeeze in the screams and the agony.

When it was all over, I pulled myself up and splashed lukewarm tap water in my face. I didn't glance into the sliver of mirror above the sink to see what physical changes had occurred during this latest episode. It wasn't necessary, anyway. My perspective is never far away from the supernatural envelope it's paired with.

My paranormal radar had increased dramatically, the differences immediately obvious in my ears and eyes. Because my hearing caresses sound at one-second delays, I find myself functioning in the buzz of background noise. I can pick out whispered conversations in a roaring cocktail party or count the hits of individual raindrops during a cloudburst. My lycanthropic sight adds to the surreal nature of my life, because this altered perception leaves me in the smear and sparkle of a world Van Gogh could have painted.

The one thing that occurred this time was a sudden ache in my gums. Opening my mouth, I didn't see any telltale signs of fangs, just my usual dentition—a space for a molar lost during a fight and a couple of silver-filled cavities.

I returned to the cubicle to find it smelled faintly of kerosene. LaRue didn't look at me when I threw him a questioning glance. Instead, he searched the database for a photo-ID match on Jerome Taggart. As he punched the keyboard he talked about synchronicity, clairvoyance, and the fact that Clement Noone was a man who claimed to heal, but was falling apart himself.

The reason LaRue and I work so well is because I let him spill his impressions. He leapfrogs from subject to subject, exploring scientific conjecture as well as invisible magic. I usually think I'm ignoring him, but I find that I often subliminally catalog his chattering to regurgitate at some appropriate point. Yet sitting there listening to his opinions on the mystical flow of the universal mind, I was hard-pressed to see how I could use this lunacy later.

Just as he ventured into a one-sided discussion on the benefits of a charm sack made of crushed black widow spiders and ground cloves, Gibson saved me from making a crude comment by calling.

"Your test results are in," he announced.

"So what do I have now?"

"Neuritis. It's an inflammation of the nerve endings. From this scan, you're a live wire. Your spine looks like a god-damned Christmas tree. Have you felt any pain?"

"No."

I could hear him take a deep breath. "What about numbness?"

"No. I told you it feels like I'm wearing inside-out fur. If anything, I'm more sensitive to things."

"What things, Merrick?"

I shrugged, as though he could see it.

"Merrick?"

"Gibson, don't make me do this."

"What things?"

He snapped the words so hard I almost dropped the phone. "All right, Doc, chew on this example. When someone is lying to me, it feels like an invisible hand is rubbing the fur the wrong way. I can tell every time."

A minute passed in silence. Finally he asked: "Do you have this symptom each lunar cycle?"

"No."

"When was the last time you had it this bad?"

I thought a moment. "Do you recall the ice storm last January?"

"Yes."

"I had a bad case of the fluffy fur then."

"It's weather-related," he said.

"Weather-related? Come on, Gibson. That's pushing the old lycanthropy theory a bit much."

"Merrick, your body is a bundle of sensory nerves. Their main function is to react to the environment, and things like cold, heat, and changes in pressure affect them. It may be the reason you responded so violently to the thunderstorm. Your nerves feed your brain's neurons and the confused sensory signals may have caused a malfunction in the way you perceive and process information."

His statement brought me to my feet, because mentally I had

run out ahead of him. "Are you saying I'm in for a challenge when this hurricane hits?"

"Being that it'll probably hit during a full moon? We may have to chain you to the floor."

26

GIBSON'S NEWS FLATTENED me. I stood in the same spot with the phone stuck to my ear long after he'd hung up. LaRue heard the honking buzz of the receiver and gently pried the instrument from my hand.

"You look like you just inhaled a noseful of peanut butter," he said.

I speared him with a sidelong glance. "There was jelly with it, too."

"Why don't you sit down?"

"I can't. Gibson said I'm a bundle of nerves and right now I feel like it. Let's hit the street and see this contact of Julie's." I turned mechanically and drove for the door, adding as I did: "On the way over you can finish telling me how to make bathtub gin."

He jumped after me, unconcerned that I'd steered him onto an innocuous subject. By the time we reached the Trabi, he had decided to start his moonshine lecture afresh and was repeating the part about how his Uncle Bosco had almost burned down the house because he'd put the still in the parlor. The flame had caught on Auntie Louise's velvet curtains and licked up the wall before his cousin managed to shoot a fire extinguisher in the right direction.

As I climbed into the car and smelled the heavy scent of kerosene, I wondered why Uncle Bosco's experience with combustible materials hadn't influenced his nephew. I decided not to ask; it was hard enough just to breathe.

Sulfuric steam exhausted from the refining factories and hung low in the streets, seemingly pushed into a thick, caustic layer by the low, dark rain clouds. The mercury had popped the hundred-degree mark at ten A.M. and the combination of pollutants made my head spin. I sat back and closed my eyes, shedding thoughts, woes, and feelings in lieu of entertaining one unattainable desire: air-conditioning.

Darryl Holt didn't have any AC either. In fact, Julie's precious contact didn't have a house. He lived among a collection of sticks, stones, and tin cans, in a neighborhood colorfully known as Typhoid Mary's Sewer. The cardboard shanties floated on the muddy edges of the Black River, extending onto a perilous sandbar. Holt lived at the far edge of this narrow tump of land and that's where we found him taking in the afternoon heat while fishing for his dinner.

"I've been wondering how long it would take before Ms. Julie sent you around," he announced.

I stared at a man wearing long, gnarled, white hair, pants too big for his bum, and a thick beard that probably held an assortment of bugs and critters. "How do you know what's going on?"

"Because I live in a shithole, you think I can't read?" he said. "I saw the obituary of your man Arkin listed on one of the bulletin boards in Washing Machine Park. It passed most people by, I suspect."

"Julie gave us your name without a lot of explanation," LaRue said as he glanced out over the water. "Who are you?"

The old boy twiddled with his fishing string, coughed up half a lung, and took a slug of greasy coffee from a cracked, stained mug. A minute following his theatrics, he answered. "I used to be the division chief for the remote-viewing section at the Office of Intelligence."

I pride myself on my snide comebacks. "Oh, yeah? When? Last century?"

He grinned at me with a mouthful of gums. "Sing that tune if you want, Marshal. It doesn't bother me in the least. You can't change the truth any more than you can change your destiny."

It sounded like he had attended the same school of life Baba had. "When were you at the OI?"

"I've never left."

"What does that mean?" LaRue barked.

"It means you can never really retire from the joint. They

come back on you when it suits them, demand your services, and threaten you if you don't cooperate."

"Why don't they just use the people on the payroll?" I asked.

"Because we're all different, honey. Each one of the monster marionettes turned out by the fright factory is a special case. We have talents that can't be exactly duplicated."

"I thought they trashed individuality with their amino dubbing?"

"They do, in a way. But no two rebuilds are alike. The human organism is unpredictable when it comes to cloning thought processes."

"What's your special talent?"

"I'm a psychic. I can tell the future by the sounds I pick up from the ether."

"I'll bet you never saw yourself in your current situation."

He laughed, spit up some more bile, and answered with a wink. "When I listened down my own destiny, I kept hearing the gentle sounds of water lapping against the shore. That's what I got."

"So, being able to read the future doesn't mean you can always see it clearly enough to know exactly what will happen," I said.

"In scanning uptime, you receive back exactly what you expect. Our thoughts are sinister that way. We see what we want to see because it fits nice and snug with the way our brain patterns work. It's the angle of our perspective, you might say."

"Perspective," I said. "Now that's a word I've heard quite a lot in the last few days."

He tugged on his line, but left the hook in the water. "Yep, the OI is heavy into perspective. That's all they got, you know. Just a bunch of loose twaddle coming from every which way, except straight down the middle. The bird's-eye view of a hundred delusional people. There isn't one constructive thing you can do with that crap. Nothing, nothing, nothing."

"When was the last time the OI used your services?" LaRue asked.

"Can't recall. Things tend to get mixed up on me lately. I've stepped into the time stream more times than a weasel into a henhouse and I've eavesdropped on a million conversations. Of course, the ones that interest me the most have to do with fishing." He hauled in his string to find he'd hooked a piece of plastic.

"Did you know Samuel Arkin?"

"Oh, sure. When he came in, there was not one man more devoted to the task of cleaning up the ghosts of our great humanitarian society." He waved at a family riding by on a flimsy, wooden raft and then changed the subject. "Word is the district opened up access to the delta. Everybody is heading out of town. This storm is going to be a real blow, you know. Most of this goddamned place is going to be wrecked." Glancing at me, he added: "And I'll be dead."

"Good that we came when we did, huh?" I said.

He nodded and tossed his hook back into the water. "I hope I catch a final meal. Hate to go out on an empty stomach."

"Did you know a man named Clement Noone?"

"Yeah. That one was a real bastard. Watch out for him."

I glanced at LaRue and back to Holt. "He's been touted as a compassionate healer. Are you telling us that's all smoke and mirrors?"

"From my perspective it is."

"What about Jerome Taggart?"

"I knew Jerome. He and Noone were a deuce once."

"A deuce?"

"Team Amino, if you know what I mean, but after a while Noone started having health problems, so they axed him. That boy has had a vendetta for the OI ever since."

"You know this for a fact?"

"He killed Taggart because of it."

LaRue and I spoke at the same time. "What?"

Holt grinned. "You betcha. Said he couldn't stand to see what was happening to Taggart."

The thought of losing a prime suspect and a couple of days of hard work tracking down confusing leads caused LaRue to transform from a mild-mannered marshal to one of hell's snarling dogs. My partner isn't a big fellow, but he's powerful, and when suddenly provoked, he can do a great deal of damage. For this display he reached down and grabbed Holt by his beard, yanking upward so the man had to follow. "You better not be stuffing us with farts, old man," LaRue threatened. "Is Jerome Taggart dead?"

Holt showed a little strength of his own and demanded his beard back, but it took LaRue more than a few seconds before he could unclench his hand. Finally he released Holt and shoved him roughly into his broken lawn chair.

"Jeez, you're a touchy sort," Holt said. "Just because Taggart is dead, it doesn't mean he couldn't have killed your Peeping Toms."

This kind of bullshit usually doesn't surprise me, but I've got to admit, this one scored my attention. LaRue's anger dropped away as well. It seemed to fall with a thunk right beside me.

"What?" he said. "Are you suggesting Taggart is a tulpa?"

Holt frowned. "A tulpa? Never heard that word, but that's not unusual. Sometimes, the uptime conversations I scan have soft spots in them, places where the sound washes out. It's interdimensional interference. So, if you know about this tulpa thing, I can't contradict you."

"This guy is totally useless, Andy."

LaRue ignored me to press on Holt. "How can Taggart kill if he's dead?"

"You have to understand that thoughts create our reality. Each thought is made merely by bending the flow of the universal vibration." He paused when we looked confused. "Physicists actually measured this frequency and found it lodged securely in the microhertz range. They say it's the tone that underpins the existence of matter. Without it, nothing in the material realm is possible. Since thought is the only thing that really exists for us, it makes sense to learn to manipulate it, right? And once you learn that, you get to be unstoppable. Hell, I've seen people so good at creating their futures that they've set up whole schedules where all the events take place after their physical selves have long departed this dimension."

27

DARRYL HOLT STOOD on the edge of eternity listening for celestial sounds, but unfortunately, he needed a hearing aide. Still, his half-cracked efforts made us move directly back to Clement Noone.

It took us about thirty seconds to have the ward cops haul him in. By the time we returned to the office, he was processed and waiting for us in the interrogation room. He came decorated in a beat-up red stocking cap, dirty white gloves, and a stained tan sport jacket. We watched him through the one-way glass before entering. Noone sat stoically in the chair talking to his crutch.

"It's a hundred and ten degrees in the shade," I said, upon entering. "Why are you wearing winter clothes?"

He ladled curtness into his answer. "Because it protects the skin on top of my head and the back of my hands from the ultraviolet rays of the sunlight. What's it to you?"

"Do you mean the color vibration doesn't somehow enhance your L-field?" I asked sarcastically.

"Not all things are mystical, now, are they?"

We slid into the chairs and started pressing his buttons. "Speaking of mystical," I said, "we've discovered that you are not. What you are is a liar and a scam artist."

His impatience gave way to flabbergasted indignation. "How dare you? I've been legal all the way. I gave you information the best I could and I've cooperated in this insanity. I'm innocent."

I flapped the photo at him. "You said you don't know this man, when you do. That makes you a liar, and the fact that you supposedly heal people for free but then have them come back for meditation sessions makes you a scam artist. Before we get

111

started on your friend Mr. Taggart, tell us: How much do you charge for your cozy, little group sessions?"

He frowned and poked a finger under his cap to scratch at his head, sighing as he did. Finally he pulled the figure up. "I ask for donations of fifty credits or more."

"Or more?"

"Depending on what the person feels they gain from that particular guided visualization." We stared at him and he added resolutely: "A guy has to eat, doesn't he? When you only have one good leg, it's hard to go shuffling around for food."

"Why did you leave the OI?" I asked.

Noone sat back and exhaled, an action that seemed to suck the life out of him. When he spoke, his voice did, indeed, sound dead. "I was an experiment that failed. A reject. It happens sometimes." He stared balefully at the smears on the tabletop.

The heat, the urgency, and my impatience got the best of me. I reached across the table and, using my lycanthropic strength, yanked him up on his one good leg. The crutch crashed to the floor and he began whimpering.

"You better get on with this explanation, Noone," I ordered. "Or I'm going to break your stick in half and throw you to the animals already enjoying our hospitality. They love cripples. If you think you're shuffling now, just wait." I paused to give him a beady-eyed look. "Speak up, Mr. Noone. What kind of failed experiment? What did the OI do to you?"

"What do you think?" he answered, through clenched teeth. "We're all slaves to the system."

I shoved him into his seat. "Were you a remote viewer?"

He snorted as he straightened his jacket and hat. "Do you think the ultimate experiments end with the remote viewers at the OI? Well, they don't. A number of us undergo extensive rebuilding—everything from amino dubbing to cellular adaptation within our central nervous systems."

"They did all that to you?" LaRue asked.

"And more. I don't know the extent of it myself." He paused to stare at his crutch. Then: "I'm not what I was. None of us are."

"What are you, then?" I asked.

His gaze met mine, and I saw the sadness and pain. "Marshal Merrick, I'm more mythological creature than I am human."

"And Jerome Taggart?"

"In terms you can understand easily? Jerome is my progeny. He is what I am and then some." He scraped his hat off to rub his head. When he did, a big wad of hair pulled away from his scalp. Noone stared at it and then cursed softly.

"What's happening to you?" I asked.

"I'm falling apart. Can't you see that?"

"What about Taggart?" LaRue barked. "Is he alive?"

Noone shrugged. "I haven't seen him for a while. I don't know for sure."

I bullied my way back into the conversation. "You said Taggart is your progeny. Explain that."

"You understand me to understand him," he answered. "Strange as it sounds, I was born with the ability to interfere with the biochemistry of another human being."

"How does it work?"

"Each cell in your body has a small electrical charge. By doing nothing more than coming into a person's L-field, I can affect the voltage strength and explode the cell. You might say I function as a human capacitor. I can also localize the target. The OI has given it the charming name of the death grip."

I turned to stare at LaRue. He massaged the stubble on his chin as he glared at Noone.

"Jerome Taggart can employ this death grip as well?" he asked.

Noone nodded.

"You're assassins," I said.

"That is what the OI intended," he answered. "I didn't have much choice about participating in this little ordeal, mind you. My father was in trouble with the government and I was the barter that pulled him out of it."

"Did they dub you?" LaRue badgered.

"Oh, yes. Right after they figured out I was a walking PK phenomenon. They wanted to create a most efficient killer, but it did't work. The thing that makes me a freak makes me sterile. By that, I mean they couldn't overcome my brain's neurological patterns with the introduction of necessary chemicals. No one responds one hundred percent to the rebuild."

"But they could copy your abilities into Taggart?"

"Yes. Some of them. It wasn't long before he was popping

blood vessels in lab rats. Yet a question in my mind has remained."

"Which is?"

"Did Jerome have the death grip before he came to the OI? I guess that's one I'll never know."

"Why would the OI let you go?" I asked.

"I wanted to use my powers to heal," he answered. "This amazing gift of mine allows me to explode cancerous tumors, affect the flow of life through the nerves, alter a sluggish metabolism. I was perfectly content to forget those horrendous days of coercion, but I found out the OI doesn't let anybody go. They build in a fail-safe by dubbing aminos they know will affect you. Change the body's chemistry and watch what can happen."

"You're suggesting that our brains are ultimately responsible for causing disease," I said.

"Everything begins with a thought, Marshal. Everything. Learn to control the brain and its autonomic nervous system, and you have the key to life itself."

Neither LaRue nor I could speak for about a minute, and like people joined at the hip, we both opened our mouths to demand the same question. I managed to get the words out ahead of his on the tail end of a microsecond.

"You've got built-in obsolescence."

"Don't fool yourself," he said. "There's not a person out there who doesn't. Whether it's introduced or natural, we're all ticking time bombs. It's only a matter of time before the organism turns upon itself." To emphasize his statement, he winced as he readjusted his stump.

"What's wrong?" LaRue asked. "Does your leg hurt?"

He nodded. "It's my foot. It aches. I don't need to hear the announcements about the hurricane; I know it's on its way. A drop in pressure always swells that ankle."

I glanced at my partner and back to Noone, and there, I found myself revising my estimation of his sanity. "Your leg stops above your knee."

He frowned, sucking on the space between his teeth. "I suppose you think you're telling me something?"

"How'd you lose it?"

"Nerve damage, if you must know."

"How can you feel a limb that's not there?"

"It's called a phantom foot. You might not be able to see my toes, but the energy is still right where it was configured."

"I take it we're talking about your L-field again?"

"The L-field reconstructs itself despite the absence of any missing limbs, organs, or thoughts."

LaRue plunged ahead of him. "Our victims have all died from apparent strokes."

"Yes. The cells are exploded in some portion of their brains."

"Is this the general pattern of assassination?"

"That's the idea. The OI wanted political deaths to look like deaths from natural causes, but with me, it proved impossible. My death grip is instantaneous."

"Are you saying Jerome Taggart can somehow delay the onset of symptoms in his victims?"

Noone paused to replace his cap. "Yes, that's exactly what I'm saying."

28

NOONE'S CONFESSION WAS more information than I ever cared to know. Our society, once the humanitarian ideal of a crazy dictator had degenerated beyond the noble paradigm to flounder in the insanity that he had ultimately unleashed. We were no longer people; we were festering wounds, and the government was rubbing salt all over us.

We thanked Noone for his cooperation, but threw him into a private cell in the lockup anyway, because he began claiming Taggart was probably dead. According to him, his built-in time bomb would have destroyed the man by now.

LaRue decided to check out another poltergeist ingredient while I stayed behind to go through the database for any clues about our suspect. Two hours went by, in which time I punched keys, picked my teeth, and worried about full moons and hurricanes. I found nothing constructive that we could use. Taggart was a nonentity, a situation we ran into more and more. His name didn't show up in any district records, and it was as though he'd been wiped from the slate. I was about to call it quits when my partner phoned to add a little glue to this sniffing game.

For five incomprehensible minutes he went on about crop circles, energy vortexes, and tulpas. When I finally managed to ask him what he was talking about, he said: "I ran across a backdoor healer who treated Jerome Taggart."

"Taggart bought ingredients for a poltergeist spray?" I asked.

"He bought a balancing spell," he answered.

I tried not to let exasperation creep into my voice, but some slipped in anyway. "What was he trying to balance—demon and human?"

LaRue chuckled. "Nope. He was actually attempting to

regain his equilibrium. Apparently, Taggart had a hard time standing up."

"I suppose this is important?"

"I don't know. I do know this, though: He gave the healer an address so he could zoom in on the particulars of the spell—Stacy Shaw's Massage Parlor. I'm heading there now."

I was already on my feet. "I'm on my way."

It didn't take me long to reach the old, stone tavern. The establishment spanned half a city block and while the whole thing violated the Pandering Laws, Miss Shaw had boondoggled a valid operating license and the blessings of the District Council.

The proprietress just happened to be in and we were shown through the glitzy lobby decorated with the weight of Victorian gilt and velvet. We passed several wealthy customers lounging around smoking expensive cigars as they waited for servicing. The sweet smell of tobacco blended with the overpowering richness of rose bouquets exploding from ornate vases set strategically about the room.

By the very nature of her business, one might think Stacy Shaw would be a mature woman, wearing deep red lipstick and a tight girdle. The fact was: Shaw was young, beautiful, educated, and carried an attitude reeking of low-life worldliness. She greeted us flamboyantly when her assistant showed us into her opulent office.

"My favorite legal eagles," she trilled. Rising from her leather chair, she hurried around the expansive cherrywood desk to shake my hand and give LaRue a quick peck on the cheek as well as a critical review. She knew of my partner's fascination with communism, and like always, she tried to use it to her monetary advantage. "Ah, but I have a new girl who hails from a district surrounding the great Volga River. She's a hardy one, strapping and strong, and because she's just started here, I'm offering her services with a discount coupon and a bottle of vodka."

LaRue grinned, but shook his head. "We're here on district business," he said. "Can I get a rain check?"

"Oh, I wish I could do that, but once I reach my minimum profit margin, I have to shift my advertising promotions. I know you understand. It's the bottom line, you see."

I pressed her with her own words. "Speaking of bottom line, Stacy, we're here about one of your employees."

"Let me guess. There's been murder and mayhem and you've traced the path to my door."

"That's right," I answered.

She pointed to a set of chairs placed strategically before a slowly oscillating fan. After we were seated, she said: "You know I run an honest business, Marshal. I can't be held accountable for what my people do on their own time."

"We understand and we're not implicating you in anything. We're simply looking for a man named Jerome Taggart."

She nodded, dividing her attention between us and a spray of roses decorating a marble fireplace mantel. "Yes, he worked for a while as one of my massage associates."

"How long did he work here?"

"About two years. He was the best rubdown man I ever had. He only had a Class-C designation, though. Not much earning potential, but the women adored him."

"Why did the women like him so much?" I asked.

"Because they came away energized. I'll tell you, his touch was magic. I'm not sure what he did, but he had so many customers, I had to start scheduling in half-hour slots rather than the usual sixty minutes."

"Sounds like things were going well. Why did he leave?"

"He got sick. It was all pretty strange. One day his muscles just refused to cooperate and he had a hard time opening his hands. From there, his strength seemed to wither away." She walked to a window and straightened a fluttering silk sheer. "It was a real shame."

"What did he do to combat his illness?"

"The usual stuff. Oil-of-chestnut rubs, hot baths, vinegar cocktails. Nothing seemed to help."

"Did he ever seek medical attention through the PHO?"

"No, not while he was here."

"Why not?"

"I don't know. I guess he had a thing about the PHO. Lots of people don't like going to see doctors. Me included."

"What finally happened?"

She sighed. "He got worse. There were days when he couldn't get out of bed. Then there was an unpleasant episode that was truly bizarre, and believe me, Marshals, I know bizarre."

"What?" I demanded.

"I came downstairs one morning and found him choking a client. He was using his left hand. Along with a couple of my bouncers, I pulled him off the woman and asked him what the hell he was doing. He kept claiming there was a demon in his arm. He swore he couldn't control it, and as if to prove the point, he went for his own throat."

"With his left hand?" LaRue asked.

She nodded. "With his left hand. I thought it was some kind of sick joke on his part, but then I realized he was really choking himself."

"How can that be?"

"I don't know. We pulled his hand down and he'd squeezed hard enough to cause blood. Well, you can imagine, I had to give him his walking papers."

"Do you know where he went after he left you?"

She shook her head. "I suppose he went home."

"Home? I thought he boarded here?"

"I mean home with his family unit. A young woman showed up claiming to be his sister."

"Did he act like he knew her?"

"I can't say for sure. They weren't hugging each other or anything. They acted like normal family members."

"Had Taggart ever mentioned his family unit before?"

"Not that I recall." She thought a moment. "I don't know if this will help you, but I suggested he visit Francesca Eugene. As bad as that guy's health seemed, I figure the best thing I could do for him was send him to a place where he could buy himself some time."

29

WHEN STACY SHAW said Jerome Taggart needed to buy some time, she'd meant it literally. The next morning we visited Francesca Eugene, a backdoor practitioner of invisible magic.

Eugene answered the door of her tenth-floor flat, surrounded in halo fashion by the brilliant sunlight streaming through her balcony doors. A stiff wind had come up during the night and it blew into her apartment to flutter linens hanging from a series of laundry lines. An old crippled basset hound came over to greet us, but when he sniffed me, he smelled my lycanthropy and backed off with a sorrowful bark.

"Ms. Eugene," I said, following introductions, "we're here concerning a murder case."

She clicked her tongue and frowned, forcing her squinty black eyes to disappear in bags and crow's-feet. "My name is Francesca, please," she said. Then, pointing to the clothes, she added: "I take in wash to help with my retirement check. I hope you don't mind if I get on with it while we talk. Being that this here storm is a-brewin', I need to get these things dried now." With that, she slung a towel at one of the ropes.

Her furniture was filled out with castoffs from cars and LaRue took a seat on an old chair supported by a tire. I found a place by leaning my butt on an orange vinyl bucket seat that looked like it came straight out of a Duvalier Classic.

"We understand you sold your services to a man named Jerome Taggart," LaRue began.

She never missed a beat. "Jerome Taggart. Polite man; quiet man; sick man."

"We believe he's killed several people."

"I doubt it."

"Why is that?"

"He just didn't seem the type."

"They never do, Francesca," LaRue said. "Did he bring anyone with him when he visited you?"

"As a matter of fact, he brought his sister. Silent woman; pretty woman; woman dripping in jewels."

"Jewels?" I said. "What kind?"

"Diamonds, rubies, emeralds. Dressed real nice. Surprising."

"Why?"

"Because Mr. Taggart wore rags. Old jeans; torn shirt; dusty shoes." She punctuated her observations by slapping another towel over the line.

"Do you know where he lives?" LaRue asked.

"Nope. The fact that he's living at all is the miracle."

"Why do you say that?"

"Bad energy. Lots of disease. He didn't look well. Never complained none, though." She whipped another towel over the rope. "He had a limp. Poor circulation is my guess."

"Would you tell us what kind of healing service you offer?" LaRue asked.

She laughed. "I don't heal a damned thing. I sell extra time to those who need it."

"In other words, you give folks a second chance by pushing back the date of their demise."

She nodded and bent to a red fire bucket to retrieve an embroidered pillowcase. "That's right. I got the gift and so I use it. Such a damned shame I can't do nothing about the quality of time spent."

LaRue frowned. "I beg your pardon?"

"I can renew someone's time on earth, but I can't put the spirit of life into it. Suffering changes the outlook. Sometimes it just isn't worth prolonging a person's days."

"And what do you charge for this service?"

"Not enough."

LaRue chuckled. "You're admitting to an illegal activity."

"So? Are you going to rush me into the slammer for it? Wouldn't matter if you did."

"Why do you say that?"

"Because I'll be dead by the time this storm passes. Where I die ain't much of a concern."

"Are you a clairvoyant?" LaRue asked.

She flipped a bright orange shirt out of the bucket, slinging water all over the dog. "Don't know for sure."

"I take it any extensions in your own behalf have finally run out."

"Yep, the credit card is done. Not all the red sevens in the world could bring my balance up to date. I'm going out on the winds of a giant wet fart."

I had to force back a laugh, so I changed the subject. "In that case, you won't mind telling us how a person can buy time from you. I mean, since after next week your trade secrets won't be any good anymore."

She flopped a shirt over the line. "Yep, you're right. Next week, my trade secrets won't be worth squat." Pointing to the dog, she said: "See that doodad my Cuddles is sitting by?"

I looked at the dog, but my gaze was immediately diverted to a large table fan, and upon closer inspection, I saw that the contraption had been modified. The front cage was missing and the plastic blades were exposed. Each was marked with a series of numbers as well as sketches of the lunar phases and drawings of the sun and the stars.

"That thing you're gawking at is my eternity machine," Eugene said. "It came to me in a dream, you see. A being of light descended one night to tell me I had the power to squeeze time with my thoughts. It told me I had to make the eternity machine so I could calculate the pop-off day for the person. From the first moment I tried it, the danged thing worked."

"You spin the blades like a roulette wheel?" I asked.

"No. The guy buying the time pushes the meter. It's more accurate under the hand of the one paying the money."

"How does squeezing time extend the date of death?" LaRue demanded.

"Think of it like rolling out pretzel dough. When you first start, you've got a glob, but as you work the dough into a rope, you realize you've got this cylinder with two ends. The end closest to me is the present day, the other is the day in question. I can squeeze time into six-month segments. No more than that."

Eugene operated a creative rip-off, I had to hand that to her—low overhead and no guarantees. If it didn't work, the customers wouldn't be around to come back on her later. "You do this all with the power of your thoughts?"

"That's right. I meditate long and hard. Takes a lot of energy to visualize my squeezing, but in my mind I press out that pretzel dough as thin as I can. Sometimes there ain't no way I can push it more than a month. Depending on the illness, you understand." She gave me a hard look. "Don't go asking for demonstrations unless you're serious about buying."

"I wouldn't think of it," I said. "I kind of like the mystery of not knowing."

"You're a coward."

The remark pissed me off momentarily, but I let the snit evaporate when I realized she spoke the truth. It was hard enough to live without thinking of the end. "Do you know if Taggart was seeking medical attention for his problems and where he might have gone?"

"Nope. When he stopped by, he mentioned he was going to see Ruchi Odell. She's a local healer who can do wonders with root beer, sea salt, and bacon grease."

30

WE FOUND RUCHI Odell at an attractive little house in the middle of Ward 97, a neighborhood known as the Greens, because right next door was a tiny park with yellowed grass, a couple of gnarled oak trees, and plenty of hungry pigeons. Mrs. Odell ushered us into her home and showed us to a couple of split-wood chairs. The windows were open and a breeze blew through, laced with the scent of jasmine as it wafted across a planter box.

Mrs. Odell appeared to be a grandmotherly type until she opened her mouth. Then I realized she was cut from the same cloth as Baba.

"Francesca said you would be here to visit me," she announced. "I want you to know right up front, I don't do anything for free. That includes answering questions."

"This is a murder investigation, ma'am," LaRue said.

"Yes, so?"

"If you don't answer our questions we can take you back to the Marshals Office for the interview."

"Go ahead," she said, patting one of her white curls in place. "The answer is the same: I don't do anything for free, including giving you information. You see, I believe my energy is valuable, and what goes out must come in. It's the Universal Law of Checks and Balances."

I shook my head. The Law of Checks and Balances—more back-door invisible magic, and from the looks of it, we had a hard-nosed practitioner. "What do you want in return for your answers?"

"Food, of course. I'm stocking up to ride out the storm."

LaRue glanced my way, and then picked into his side pocket, producing an expired package of chocolate candy.

Odell snatched up the treat with a quick thank you and turned to stare at me. Reluctantly, I passed on a small cellophane bag of tea crackers. She studied the crumbled contents for a moment before agreeing to the parley with a sharp nod.

"Pretty danged meager for a couple of Class-A designations," she said.

"Life is tough all over, Ms. Odell," I answered. "We want to know about a man named Jerome Taggart. He came to see you within the last six months, I believe."

She tossed her prizes into a cracked plastic trash can sitting beside her chair. The container was brimming with other supplies: jars of black malt, a couple of oranges, a small bag of flour, and some cookies. "Yes, Mr. Taggart showed up here."

"What did he want?"

"What everyone wants from me."

"Which is?"

"Health."

"And how do you do that?"

"I make up special tinctures and poultices and then I lay some special spells onto them."

I shook my head. We'd walked into another mustard-plaster scam.

"You don't understand it, so you discount it," she said, seeing my expression.

"I've explored my share of back-door voodoo. So far I'm not impressed."

"That's because you don't understand what's behind it. I might use a mixture of chimney soot and lard, but that's just so I can focus the spell. It's the thoughts and attitudes behind the words. You have to believe in the power of your own mind. When you can do that, you have your saving grace right there in the palm of your hand. I can slather on goo all day long, but if you believe you're going to die, then that's your fate." She paused to study me. Then: "Most folks have rotten mind-sets. They know about pain and suffering. What they don't know is to change it, they have to change their feelings toward the world and know right from their hearts in the power of positive emotions. It takes a lot of work to become a joyful person in the midst of daily strife, but it can be done. I mean, look at me for an example."

I did look at her and I saw an old lady in her sixties. "How are you different now that you have a happy mind-set?"

"When I was fifty-three years of age, I got an awful diagnosis from the PHO. Those quacks said I had cancer of the throat and they wanted to cut my tongue straight out of my head. Well, I came home and prayed on it and then I was answered with enlightenment. All I had to do was believe that my desires were instantly and constantly granted. It worked. I practiced my positive thoughts for days and used some liniment rubs and drank down plenty of white whiskey and petroleum jelly. When I went back for another checkup, the Big C was gone. The doctors told me the rubs and stuff didn't heal me, so that means the thoughts did it."

"And you've been selling this package ever since," I said.

"That's right," she answered matter-of-factly. "There's no universal law which says I can't."

"Maybe not, but there is a district law against it," I told her.

She blew me off with a flap of her hand. "Pish-posh. Those laws are made by greedy bureaucrats. They can't stop stuff sent down from the angels, now, can they?"

"They will certainly try," LaRue muttered. Louder, he added: "What type of cure did Jerome Taggart request?"

"A whole body healing," she answered. "The poor man was in crippled shape when he came to me, but when he left, he was cured. I made him a poultice of Epsom salts, potato skins, cooked rice, and primrose oil. The spell took a long while, I'll admit, but once I did my treatment, the healing was in the bag."

"A whole body healing must have cost a lot of energy in return," LaRue said. "What did you charge him?"

"Well, there was a woman with him. He introduced her as his sister. She did the paying."

"What was her name?"

"I don't know. I never heard him call her by a name."

"What did she look like?"

She shrugged. "I can't really say for sure. She wore a scarf around her head, so I couldn't see what color hair she had, but I remember she was pretty in the face and wore nice clothes and lots of expensive jewelry. In fact, that's what she used to meet the price of the healing."

"Jewelry?" I asked. "What kind?"

Odell rose from the chair and stepped to a rickety sideboard. Opening up the drawer, she pulled out a shoe box, and rifling around inside of it, she produced a large cameo brooch. "This was supposed to be made by some dead Italian artist. I don't know if it was or not, but the energy was good around it, so I took it. Isn't it beautiful?"

It was at that.

31

WHEN RUCHI ODELL showed us the cameo, I called dispatch immediately to have a couple of ward cops fetch Andrea Pio back in for another interview, but as we left the spirit healer's residence the word reached us that it was impossible. Apparently, Ms. Pio had winged off to a safer locale, because her house was buttoned up tight. We had no choice but to follow Mrs. Odell's recommendation to visit a woman named Zela Tooph.

We tracked down this particular back door swindler and discovered she worked out of a tattoo parlor. We also found her doing a brisk prehurricane business.

The place took up the rear storeroom of an abandoned vid-repair shop. People shoved and squeezed, trying to form a loose line inside the building. Although tattooing is illegal, and we were dressed in our black uniforms, no one seemed prepared to bolt and run. There comes a point in hopelessness when even the fear of authority no longer matters.

After five minutes of being patient, my indulgent mood fled down some rat hole and I pushed my way through the crowd with my weapon drawn. The folks cleared away like a fork in the Black River and LaRue and I drove our way into the spider's web.

Zela Tooph turned out to be a voluptuous, dark-haired vixen, wearing heavy makeup and jangling bracelets. Beyond that, she had her big ass poured into a pair of shorty-shorts and her feet crimped into black stiletto heels. She sweated over a customer, diligently operating a battery-powered tattoo wand and applying a dab of red ink to the man's arm.

When we walked in, she didn't stop her chore and didn't look at us. Still, she'd gotten the word we were in for a talk and so spoke accordingly. "Don't hassle me, marshals. I'm busy."

"We can see that," I said, stepping over to the chair to watch her work.

The man she decorated glanced at me, but appeared as unconcerned as she. Studying the design, I was surprised it contained the name Charlie Smathers and a nine-digit number that was most certainly his district identification. "How come all the business? Running a special or something?"

She snorted. "Running a special. Yeah, you might say that. With the storm coming, I'm giving fifty percent off. I figure this old store ain't gonna be here after the wind blows, so I might as well use up my supply of ink before I crawl into my bomb shelter."

LaRue worked his way into her view, too. "ID tattoos?"

"That's right." She paused to dip ink from a smudgy glass and took a second to give us a quick once-over. "You know, the government should provide this service, but hell, they ain't gonna give nobody a hand. Leastwise willingly."

"So you're marking folks in case they die in the storm," I said.

"Yeah. The cleanup teams will know their names and numbers, and if the bureaucratic bastards have a mind to, they can contact the family units. I don't think they will, but it's smart to be prepared." Returning to her client, she began filling in her design. "I take it you two don't want a tattoo, since all the cops will be safe and sound. After all, everybody knows the government takes care of its own first."

"I wish we had that in writing," LaRue muttered. Then, louder: "We're investigating a multiple homicide and we understand you did a tattoo for our prime suspect. His name is Jerome Taggart. Do you remember him?"

She shook her head and pointed a long red fingernail at the fellow in her chair. "I can't remember who I did an hour ago."

"Do you keep records?" I asked hopefully.

"Nope."

"He was sent to you by Ruchi Odell."

"Ah, Ruchi, what a sweet, old broad. She fixes me up right when she can." Charlie Smathers flinched when the needle hit a nerve and she patted him on the shoulder. "We're almost done here, friend."

He nodded and closed his eyes against the pinprick pain of the stylus.

She rolled the name around on her tongue. "Jerome Taggart. Jerome Taggart. I don't recall. What was the matter with him?"

"We're not sure," LaRue answered. "He was ill and perhaps was worried about dying."

"Everybody is worried about dying. The tattoos I give for healing keep specific diseases away."

"Do you explain this to people?"

"Try to. I don't want to take nobody's money dishonestly. Of course, lots of folks are already sick and got it in their heads that a little ink under the skin is going to help them."

"What kind of designs qualify as healing tattoos?"

"That's up to the person. I usually counsel them beforehand. They can choose some of my pictures or they can bring one that has special meaning. Most people draw up an idea and then I use their plans to make a real nice tattoo. Color is important. It expresses the energy behind the pictures."

"It doesn't matter which designs they choose, then?"

"No." The moment she made the statement, I got an idea and pulled out the tulpa card, flashing it at her. "He may have wanted this particular design. Does it look familiar?"

She stopped instantly upon seeing the card. "Oh, yeah. Now I know who you're talking about. He wanted this design placed over his heart." Frowning, she put a finishing touch on Charlie's bloody identifier and turned away to fetch a gauze pad lying on a nearby table. "Well, I should say his sister wanted it placed over his heart. It was real important to her."

"His sister, huh?" I said. "Did she give a name?"

"Nope. She didn't say much except about the location of the tattoo."

"What did she look like?"

She shrugged. "Pretty. She had good skin for inking, but that's all I can remember for sure."

"Did you tattoo this design on him?" LaRue asked.

"Oh, sure. It was a complicated picture. I had to draw it out freehand and then transfer the design to his chest before I could even get started. I usually just use my art skill, but I was afraid I might make a mistake on this one."

"Did you do this all in the same day?"

"Oh, no. It took me a week to draw the picture up right. I called him and he came back in with his sister. Poor guy was in the chair for hours."

"You called him?" I said. "Do you still have that number?"

She laughed. "Listen to you. Of course not. I don't keep stuff like that around. Bad luck, you know."

"Bad luck?"

"Evil mojo. When someone is worried about being sick, they draw that energy pattern to them. After the tattoo is inked, this energy has to go somewhere, and since it can't get by the healing design, it can stick to the tattoo artist before the picture is done. I burn everything connected to sick people. I also wear my own healer." She lifted her filthy tank top to show us an elaborate colorful painting of a hawk floating just above her navel. "This here is my symbol for health. The hawk is a powerful bird."

I could feel myself getting exasperated. "When you called, who answered?"

"As I remember, it was his sister. She took the message and brought her brother around the very next day. It's a good thing, because they hadn't paid me for the prelims, and I went and tossed the number in the fireplace right after I gave them the word that the picture was ready for inking."

"Did everything go smoothly when they came around?" I demanded.

She slapped Charlie on the thigh and stopped in her explanation to give him directions about keeping his tattoo clean. With that, the old boy climbed out of the chair, paid her with cold, hard credits, and before we could speak another word, a new client entered and flopped into the seat for service. This fellow handed her a slip of paper and completely ignored us.

"Everything went real nice between him and me, at first," Tooph said, returning to the subject. "I was just about finished coloring in his design when he started acting real strange."

"What happened?"

"His hand started doing all kinds of funny twisting and stuff. I mean, it didn't look like it had the constraints of any bones. Turned in on itself at an odd angle and then, right as I was in the middle of doing a lovely, yellow cream accent, he attacks himself."

Obviously, she'd been drinking her tattoo inks. "What?"

"You heard me. His hand went to his throat and he starts to strangle the life out of himself. The sister managed to calm him down, but I'll tell you, it put the jitters in me."

"I'm sure it would," LaRue offered sympathetically.

"Did he come to his senses and apologize for his display?" I asked.

"Well, yeah, he did. He kept saying it wasn't him causing the problem. At that point I didn't care. I just wanted him out of my chair."

"Did they pay you for your services?" LaRue said.

She nodded. "In fact, they paid more than I asked. This lady had jewelry dripping off her, and she offered to complete our business by giving me a big cameo brooch. It was for my trouble and all, you understand."

"Did you take it?"

She laughed. "Why, of course."

32

AFTER LISTENING TO the weird crap these back door healers spewed, I didn't think I could listen to another interview steeped in the occult, so I begged off for the day, deciding to confront Gibson with some distasteful suspicions I was growing.

Though the day leaked slowly into evening, the heat and stink still lay thick in the streets. It was as if the whole world sweated, panted, and anticipated the coming death of District One. This sensation crept into me, perhaps hanging on to some unnamed lycanthropic sensibility. Whatever it was, by the time I arrived at the free clinic, I had become annealed by melancholy.

Gibson was nailing pine planks over the smudgy bay window of his little kingdom. He nodded in greeting and immediately started muttering about having to keep a medical warehouse in his apartment, and now it seemed he should stock wood, fiberglass, and exterior doors, too.

"I take it the district said no to any kind of emergency allowance," I greeted.

"It comes out of my pocket," he grumbled. "Everything eventually comes out of my pocket." Grunting, he thrust his chin toward the end of the board. "Would you help me balance this?"

I grabbed the hammer instead of the load, and while pounding I broached the subject of my visit. "Tell me the truth, Gibson. Did you want to parade me in front of those PHO quacks for an entirely different reason than securing your research job?"

He almost dropped the board, but recovered in his usual manner by trying to defeat my curiosity with an impatient expression. "It's like I told you."

133

I snorted. "You know that inside-out fur of mine? Well, it's itching, and when it does, I know I'm not going to like what I'm about to hear." I paused to study him, looking for something in his face that would prove me wrong. Unfortunately, I couldn't find it. "The way I see it, there isn't much call to find a cure for lycanthropy. How many people in the world actually claim the same problem? I'm sure it's not enough to worry about."

"What are you driving at, Merrick?"

I pounded a final nail and said: "There's no grant, no job, no hint of the possibility. Is there?"

He stepped away to squint at me. "Why are you suddenly so concerned?"

"Suddenly concerned? What dimension have you been living in, Gibson? This whole goddamned association is my concern and it's about time I'm included in all the nasty secrets."

"I'm helping you of my own free will," he snarled. "It's my money that keeps you in a job and my time and care that keeps you sane, so do me a favor—don't ask questions."

"You've thrown that threat at me so many times, I've stopped listening. If I walked away tomorrow, I wouldn't be worried. You've been completely dishonest with me, haven't you? You've juggled the truth from the beginning."

He tagged on an innocent look. "I'm not lying to you."

"Oh? How thick is my medical file by now? The one the shrink keeps has got to be a foot deep at least. It took me a while, but I understand now."

"Merrick, you don't understand anything."

"Well, let's see just how much I've figured out," I answered. "You're planning on selling new brain technology to the government. That's why we've been playing these different games—the biofeedback, the hypnosis, the scans, the blood tests—all of it." I stopped speaking, hesitating for an awful second, in which time I knew I had to face the rotten truth. The words scratched my throat as I spoke them. "How long does it take to invent something the government will buy? And speaking of buying, what exactly are they looking for these days and who might be the highest bidder—the Office of Intelligence?"

His face fell flat, gone from innocence to anger to an expression of severe indigestion. He turned, picked up the box of nails, walked by me, and opened the clinic's door. Standing there, he silently waited for me to precede him. Gibson is as good at the stall as I am.

The clinic was empty and without electricity, deemed temporarily unnecessary by the government. He locked the door, tossing the tools beside it. Then, with hands on his hips, he faced me.

"Whatever gave you the idea I'm a rich man?" he asked.

I hadn't expected this tack. "You come from a wealthy family unit. You were rated high enough to attend the university and you're a physician."

He sighed and flopped heavily onto the ratty couch. "Didn't I tell you once that coming from a wealthy family unit means nothing? Do you see how I live? Where's my nice mansion, huh, Merrick? No one gives me a thing I don't earn first."

"So, you admit running a scam on me?"

"Yes, I admit it." He stared at me for a moment before continuing. "You're right. There is no research grant, no job, no hint at the possibility. There never was." He stopped again to rub both of his hands down his face. When his fingers passed his chin, I saw a defeated expression magically appear. "Do you know how many doctors there are?" he murmured.

I shook my head, remaining steely by remaining silent.

"There are more than the government needs. Most of us survive at the grassroots level, and as you know, down here in the dirt, the pay stinks. I have the additional problem of having deep-seated feelings about my humanitarian responsibilities and I go out of my way, physically, mentally, and financially to help people. You can thank my lovely father for those ideals. He raised me to be a Good Samaritan, but although my soul knows it, my stomach doesn't."

I never thought I would be in a position to give Gibson my compassion. It worried me a little that he might be stapling up the rip in his plan by hitting me with more half-truths, but I'm a sucker for his theatrics, and after a minute of indecision I gave him the benefit of the doubt. I slid onto the sofa. "Why weren't you honest with me in the first place?"

"Greed," he answered. "I didn't want to share the money

with any more people than I had to. This was for me; for my future."

My sympathy evaporated at hearing his reply stated so succinctly. "The money would have still been for your pockets and yours alone, had I not started asking these questions. You would have kept me purposely in poverty, so long as you had plenty."

He stared at me and then dropped his gaze to his lap. "I don't know, Merrick. I really don't know, and that's as honest as I can be."

33

IT'S FUNNY HOW we demand to know the truth, even if we die by inches upon hearing it. My own small death held plenty of tears, but I've never been one to cry. I rely on anger to see me through hurt, but in this case, my rage had pushed through my L-field and I didn't know it until it was too late. The space it vacated was quickly replaced by bitter understanding.

I am intimate with the fear of poverty. I know it better than anything else, and though I had the wind knocked out of me over this betrayal, I empathized with Gibson. Had I had half the chance, I would have done the same thing. Maybe, when all was said and done, it was this realization and not Gibson's admission that bothered me so much.

I didn't get an opportunity to reflect upon this latest dilemma of conscience. The nagging voice of the dispatch operator blasted over my com-node and nearly deafened me with a relay message to call Angela Whitehead as soon as possible. When the transmission was done, I tapped the pager stud so I wouldn't have to go to the trouble of pulling the mike up to my lips to respond.

Gibson gave me one of his intense expressions, waiting for me to make the next move. I did, too—by pointing to the telephone.

"Do you have communications?" I demanded.

He nodded. "Last time I checked."

I went for it, and dialed Angela. She answered immediately.

"I did some asking around for you," she said. "Talk to a fellow down on the Verrazano by the name of William Zane."

"Who is he?"

"He's an artist. Not designated or anything. He does it to supplement his retirement."

"Why this guy, Angela?"

"He might know your remote viewers."

I smiled despite the current crack in my emotions. Thanking her, I dropped the phone with a clunk and turned back to Gibson. He still watched me with that familiar fierce squint of his. "Have you been dealing with the OI?" I asked.

"Off and on for a couple of years," he answered quietly. "Like you said, they're the best game in town."

"What have you sold them so far?"

"Nothing."

A fissure started to grow in my patience. I walked over to him and matched him with a furious stare of my own. "You better not be scaming me again, Gibson. If I find out you are, I'll be plenty pissed, and contrary to what you believe, I don't have anything to lose. To be honest, after this storm comes through I'll probably have even less. So don't hand me the same old crap. I'm not buying it anymore."

He didn't reply. Instead, he leaned back, crossed his arms, and pulled a heavy breath.

Since I traveled on his highway of guilt, I pushed the speedometer. "Do you know anything about the PHO collaborating with the OI on a program involving traditional healing?"

"What does that have to do with this?" he demanded.

"Not a thing. I just want to know."

He took a moment to reevaluate where the conversation was heading. When it looked safe, he said: "They've got a backroom setup in Ward One Hundred."

"Have you been there?"

"No."

"Do you know who operates it on the PHO side?"

"No."

"We're running out of time to do this shit legwork. Can you find out and get an address for me?"

He studied me openly, letting his gaze pass over every inch of my body, as though this might give him some clue to my thoughts. Finally he said: "You make me crazy, Merrick. That should be better than all the gold you could possibly ever want."

"It is," I answered. "Unfortunately, my stomach doesn't know it."

Gibson flashed me a small smile. "I can have the name and address for you tomorrow morning."

"Thank you," I answered, sitting down again. "Tell me, do you happen to know an OI contact by the name of Casper Conrad?"

"Conrad is the guy I've been trying to sell to."

My throat suddenly dried up on me and it was hard squeezing the words out. "Does he know about me?"

Gibson nodded. "Yes, Merrick, he does."

34

I WAS GRATEFUL for the intermission in my little drama with Gibson. I told him I would see him in the morning and rushed off, leaving him to his boards, his nails, and his concerns about my future cooperation. Twenty minutes later I walked into central lockup and Clement Noone's cell.

I probably should have worried about what this character could do to me if he got close enough, but caution isn't high on my list of priorities. So, sitting down beside him, I placed my hand gently on his shoulder and said: "Clement, I understand what you're going through."

He nodded. "I know you do. You're a live wire, just like me. I saw it from the first. I didn't need a voltmeter to tell me that. Did the OI get to you?"

"Not that I'm aware of, but I have a feeling they're just waiting to yank my number."

"That doesn't frighten you?"

"It makes me mad."

"Just wait. Terror has a way of entering the equation."

I shivered, but kept the creep of uncertainty to myself. "Thanks for the warning. Tell me, do you know a guy at the OI named Casper Conrad?"

He scowled. "Yes. He was responsible for my involuntary incarceration. He's an SOB. Don't let him fool you."

"It seems Conrad is responsible for all kinds of things over there. Did he bring Jerome Taggart into the program?"

"He introduced us. I don't know anything else, but I assume he did."

"I understand there's a free clinic in Ward One Hundred that is supposed to offer patients traditional healing options."

Noone stared at me, and then blew a hard sigh. I was washed in his sour breath. When it threatened to knock me off the bench, I dug my fingers into the scaly mattress and held on to get the info I needed.

"How'd you find out about that place?" he asked.

"Never mind. It's a front, isn't it, Clement? It's more of a screening room than a clinic. It's how the OI gets its human material for experimentation."

"That's right."

"Is it how they got you?"

"Yes. I didn't go there for care in the beginning, though."

"You weren't born with your incredible abilities, I suspect."

He glanced at his gnarled, dirty hands. "No. I lied about that."

"Why am I not surprised? How did your miracle really happen?"

"I used to work as a roofer. One day I fell thirty feet onto a concrete foundation. I shattered my leg and hit my head. They tell me I was in a coma for two weeks." Pointing to his stump, he added: "When I woke up I discovered this."

"What led you to this clinic for traditional healing?"

"The recommendation of my neighborhood doctor. They all have standing orders to report 'irregularities' to the government, it would seem. I mentioned during a follow-up exam that I thought my head injury had caused a problem in my eyesight, because I kept seeing colorful auras around everything— organic and inorganic things. A day later I was at the freak clinic being checked out. A day after that I met Conrad and lost my freedom and my life."

"You said your father was in trouble with the government."

"He wasn't until the OI wanted me. Then, suddenly, all his environmental tax returns were erased from the system and he was charged with evasion. They were going to send my whole family unit to a labor camp. By cooperating, the tax forms magically reappeared and everybody was happy. Except me."

I sat back and tried to sort through some end pieces in this whole affair, but Noone interrupted me. "What's wrong with you? Maybe I can cure you."

I angled my look toward him. "I doubt it."

"Why?"

Standing, I used the dim light in the cell to conceal my face and any beleaguered emotions that might cross it. "You can't help me, Clement," I whispered, "because I'm more a mythological creature than even you are."

35

THE NEXT MORNING came earlier and hotter than usual. Baba was at her loom, clacking away on a pair of "summer" curtains she intended to hang after the storm blew the windows out. The weather reports coming over the array were growing more dismal by the hour, which meant we would have to step up efforts if we were going to get anywhere near Jerome Taggart before the district turned to rubble.

To this end, I left a few minutes after my roommate's noise began. I took the subway to the Verrazano to visit William Zane.

The shopping plaza was crowded with folks looking to trade provisions for the hurricane. The district bakeries, butchers, and dairy shops were doing brisk business, too. Along the way, I bargained a pair of my old uniform boots and a thermometer I'd kiped from Gibson's clinic while talking on the phone to Angela Whitehead. My parleys netted me three cans of Sterno, a pound of white beans, and directions to Zane's flat.

He lived in a small duplex at the far end of the plaza. Zane's wife answered the door, introduced herself, and led me into their tiny home. From the way Angela had talked, I'd gotten the impression that Zane was wealthy, but this house, though clean, was nothing remarkable. In fact, it was pure kitsch. The tables and chairs were pine packing crates and the wall coverings leaned toward a South Sea island theme, with the decor filled out by strands of plastic patio lights hanging from the low ceiling. Greeting me in the midst of this tropical paradise was Zane, dressed in red Bermuda shorts and brandishing coffee in a beer mug.

"Angela said you would stop by," he said. "It's about my paintings, isn't it?"

"Yes. She thinks you may have been the subject of a paranormal scam."

"I suppose there's no good way to explain it, but I don't think it was a scam. There isn't a lick of evidence that can prove it. Whatever happened to us, it was so good, I wish to hell it had never stopped."

I couldn't contain my surprise. "You didn't want this interference to stop?"

"No. It was the best deal we had going."

"From the beginning, please. What happened?"

"You have to realize first that I used this money to supplement my retirement income."

I nodded. "I'm not here to haul you in for undeclared earnings."

"That's good to hear." He slugged his coffee before answering. "I've always fancied myself a painter. For years I worked on my own stuff, trying to sell my canvases on the side." Holding up his hand, he rubbed his fingers against his thumb. "The talent is here. It just never got out on the canvas like it should."

"I keep telling him to be patient," his wife said. "He'll get it one of these days."

He frowned at her. "St. Ophelia, Jerdine, I'm sixty-three years old. One of these days might be too late for me."

"What happened?" I demanded, charging the statement with a growl.

It was enough to bring Zane back into focus. "I was busy doing a series of landscapes in oil. They really weren't much, I have to admit. There aren't many pretty vistas in this damned district, but I still try to find the light, if you know what I mean. I'm nothing if I'm not diligent. You see, I keep my workshop in the basement and go down there to paint every day."

"Lord knows, I don't get to see him any," Jerdine commented. "He locks the door and I can't even fetch my canned goods while he's creatin'."

"That's why we've been an item all these years, woman," he answered. "You can't drive me crazy when you feel like it."

"Well, crazy is what you was going, even without me," she fired.

If I didn't get Jerdine out of the room, I would never get this interview done. "Mrs. Zane, that coffee smells good. Is that molasses and lime I smell?"

"My, my, look at that William, a marshal who knows about the finer things in life." She rose and I saw my plan had worked. "I'll get you a mug while my husband tells you the rest."

I smiled a thank you and then laid a hard squint onto Zane. "Go on, please."

"I was standing down in my basement and it was like something popped in my head. Suddenly I was the master of masters."

"I beg your pardon?"

"I was channeling the great works of art done by the finest painters in history."

I thought of Fraley's disincarnate friend, Manu. "Channeling?"

"Yeah. My natural talents were being used, but my hand was guided by someone else."

I've heard of some creative rip-offs, but this was a new one. "Did you hear voices or anything?"

"Funny you should mention that. While I was working on the paintings I could speak the old languages of the masters. My Picasso period had me speaking Spanish without a problem at all, and when I did my Rubens, I could lay out Jerdie with Dutch. After I finished the paintings, the ability just left me."

"How long did it take you to do a canvas?"

"About a week total for each one."

"What happened next?"

"I told him to get out there and try to sell this stuff," Jerdine said, entering with my glass. "But we didn't know where to sell them."

"That was until a man approached me one day," Zane said. "I'd taken my canvases out onto the front patio, hoping someone would see them, and like an angel from the sky, along comes this guy who changed our lives. At least for a little while."

"What was his name?"

Spearing me with a look, he said: "His name was Drake. I don't know if it was a first or last name. He was a godsend, though."

"Why?"

"He sold my paintings, of course."

"He did? To who?"

"He never did tell me and I didn't care so long as the credits were coming in."

"Drake kept saying William was blessed," Jerdine said. "He said all those dead artists favored my husband and wanted to help us."

"How much did he sell your paintings for?"

"Well, I'm not sure, but we got a nice little cut. It was enough to buy us some things we needed. The money wasn't no millionaire's purse. Still, we're grateful for what this man did with the canvases. I mean, you can't expect too much since they were all copies."

"You couldn't tell them from the real thing, William," Jerdine said. Then, staring at me, she added: "He got to painting this one—a pretty, pretty picture by an artist named Monet. Our daughter brought us a picture book and showed us the very same painting. I studied and compared them, I did. No difference."

"Did this man ever introduce you to any of his friends?" I asked. "Perhaps a man named Ford or one named Arkin?"

He shook his head. "Drake is the only one we ever met."

I shifted the course of the interrogation and gained some surprised looks in the process. "Do you create jewelry in this same fashion?"

"No," he answered. Then, glancing at Jerdine, he continued. "A friend of ours—Beatrice Tice—she started channeling the old jewel smiths and such."

"She's done some lovely work," his wife added.

"Did she come up with this talent about the same time you did?"

Zane sucked at his drink. "For a fact, she did. We were part of a small, underground group of local artists. The stuff we paint and sculpt isn't preapproved by the Agency for the Arts and Humanities, you understand."

"Did anyone else in your group share your good fortune?"

"Probably. Since I've been channeling, I haven't spoken to any of them."

"Why not?"

"Because Drake thought it wouldn't be a good idea. You know, petty jealousies and things. They can really dent your perspective."

"Are you still painting?" I asked.

"Well"—he sighed—"it seems I've temporarily stopped pulling in the talent of the masters."

"When did this occur?"

"Last week. My colors just up and ran dry. It's a damned shame, because I was right in the middle of a nice project. Still, I'm sure all those dead artists I've come to know so well will get back to me when they can."

"When was the last time you spoke to Drake?"

"A couple of weeks ago. He came by to pick up a Degas I painted."

I slugged the coffee and tasted the flavors my nose had identified. "Can I see your most recent canvas?"

He grinned. "Why sure." Rising, he led me to a small, brown door in the tiny kitchen.

The basement was windowless, damp, and filled to the rafters with paintings. He saw me staring at a large watercolor leaning against the side of the wooden steps. "Oh, don't bother with that one. It's just some of my own work. Not very good, either."

In fact, it was exquisite. Zane was right: his talent was there. It was too bad he didn't give himself credit for it.

He worked his way over to an easel covered with a bright blue bedsheet. "This is what I wanted to show you," he announced. Pulling the cloth away, he revealed a half-finished painting.

I stood there in awe and, admittedly, was confused. Had I not seen it for myself, I might have discounted this amazing story, but when the stained shroud protecting the canvas was removed, I saw the strange landscape of Edvard Munch's *The Scream*, an expressionist masterpiece that had disappeared from public view forty years before.

36

WILLIAM ZANE'S EXPERIENCE was odd, but the implications were startling. As I hurried to the subway to meet LaRue, I couldn't stop wondering if it was possible to tamper with someone's God-given talent. Could an outside influence change the firing patterns of a person's brain and turn the mediocre into the master? Worse than that, could these interlopers control the flow of the energy for their own gain? My ideas about Arkin and his team had been far too simplistic; it was evident now.

After Duvalier changed the world, he sold off the museums to the highest bidders and with vases and sculptures went the paintings. Art experts became a thing of the past and art critics took their places. It would be damned hard to tell what was a genuine Erté and what was not.

I met LaRue at an address in Ward one hundred that proved to be a ragged building with dingy furnishings, and despite the fact that all other free clinics were closed for storm preparations, this aide station was going at full tilt. Stepping into the crusty waiting room, I planted a look at the patients, secretly hoping to find a lycanthrope among them. It was a useless game, because not even my inside-out fur itched enough to alert me.

LaRue took the con and approached the receptionist. "We've got an appointment with your administrator."

She nodded and waved us down a hallway. The size of the clinic proved to be illusionary, because when we reached the end of this stretch, we were escorted down four flights of steps and into a large white laboratory. It's here we were introduced to Dr. Margaret Quinlan, a tight-assed old biddy with a peppery attitude. When we identified ourselves, she gave us a quick nod, pausing to let her gaze linger upon me. I got the prickles during her momentary review, certain she could see my supernatural disposition barely contained by my shrunken uniform.

We slid onto stools by the fancy lab tables and kept silent for a minute as we watched a couple of beefy assistants help a naked young woman into a large steel cylinder. She tossed us an embarrassed look, and to be kind, I glanced away. LaRue, on the other hand, checked out every inch of her skinny body. The men locked the door behind her, but she turned and stared at us through the viewing glass.

"What's that thing?" I asked.

"It's a hyperbaric chamber," Quinlan answered with smart efficiency.

"What does it do?"

"It raises the atmospheric pressure. Classically, it's been used as a method of treating decompression sickness and as an antiaging process." She paused to lean over a microphone attached to her desk. "How do you feel, Becky?"

Her response whined over a small speaker. "I'm fine. Are you sure this isn't going to hurt?"

"Quite sure." Quinlan nodded to her associates, one of whom fiddled with the buttons on the front of the box. I heard the hiss of a hermetic seal. The doctor sat down next to me and touched a stud on a control panel by her computer.

"What's this woman's problem?" I asked.

"She really has no problem at all. She's here as an experimentee." After motioning to her assistant to flip a switch, she then added: "If you have concerns, you should know she's been paid well for her cooperation."

"What kind of experiment is this?" LaRue said.

Quinlan grunted as she studied a scrolling readout on her monitor. "You're not here because of this, Marshals."

Her petulance hit a raw nerve in me and I reached across the table to grab her wrist. She snapped her head around to glare at me and tried to wrestle free. I enjoyed her struggle for just a moment before speaking softly. "Dr. Quinlan, we're law-enforcement officers actively pursuing a murder investigation. This situation requires you to answer any questions we put to you. Failure to comply can and will lead to incarceration."

She tried on a defiant expression, but lost it to pain as I squeezed. "You're hurting me. Please. Stop."

I didn't let go. Instead, I pulled back on my strength, maintaining just enough to make it clear how vulnerable she really was. When I was sure everything was copacetic, I released her. "Answer Marshal LaRue's inquiry."

Quinlan rubbed her arm and some feeling back into her fingers. "This woman has the ability to maintain her body without material nourishment."

"That's impossible," I said.

"It's true. We've been documenting her since the age of sixteen. She's now thirty-six and has taken no food or water for the past twenty years."

"How do you know this?" I asked.

"Because she's been in government custody since that time."

"No one can go twenty years without eating."

"It's hard to believe, I know." Quinlan paused to stop the rise of pressure in the container and then pointed to a thick paper file sitting on a nearby stool. "That is her dossier. If you open it to the first twenty-five pages, you'll find my report of this past week. She's been here in the clinic and has been closely observed by two independent PHO physicians. During that time she took no food or water, but she passed blood and bile and urinated a total of thirty-six cubic inches. Her weight was at one hundred and twenty-eight pounds on the first day and dropped to a hundred and eighteen pounds by the third day. On the fourth day, she was down to one-fifteen, but on the fifth, she was up to a hundred and twenty-three pounds, and by the time Saturday rolled around, she was right back to where she'd started."

"How can that be?" LaRue demanded.

"We're not sure," she said. "There could be several explanations, the simplest being that we exist in an ocean of life-sustaining energy, but for whatever reasons, only a few people in millions can access it."

"Others can do this?"

She nodded. "In fact, the first documented case was in the early part of the last century. A Russian woman claimed not to have consumed food and water for forty years. At one point she came under close scrutiny of the German SS during World War Two. They couldn't detect any fraud."

I understand about strange metabolic forces. My own burner

runs as hot as the Trabi's engine. Gibson believes this is the very reason I heal quickly, run faster, and have more brute strength than my size should allow. Knowing this, I've often wondered if it will cause me to die an early death. How much heat and friction can the human body actually take before the insulation wears thin?

Sliding from the stool, I approached the cylinder and glanced through the window. The patient seemed unconcerned and had settled into a soft chair, covering herself with a blanket. She diligently stared at the pictures in a glossy magazine. "Why the pressure chamber?"

"We're attempting to see if an increase in oxygen pressure changes her ability to sustain her body in this manner."

"What would that show?"

"Well, it could be that the pressure affects the flow of undetected energy. We can't measure it, obviously. So we make our calculations according to inference. In other words, what changes do we see in the patient?"

I shot a look toward LaRue and he asked the question I was thinking. "What do you believe, Dr. Quinlan?"

She shrugged. "I don't know. For myself, I'm hoping to understand how she converts oxygen and other gases. This might give us some useful clues."

"Why are you doing this in the first place?" I asked.

Her reply sounded hollow, though the words had a rather ominous ring to them. "Our world is woefully lacking in resources, Marshal. Can you imagine being able to transmit this ability to the starving masses?"

LaRue simply stared at her. My stomach decided to mock the outrageous idea by growling.

Quinlan heard it and managed a chuckle. "Since you understand the importance of this test, I hope you'll keep this information to yourselves. Now, what did you really want to talk about?"

"We know this place is an OI clearinghouse," LaRue began. "We understand many of the individuals who stumble in here think they're getting an acupuncture treatment to clear up their acne, but, instead, end up having their psi-abilities exploited."

Like a fitful neon light, she flashed us a resigned expression.

"I'm right on the doorstep of my retirement, Marshals. Please don't complicate matters for me."

My partner continued to play it hard. "It's a shame, but we don't have time to do this gently. We need to find a man named Jerome Taggart. Did he come through this establishment?"

She stalled again. "You said yourself it looks like business is good. Well, it is. I don't see every patient personally and I don't read every file personally. We transmit data to the OI that fits within specific parameters set by the government. Beyond that I don't ask any questions. It's none of my business."

"They've threatened you."

"Life is a threat, Marshal. You deal with it."

"Yes, by closing your eyes to the flagrant disregard for our humanitarian rights." I leaned toward her. "Do you know Jerome Taggart?"

She sighed, yanked at the collar of her white coat, and pushed back from the desk. "I knew that bastard would come back to haunt me one of these days. Jerome Taggart is a very disturbed man."

"When did he come here?" LaRue asked.

"The first time? Four years ago. He suffered from undefined seizures. Each convulsive episode would leave him with temporary amnesia, various disassociative symptoms, and delusions."

"What was so remarkable about him?" I asked. "It sounds like epilepsy."

"It was. The remarkable part was what happened after he received electroshock treatments."

"You gave him the juice?" LaRue said.

"Not us," she answered. "A clinical physician somewhere on the PHO circuit. I can't recall who it was off the top of my head."

"What happened?"

"Taggart was only supposed to receive a small dosage, but the tech apparently misread the prescription. It was a strange accident." She paused to insert a sigh. "He was sent here, because the excessive shock changed his L-field."

I glanced at LaRue and back to her. "So, there *is* an L-field?"

"Oh, yes. Science has known about it for decades. In most people, it acts like an insulating shield against the environment.

It can be measured and in normal ranges displays a small electrical charge. The shock Taggart took boosted the charge. He could walk into a room and make people's hair stand on end. It was uncomfortable to be near him, because you were aware of this intensity he had." She paused to gain momentum again but ran out of steam after one sentence. "I'll never forget that guy."

"So you sent him to Conrad," I said.

"Yes." She clicked her tongue and stared at me uncertainly.

"Dr. Quinlan, if you know something, please tell us."

"I've never spoken about any of this," she answered. "I'm afraid."

"Of OI retribution?"

"No. I'm afraid of what the OI will use me for next, should they find out I spoke with you. Casper Conrad is a dangerous, powerful man who comes off like a real nice guy in a rumpled suit. He's a viper, Marshals. Don't forget it."

My heart took an extra bump upon hearing her words. Gibson had unwittingly offered my lycanthropic soul to the head demon himself. I pushed this thought away and continued to press Quinlan. "We have eyewitness accounts of some bizarre behavior demonstrated by Mr. Taggart. He apparently has a problem with his hand."

"Mr. Taggart had a condition known as alien hand syndrome."

I glanced at LaRue and found him staring intently at the doctor. "His left hand, I assume?"

"Yes. Alien hand is a neurological dysfunction caused by damage in the switching centers between brain hemispheres. People with this condition report a lack of control when a seizure begins. The hand actually seems to move of its own accord, no matter what the person tries. It feels like they're not alone, that an alien within them is guiding their actions."

I kept a gasp in check, but it wasn't easy. My paranoia meter was on full tilt as I considered the myriad displays of a crippled brain.

"I performed a few tests on Mr. Taggart before I called Casper," Quinlan continued. "This man was sick with a host of problems. The disproportionate electrical field had begun to fry his nervous system. At least that's what I assumed."

"Why?"

"I found the signs of demyelination." We both tossed her confused looks, so she explained. "The myelin sheath is a layer of insulation that coats the axons of nerves. It's responsible for the transmission of the electrical impulses within the system. The brain is made up of myelinated nerve fibers. Victims of multiple sclerosis suffer demyelination in the brain and spinal cord, but it's thought to be caused by a virus picked up early in life."

"Still, Conrad wanted him," LaRue said flatly.

"That's right. I don't have the facilities to do a full-scale scan, you understand, but I have experience in neurology. At the rate he appeared to be deteriorating, I wouldn't give him more than ten or twelve years."

"Conrad considered ten or twelve years a good return on his investment," I said.

She nodded, hesitated again, and finally punted the ball. "The reason he was worth fooling with was because the shock treatments left Taggart with amnesia."

"So, he could tell this guy anything about who he was and he'd believe it?" LaRue asked.

"Well, no. Drug therapies have made it possible to recover missing memories. They've also made it possible to replace them."

37

WE RETURNED TO the office long enough to be grabbed by Julie. She invited us into her private cubbyhole.

"That tip you got from Fraley paid off," she announced, pointing to a thick manila file open on her desk. "The cleanup team on the case found these in a storage locker rented to Arkin. Seems we've got a man who not only kept his apartment fastidiously clean, but believed in neatly organizing information on his work assignments."

"Cover your ass, huh?" LaRue said.

"I'd do the same thing in that business," she answered.

I have to admit, Fraley's hit unsettled me, but I didn't mention it. "I take it a lot of familiar names came up."

She smeared on a lizard smile. "His little peekaboo teams were heavy on the personnel. Everyone from psychics to photographers to actors to teachers to hit men. Most are temporary employees who have no idea what is going on. It looks like they receive their assignments and compensation through a third party."

"Was the third party mentioned?" LaRue asked.

"Our friend Casper Conrad's name came up quite often."

"Twenty people," I said. "That's a lot of varied perspectives."

"And the results of an investigation are open to all kinds of subjective analysis." She pushed the folder toward me. "Take a few minutes and do some reading," she ordered. "When you've got something to work with, haul this file back in here before you hit the street. I don't want anyone looking at it except you two. Clear?"

We did as she asked and hurried back to our cubicle, where we spent a couple of hours perusing pages that were as extraordinary as they were unsettling.

There were in-depth notes on how the OI manipulated William Zane and several other struggling artists. The trick was to find people who had extraordinary talent, strong beliefs in spirit guidance, trust in invisible magic, and a pound of gullibility. Arkin explained how difficult it was to convince people of their inherent worth; self-esteem, apparently, being the barometer for success.

He gave names of associates who helped with his various scams, what he paid them, and when. Arkin had a ying full of contacts, too many for us to check out. I was beginning to despair when on the next to the last page, he mentioned someone we knew already—Teresa Yarnell.

I grabbed LaRue by his sweat glands and off we went for a visit.

We found her at home in Ward 26. She had a modest house with a tree in the yard decorated with gold lamé prayer banners and sparkling green tinsel. We entered her screened front porch to see this glittering theme repeated, with the addition of aluminum cans and garland. Yarnell came to the door, but instead of inviting us in chose to hold the interview on the stoop. We obliged her by settling onto the moldy wicker furniture. LaRue immediately pounded her with questions about her taste in exterior design.

She hesitated in answering, but finally fessed up. "I use them to block out psionic transmissions."

"Incoming or outgoing?" he asked.

"Both."

"Are you afraid you're being watched?"

"I am. You're proof of that."

"We're here to ask you some questions about your remarkable abilities," I said soothingly. "We're not watching you."

She didn't reply; instead, she leveled a frown my direction. "My kids will be home from school soon and I don't want you to be here. You might upset them. Tell me what you want to know and then please leave."

Her attitude pissed me off and I lost all my sweetness. "Don't you know why we're here?"

Suspicion dallied with her frown. "What are you driving at?"

"You're clairvoyant and clairaudient. Didn't you see us or hear us coming?"

"I told you I'm psionically protected while I'm here."

I glanced around. "A soup tin can do all that? Imagine it, Andy. Not only does it hold chicken noodle stew, it can hold bad vibrations, too."

Yarnell came to her feet and paced the length of the porch. "Please," she begged. "This is no joke."

"The joke is seeing the future," I answered.

"You don't believe in any of this, do you?"

I stretched against the turn of the chair, crossed my legs at the ankles, and studied her with a lazy expression. She immediately hopped back to her seat, as though my thoughts drove her there.

"How were you enlisted in the OI?" LaRue asked.

"I was sent to the clinic in Ward One Hundred."

"What was wrong with you?"

"I had viral meningitis. The doctors treated it with antibiotics and after a short stay at the hospital, I was cleared of the problem, but a few weeks after I came home, I started having these visions."

"What were they like?" I demanded.

"They weren't like anything. They didn't come to me in bright colors and loud noises." She stopped speaking and started massaging her temples. When she continued, her sentences sounded dry. "The first time it happened, I was listening to the news report on the vid one morning while cooking breakfast for the kids. The announcer said Minister Ash Kester had been shot in the head. The protective service people had caught the murderer before he could leave the Science and Technology Building. The shooter's name was Donna Fegan. I watched the report and then I watched it again when they repeated the bulletin an hour later. For some reason, it caught my attention and I called my girlfriend to tell her. I also called my husband at work and my mother and father." She paused again, but this time I couldn't tell if it was for effect or not. "Minister Kester was shot two weeks later, but the circumstances of her death were the same."

"Did you have these episodes frequently after that?" LaRue asked.

"Yes. It was getting so I couldn't tell what was reality and what was a future event. I went to the doctor at the local free clinic. She saw me and then sent me to Ward One Hundred."

"Who brought you in? Casper Conrad?"

"Yes."

"Did he bring in Sam Arkin and his crew that way?"

"No. Sam started at the OI around the same time Casper did. They're old timers."

"Did Ingrid Calloway bring them in?" I demanded.

She dropped her gaze to the floor. "I'm not sure."

"Mrs. Calloway did more than the taxes, huh? Did she bring in Amarilo Valquez and Dixon Emery?"

"Yes, I know that for certain. They came on board a while after I started. She brought in Andrea Pio, too, but Ms. Pio was initially recommended by Casper."

"Tell us, Mrs. Yarnell," I said, "do psychics work with the remote-viewing groups, just to make sure nothing unexpected happens?"

Her head came up and bounced around the same way LaRue's spring-necked Lenin doll did. "That's classified information," she snapped. "How did you find out about that?"

I lied, and made it sound intimidating. "OI employees aren't the only ones who have to pass psi-tests."

It was enough to frazzle her one remaining nerve. She jumped from the chair and took a furious turn around the porch, finally stopping to cross her arms and tap a staccato beat with her foot. "You want to know if I worked with Sam."

"That's not a necessary answer. We already know you did."

She scowled, taking a moment more to sound out an SOS on the floorboards. Then: "Sam needed a clairvoyant. He was impulsive and prone to interfering in situations best left alone."

"Does that mean remote viewers have the ability to affect the target?"

"Yes. Sam's team were some of the hottest peekers around."

"Peekers?" LaRue said.

"Yeah, it's a play on PK. You know, PK—peekers?"

LaRue nodded. "What made them so hot?"

"With a little selective help, they could make a person think and do practically anything they wanted. You have to understand that the human organism is wide open to invasion. Certain nerve sensations can become learned responses and psychokinetic energy can affect the central nervous system. I saw Arkin and his team turn a criminal into a priest once, just by making him believe he was receiving regular visitations from St. Ophelia. When she appeared, it was a signal for his brain to release endorphins, hormones that stimulate certain areas of the brain."

"You're talking about stimulating the pleasure areas in the brain," LaRue said.

"That's simplistic," she answered.

"How so?"

"By training the brain to release certain chemicals upon command, be it induced by a hallucination or by an actual event, you can get any response you want." She stared at me with a sudden wild expression. "What if I told you just the right vision and just the right nerve response would place you within a state of rapture which could go on for hours?"

"I'd say I wish I could do it."

"Be careful what you ask for Marshal Merrick. You just might get it."

LaRue banged away at the subject. "These people are conditioned from beginning to end without them even realizing it."

"That's right. As expensive as it is, it's still cheaper than prisons and labor camps."

"I take it, once a person has been conditioned, other PK controls take over in a maintenance capacity."

"Yes. Peekers look in at assigned intervals and report back if further stimulation is warranted. Call it a booster shot, if you will."

Hearing this horrendous confession, neither LaRue nor I could speak for a minute. I finally summoned my voice. "We're assuming they needed to work the street angles on these setups."

"Yes, depending on the target and the situation, but the remote viewers never leave the safety of the office. The OI hires con artists of every description to round out the ballgame—who and whatever they need to get a job done. All Sam and his peekers were concerned with were the brain changes."

"Did they use other methods besides telepathy to coerce an individual?"

"Yes. They were very good at inducing all sorts of PK

phenomenon remotely. These were powerful men, Marshal. They used at least sixty percent of their brains as compared to the odd ten percent the rest of us manage. Maybe that's one of the reasons they burn out so quickly."

"What did you do as part of the RV team?" LaRue asked.

"I did a foresight and a hindsight scan. In other words, I looked to see where the person headed without the OI interference and where he would head with it."

"That's suggesting time has several different lines to choose from," I said.

She nodded.

I used the opportunity to hit her with the big guns. "Did you ever work Arkin's collateral scams, Mrs. Yarnell?"

The question shot her rockets again and she walked back and forth several times before replying. "I kept trying to resist him."

"Did he ever attempt to convince you by using his team's abilities for persuasion?"

"No," she whispered.

"Are you sure?"

She hesitated, so I filled in her answer.

"The way I see it, something happened to you during one of his rip-offs. You transferred out of the remote-viewing section to get away from him. What went on?"

She sat back down again and faced me directly. "Part of my duties was to serve as a psychic power reader. I could actually plot the occurrence of a future event by relating it to something in the past."

"Working the possible time lines?" LaRue asked.

"Yes. There's more to it than that, though. I've never been able to adequately control my psi-abilities. All the training I've gotten hasn't made it any easier to know the difference between the past, present, and future. What it did was allow me to psionically step clear of the fourth dimension, that of time."

LaRue grunted. "What you're suggesting is that you stepped into the fifth dimension, that of eternity?"

She nodded. "I took a trip into eternity each time I had a peek. It's taxing on your psyche. It changes your perspective—and not always for the better."

"I should say so," I answered.

"At first I was on a schedule, but then things got busy and

they upped the number of times I took a dip. Then Sam started hounding me for favors."

"Did you do them?"

"Yes."

"Because you were afraid of him?"

"Yes. I was dipping so much after a while I found myself with a backwash problem. I'm constantly flooded by images and sounds until I don't know what's real anymore. That's the reason for all my danglers. They really do seem to help." She scowled at the floor. "Perhaps I'm deluding myself, but I have to do something or I'll go mad."

LaRue was ready with one of his metaphysical proverbs. "Some wise old fellow once said: In a world of illusion all living things are deluded."

To hell with that philosophy. "You worked with Arkin in a scam involving Jerome Taggart. What was it?"

She shook her head emphatically. "No, I didn't."

"Don't lie, Mrs. Yarnell."

"I didn't. The last scam I helped Sam with involved Andrea Pio."

I glanced at LaRue, who absently fingered the end of his hair braid as he studied the woman. Then, in a quiet, husky voice, he said: "What did Ms. Pio do to deserve their attention? I thought she was their boss."

"She was, but Sam was crazy with the need for revenge. His health was failing and he thought he deserved more from the OI than a boot out the door."

"He was fired?" I asked.

"The whole team was disavowed a few months before they were due to retire with a full pension. It's a cost-saving measure for the government."

"The lousy bastards," LaRue muttered.

"What was Arkin planning for his revenge scam?"

"I don't know. Drake asked me to scan ahead. He wasn't looking for a power reading; he just wanted me to have a peek to make sure everything would be all right for the scam. He gave me the date it would be completed and I checked for him."

"You saw Taggart?"

"Yes. I saw him and Ms. Pio. The backwash was bad, Marshal. I kept getting disjointed messages. At one point I saw

Sam and his team sitting around a table, and in my psionic state, I didn't hear them breathing. They were dead."

"So, what did you do?"

She shrugged. "I lied to them."

38

WE HAD JUST reached the Trabi when dispatch called about us seeing a man in Ward 67. It was across the district from where we were, but Julie had gotten on the horn to stress the importance of this interview, so off we went, working through detours and barricaded streets until we pulled up to a large cinder block house washed in flamingo pink, turquoise, and sunflower yellow. We found the fire-engine-red front door slightly ajar and poked our heads in to see a tiny waiting room done in garish tones, suggesting the painter had either bought his acrylics on sale or had a rather unappealing sense of beauty and harmony.

A young woman dressed in white harem pants and a diaphanous blouse greeted us as we stepped inside. "My name is Amy," she said. "How may I help you?"

LaRue was too busy ogling her tits through her filmy shirt to answer, so I did the honors by asking to see Randolph Inghart.

She bowed and led us quickly down a long hallway to the last room on the left. Inghart proved to be a tall, reedy, long-faced fellow whose outfit matched his receptionist's, and at the moment of our arrival he was busy clipping a piece of hair from the head of a young boy lying on an examining table. He worked with an assistant, who placed long, golden, acupuncture needles into the child's midsection. The kid stared like a zombie at the flecks in the ceiling tiles.

"Thank you for coming, Marshals," Inghart said. "This is my colleague Jan Wyatt."

"What is this place?" I asked.

"We're a traditional healing center," he answered. "We're fully licensed, of course."

163

"We understand you have information pertaining to a murder investigation?"

"Yes. You talked to Dr. Quinlan about a man named Jerome Taggart."

"That's right. How did you know that?"

"I was in the next office. The walls at the clinic are thin."

I glanced at LaRue and discovered him studying the child intently. "Do you both work at the free clinic?"

"Yes, and we're concerned. We know the OI is taking experimentees from there."

"So what's your gig?" I asked.

"I'm a specialist in radiesthesia."

"Which is?"

"Radiesthesia is the process of diagnosing illness with the use of a pendulum. It's a form of dowsing."

"I've heard everything now," I said, adding a sigh for emphasis.

Inghart smiled. "No, you haven't. The OI has experimented with so-called occult cures for years. The free clinic exploits the traditional arts, hoping to collect esoteric knowledge for its own ends."

"We understand. Do you know something about Jerome Taggart?"

The woman answered. "We've both seen him on a professional basis. Several times."

"And so you think there's something fishy in the perfume factory, huh?" LaRue asked, finally wrenching his gaze from the child.

"Most definitely," she said. "We're not privy to secret information, you understand. We work as consultants, so what we're about to tell you is subjective as far as that goes."

"Don't keep us in suspense, then," LaRue said.

Inghart took the lead. "Quite simply: Casper Conrad is the problem. He would have made an efficient Nazi during World War Two." He paused in his explanation to step to a white metal cabinet. When he returned, he brought a silver, cone-shaped pendulum strung on a delicate black thread. He used his thumb to flip open a tiny lid on the medallion and then stuffed the wad of hair inside. "Conrad has most people frightened and Dr. Quinlan cowers at his approaching footsteps."

"But not you two?"

He shrugged, giving me a sideways glance as he did. "Dr. Quinlan lied to you. Jerome Taggart has been coming to the clinic once a week for treatment."

"When did it start?"

"About six months ago. I did a reading on him the first time he showed up."

"And?"

"And, the dowsing showed systemic nerve dysfunction."

"Dr. Quinlan told us about his symptoms," I said. "What's the matter? Weren't the walls thin enough to pick up everything in our conversation?"

"We heard you," he answered. "Radiesthesia goes deeper than any nuclear scan. It measures the invisible."

I forced my biting sarcasm into the corners of my teeth before answering. "Mr. Inghart, we don't have time for this."

"I'm talking about science, Marshal Merrick," he snapped.

I took a step toward him, waiting for him to flinch. He didn't, but I never let a good intimidation ploy go to waste. "You better cough up some real microbes, mister, or I'm hauling your ass back to the shop. Now spill it."

He jumped into an explanation at light speed. "His symmetry was all wrong. I intuitively divine the psychokinetic energy captured within the body and I found clots of measurable electrical resistance throughout his system. Besides that, his magnetic polarity seems to be shifting back and forth."

"You can tell all that from hair?"

"By asking yes-or-no questions and seeing which direction the pendulum swings or rotates, I can make a diagnosis. I'm telling you, this guy is starting to short out, and until a couple of weeks ago he came in here regularly for isoelectric stimulation."

"Let me guess," I said. "Isoelectric stimulation gets the juice flowing again and breaks up the energy dams."

Wyatt nodded. "That's what I do with the needles. The body is composed of several meridian points. These are places where electrical conductivity within the nervous system converges. By inhibiting or stimulating the natural flow in these areas, we can treat people for a variety of medical problems. Acupunc-

ture has been an effective treatment for stroke victims since
early this century."

LaRue ignored the malarkey and asked: "Did a woman
accompany him when he came for his appointments?"

Inghart nodded. "His sister, so she said. I'm sure she was his
control, though."

"What was her name?"

"She never offered and I never asked."

"Did you cure him?"

"No," Wyatt said. "He claimed we did, but our tests proved
his condition had done nothing more than stabilize."

"I assume you use some sort of objective quantitative
method to gauge changes?" I said.

"Yes. You can measure electrical conductivity." She paused
to wiggle one of the needles sticking out of the kid's stomach.
"He had a bad limp, the result of poor circulation in his leg. I
asked him if he was in pain one day and he denied he was."

"He should have been?"

"You don't understand. He denied there was anything
wrong. In fact, he appeared stunned when I mentioned it. He
claimed he felt fine and that his energy level had never been
higher."

Inghart added to her statement. "We're aware the OI does a
conversion process of some sort. Whatever they do, they
obviously have this guy convinced that he's in perfect health."

39

After meeting with these two wackos, we headed up-district to work another angle. Halfway there, the heat and the smell of kerosene forced me into a stretch. I yelled for LaRue to pull over, because between the fumes and the pain in my solar plexus, I couldn't breathe a teaspoon of air. He wasn't to a complete stop before I shoved the door wide and launched myself onto the street, panting like a wolf after a long run.

Some stretches come on with a premium of dead time loaded into the schedule. During these seizures, my thoughts become so quiet, I fear they've fled for good. The components of language slowly dissolve and I'm left with tapioca for brains. Once the agony is over, it takes several minutes to regain my composure, and of course, all this was happening in the middle of one of the worst neighborhoods in the locality.

When I finally came around, LaRue had dragged me into the shade of the only tree on the block. There were pigeons all around us and a couple pecked at my partner's hair braid.

"Ty," he whispered, "I don't mean to hurry this along, but we need to get into the car as soon as we can."

I nodded, tried to stand up, and fell back on my tush. Dizziness swamped me in the midst of a sudden, blinding headache. It was then I realized we weren't alone.

Three bruising street thugs had joined us. I squinted at them, but against the glare of the sun and the light sensitivity brought on by the migraine, all I saw were shadows. It was bad news: we were going to get rolled and the only thing I could do to help my partner was puke on the creeps' shoes.

One of LaRue's most effective weapons is his ability to talk the tail off a comet. Instead of immediately going for his service revolver, he will first try to defuse the situation by suggesting topics of paramount interest to the listener.

"Hello, boys," he said languidly. "Right hot day, wouldn't you say?"

The bruisers each took a step closer. "Looks like the heat has got your pretty partner," someone growled.

LaRue swatted at a pesky bird before answering. "No, it wasn't the heat, fellows. It's the plague."

The man answered, but this time trepidation had entered the picture and he no longer barked belligerently. "What kind of plague?"

"The kind that's airborne." I could feel LaRue settling into lecture mode. "You see, after you breathe the same air as a plague victim, the virus gets into your lungs. At that point it forms a pusy paste that fills up your bronchial system. From there, it leaks into your chest cavity, where it begins to sludge up your organs. This whole time, the plague worms excrete an enzyme which eats away at the very flesh of your body. In about two weeks your skin rots and your meat falls off the bone."

Silence followed this introductory explanation. Then: "Well, why ain't you got it?"

"Because I've been vaccinated," LaRue answered. "Now, if you gents don't want to experience the burning regret of getting too close, I'd suggest you just take it on down the street." With that, he stood up, patted the dust from the front of his cammies, and then hoisted me to my feet.

Once up, I witnessed the quick retreat of the goon squad. "Plague?" I said.

"It worked, didn't it?"

I tried to nod, but the movement aggravated the delicate balance between the pain in my head and the biliousness in my stomach. LaRue guided me to the Trabi and took off at a fast pedal. Each bump and chuckhole seemed to rattle my brain and I had to finally confess my weakness. "Andy, I have to go home for a few minutes and lie down. The heat has really beaten me up."

He nodded, but said: "Do you think it's just the heat, Ty?"

His question made my head hurt more as I tried to concentrate. "Why do you ask that?"

"You've had three stretches in quick succession."

"So?"

"What if we are in the middle of a paranormal scam with this poltergeist stuff, and what if it is coming in from the OI?"

"Are you saying my stretches are being induced remotely?"

He glanced at me. "Maybe it's too farfetched, huh? You've had bad cycles before."

I just stared at him, able to comprehend the possibility, but unable to express the horror of it. He turned back to the road, gunning the Trabi, and as we headed toward my apartment his words grew with intensity in my thoughts.

We were three miles from my building when LaRue's communist car cut out. The thing stopped like a watch: the steering wheel froze, the wheels locked up, and the trunk popped open. LaRue tossed me a look and I saw a suspicious glint in his dark eyes. He slowly opened the door, trudged to the front of the car, and snapped the hood. I expected his usual curse, but this time I didn't hear a word. Instead, he propped the lid back and motioned me with his hand. I joined him, glancing at the engine.

"What's wrong?" I asked.

"You're kidding, right?" he said.

"Andy, I don't know anything about cars. What blew?"

He blinked at me. "You can't see it?"

I turned back to check again. It was the same greasy lawnmower motor it had always been. "No, what am I supposed to see?"

"It's oozing tapioca," he said.

40

I STOOD THERE as stunned as if a fly had zoomed up my nose. Had our poltergeist read my thoughts? My expression cast doubt on LaRue's assessment of the situation and he groaned.

"You don't see it, do you?" he said.

"No," I answered, unable to keep the huskiness from edging my voice.

He squinted at me. "What else, Ty?"

I wanted to shake my head, but that hurt too much, so I shut my eyes and sighed. Without opening them, I said: "Andy, I was just thinking how some of my seizures turn me to tapioca." I chanced a peek to see his reaction and it was what I expected.

He looked toward heaven and wailed: "Oh, shit; oh, shit; oh shit!"

I glanced at the engine. "Is the tapioca still there?"

"Yes," he answered dismally. To prove it, he reached toward the makeshift air filter and yanked out one of the nylon pot scrubbers he used to catch the dirt. Holding it out in front of him, he studied it. "Why can't you see this?" Then, before I could answer, he took a close-quarter sniff of the item. "And why can't you smell it?"

"What does it smell like?"

"Like vinegar."

"Maybe my stretch had something to do with it." I paused to coax the head knocker out of my skull by massaging the bridge of my nose. "Maybe this last jolt changed my perspective somehow. Maybe the neurons in my brain are funneling down different tubes."

"Are you saying my thoughts are keeping this car from running?" he asked.

"I don't know what I'm saying, Andy. I'm the last person

who would admit the possibility, but maybe it does have something to do with your brain's biochemicals. The fact that I can't see this doesn't mean it's not real to you."

He nodded. "But what can I do to change it?"

I hung out a theory to dry. "Bowen told us Noone healed by incorporating the interaction of the physical brain and the thoughts of the subtle mind. If that's right, then it doesn't matter which comes first—the thoughts or the electrochemical process."

My partner is quick, even when he's dealing with metaphysical tapioca. "So, if I change my thinking and somehow deny the existence of this goo, it could change the way my physical thoughts work and make the crap go away."

"Exactly," I answered. "Still, you're natural resistance might play against your efforts."

"Well, let's try." LaRue replaced the pot scrubber and then ceremoniously lay both hands across the battery. He made a show of concentrating and repeating the sentence: "I'm imagining this whole thing." After five minutes of intoning this mantra, he gave up. "It's not working."

"It might be that you can't convince yourself."

"So, what will convince me, then? If I can't figure this out, we're on our way for a long walk, and I know how much you feel like doing that right now."

I squinted against the bright sunlight and dipped my chin in an effort to nod, but a piercing pain drilled my resolve. Cutting the movement short, I replaced it with a suggestion. "What about your poltergeist spray?"

"What about it?"

"Spritz it on the car."

"But it's not done. I don't have all the ingredients yet."

"Didn't you tell me your mother said the act of putting together the spray was just as important as the stuff itself?"

"Yeah, so?"

"Andy, don't you believe the spray will work?"

He stared at me a moment and then I saw the bulb go on. "I believe it will work."

"It doesn't matter if all the ingredients are there or not."

LaRue dove into the backseat of the Trabi, coming up after a few seconds with a spray pump bottle. He returned and aimed his poltergeist eradicator at the grille. Muttering curse words in Russian, he layered the front of the car with a steady stream of rum and frog hairs. He glanced at me. "How long should I wait before checking?"

I flapped a hand at him as I climbed into the passenger's seat. "Don't check," I called. "Just see if she'll start."

He did as I asked and the Trabi chimed to life after only a few ragged attempts. "This really weirds me out," he said. "If it's that easy to change thoughts and biochemical thought patterns, why haven't I had such success in the past? St. Ophelia, it must have taken me three years to wean myself from artificial sweetener."

"That doesn't bother me so much as the fact of how insidious this whole mess really is," I said.

"Yeah. You can't exactly look over your shoulder to see who's doing it, either." He gunned the car. "Worse than that—it doesn't matter if it's a goblin or a person playing these games. The result is the same."

Upon stating the reality of the situation, LaRue wound down into silence. He also didn't take any chances by turning the engine off when we reached my building.

I told him I'd be back before our next interview and entered the walk-up with a sense of relief. The darkness in the stairwell seemed to ease the pound in my head. Unfortunately, the respite I longed for was not to be. Gibson was over for a visit.

I found him layering trash blankets against the big window while Baba supervised. It was hotter than the inside of a chili pepper because of it, and seeing the good doctor did nothing for my fractured mood. I must have looked as bad as I felt, because he came to me instantly, stopping short to touch me with his intense scrutiny.

"Couch," I mumbled, and headed for it.

"Stretch?" he asked.

I rolled onto the sofa and felt the ache in my head track down my spine. "Yeah. What are you doing here?"

He flopped into my lumpy recliner. "We need to talk."

"Baba, could you pour me some water?" I begged.

She nodded and turned away to fiddle with the pressure gauge on the sink while Gibson continued.

"I was wrong," he announced. "I should have been up front with you from the start."

I pulled a deep breath, but didn't answer.

"If Myra and I make any money, we'll split it with you."

Enough. "Go away, Gibson. I'm not in the mood for this right now."

"I'm trying to apologize here."

"I don't want your apology. It's just a lot of stinking wind." I could feel him tense without even glancing in his direction. "You're afraid I'll call your bluff and walk away from these experiments in misery."

"I'm trying to be reasonable," he husked.

Baba stepped over with a glass, giving me the eyeball for not cooperating. I took the water with a thanks and then ignored them both by quietly sipping my drink. The day had further frayed the ends of my inflamed nerves. I hurt all over, physically and emotionally, the range of this pain beginning in my spirit and ending in a sore tailbone. Turning toward Gibson, I said: "I don't want your precious money."

He grew suspicious in a heartbeat. "What else is there?"

"You don't get it, do you?" I spat. "The simple fact is I want to be able to trust you. That's all there is and nothing more as far as I'm concerned. Now that you know what's behind my questions, do me a favor and give me some space so I can let the wolf finish ripping my guts out."

He squinted at me and then rose woodenly, nodding to Baba before leaving. I was grateful for his silence this time, but the moment he was gone I was forced to stand down my roommate, an opponent who can slather a statement with such ferocity it makes your skin shrink. What better time to assault me than when I'm feeling like I'd just been tossed into a food processor?

"He told me what he did," she said. "You're a goddamned fool for not taking the money, my dear."

41

I DIDN'T INTEND to, but I slept straight through the night and awoke the next morning to Baba's continued observations about my sanity. Thankfully, the headache was gone, replaced with a tight feeling in my scalp. I escaped my roommate and headed back to the office. Our cubicle smelled faintly of alcohol, so I knew LaRue had deloused our habitat with his poltergeist spray. I found him with his legs propped comfortably upon his desk, eating his brown-bag breakfast of cold rice, pickled limes, and chocolate cake.

He'd diced the dessert onto a dirty paper napkin. I inhaled the sweet fragrance wafting from it and was suddenly ravenous. It was then I realized how badly I'd screwed up by not eating the day before.

The wolf strikes hardest on the full moon and my ability to take in nourishment is confined to fantasies about rare steaks and french fries. According to my partner, I attract a form of supernatural rabies. He thoughtfully explains his conclusion every month, adding a touch more metaphysical charm each time he does.

As far as Gibson is concerned, my problems stem from a brain that turns on a fail-safe to make sure the lunar stretch occurs. He's sure if I ever managed to get food and water past my lips, I might actually find a way to break the lycanthropic cycle. But then, everything is easy in theory.

"Andy, I'm sorry about yesterday," I said quietly, sliding into my seat.

"It's okay, Ty. I understand."

I stared greedily as he popped a pickled lime. "No, it's not okay. I'm concerned I'm going to leave you in a lurch. I can't seem to get a handle on my lycanthropy anymore and you need a partner you can depend on."

He stopped sucking to consider me. "I can depend on you. I have in the past, and when it counts, I can in the future."

I didn't reply. LaRue's ability to encourage trusting, personal relationships was just as weak as mine. For most people, he talks too much, but more than this, the subjects he chooses usually put folks on the defensive. Besides that, he occasionally leans toward unnecessary violence, heavy bouts of paranoia, and the habit of wearing charm sacks that smell like garlic and cinnamon. His truth was as sour as mine: we were joined not so much by a badge and a work assignment, but by the uncompromising loyalty created by the acceptance of our individual oddities. Simply put, no one would willingly work with us.

Nodding, I said: "What's on tap for today, partner?"

He grinned, relieved I was done looking out for his professional welfare. "Kelly Bates."

"Is she still in town?"

"According to a couple of ward cops doing a little extra surveillance duty for me. Guess where she went last evening?"

"Where?"

"To see David Bacon at his home."

"Oh, now that is interesting. Did you send a couple of cops around to escort Mr. Bacon in for an interview?"

"I went along to help muscle the guy, but when we knocked on the door, he was gone. I'm of the opinion the bastard knew we were onto him."

"Kelly Bates being the one who warned him?"

"I can only imagine. After yesterday, I suspect every paranormal freak at the OI."

"Did you have a search warrant to check the premises?" I asked innocently.

"Oh, sure. It's called the flat edge of a coupon book."

I smiled, but didn't remark on his lock-picking skills. "Did you find anything?"

"Did I? Well, you tell me." With that, he handed me a dog-eared shoe box.

I flipped off the top and to my amazement found a stack of

tulpa cards, each one etched exactly like the one we had. "A Manjinn factory?"

"Looks like it. He had a drafting desk set up and there I found a card partially painted."

"Anything else?"

"A jar of black Russian caviar in his pantry. Imagine that?"

"OI employees must get some nice change for their jobs."

"Yeah."

"Do you think Bacon was playing both sides against the middle?"

He shrugged. "I keep replaying the story about amino dubbing and the variety of ways you can convince a person he's something he's not."

"Do we have an APB out on this guy?"

"The minute we find him he's ours." With that, he dropped the discussion in favor of passing on info pertaining to ESP experiments performed by the long-dead Soviet Union. By the time he'd scarfed up his cake, I was ready to bolt for the door, having grown more hungry by the minute. I wished with all my brain's might to let me just get a little food into my complaining belly.

Yet for all the urgency to beat the hurricane, LaRue paused to hook his spray bottle to his utility belt. Armed to the paranormal hilt, we traveled to the north side of the district, where Kelly Bates lived in a shabby high-rise.

We were forced to climb the stairs, past the temporary encampments of refugees swept from their tents and shacks. Kelly Bates answered our knock by tentatively cracking open the door of her flat. When she saw us, she stepped back, flinging it wide and rushing us inside the large room. Before we knew what happened, she'd barred the entrance behind us.

It looked like she'd studied decorating and design with the same teacher as Teresa Yarnell. Tin cans and tinklers hung from the ceiling, wind chimes dressed the windows, and chains of old mercury thermometers strung on red and green ribbons hung like leis around the refrigerator and stove. Her camera equipment took up one corner of the flat and was marked off with an encircling ring of baking soda.

Bates made skittery movements as though she expected an assault from every direction. In a strange fashion, she remembered her manners and jabbed repeatedly toward a recliner and footstool. She waited until we were seated before firing a question at us. "Did you see anyone lurking out by my apartment?"

I swung my leg over the ottoman. LaRue stood up and stepped toward her camera gear, an action that jittered the woman even more.

"Be careful," she screeched. "I don't have the money to replace anything."

"Who would be lurking outside your flat, Kelly?" I asked.

She swiveled mechanically back to me. "I don't know. I don't know. Could be anyone."

"What are you afraid of?"

She blinked at me and then it seemed her eyes lost their focus. Incoming telepathic transmission?

"Kelly," I snapped. It was enough to bring her back, but without her earlier resolve.

"The itinerants in the hallway. One of them has been following me." She flexed her fingers and scratched her arms. It was then I noticed she had rubbed herself raw.

I got that familiar itch crawling through my inside-out fur. "You're lying," I growled.

Her attention pivoted to me immediately. "Why do you say that?"

"Well, you have all these bangers hanging from the ceiling. Teresa Yarnell had the same thing. She was concerned about psionic invasion. Are you?"

She took a deep breath and stepped further into her own dread. "Yes."

"From who?"

"I can't tell you. If I do, I'm dead."

"More OI secrets?" I paused to massage a growing ache in my neck. "You were so helpful only a few days ago."

"That was then. I've done everything I can for you."

"No, you haven't. Who threatened you? David Bacon?"

She frowned and cut a path to the door and back. "No. David wouldn't hurt me."

"Who then?" I said sharply.

"The killer," she whispered.

"Why would the killer want to hurt you?"

"Because I know too much."

"Tell us what you know so we can help you."

"You can't help me. You can't save me from a tulpa."

Was she tightrope walking, controlled on the high wire by an invisible source? "You don't believe in demons, do you?"

She didn't respond. Instead, she checked the door, bellying up to the peephole.

My patience refused to cooperate one moment longer. I looked for some help from LaRue, but his pecker had gotten hard when he saw all the electronic equipment, and so I was on my own for the time being. "Sit down, Kelly," I ordered.

Like a frightened fawn, she obeyed me immediately. She tripped her stare between us, and for a second I thought she might start weeping. I pressed the last point, taking this horror show toward its inevitable end. "Kelly, has Casper told you about me?"

She nodded. "I'm aware of what you are."

"Which is?"

"An OI secret project."

Her statement snagged LaRue's attention. It was a good thing, because if I did have fangs, they would have been showing, gauging by how far my jaw dropped.

"What kind of secret project?" he asked.

"I don't know. Casper wasn't specific. It was all need to know."

"Has he been studying Marshal Merrick for long?"

"Awhile, I think."

I felt like the cartoon character who eats a lit stick of dynamite and gets his shorts blown off. Gibson had inadvertently paraded me naked down Main Street. I was vulnerable to a new kind of invasion now, one that involved the intrigue of psyche and soul. This violation enraged me and to save myself from having to hear more, I pounded on Kelly Bates's own fractured ego. "Then, as I'm sure you are aware, I can be nastier than any tulpa David Bacon might conjure up. I want to know if he's behind this lunacy?"

"No, I told you. David wouldn't hurt me."

"We think he's controlling Jerome Taggart's will."

"No. He did a conversion on Taggart."

"The conversion made this man believe he was a tulpa?"

She nodded.

"That's obscene," I spat.

"I know. Believe me, I know. Taggart's was the most amazing transformation I'd ever seen. They were using new brain technology, amino dubbing, harmonic destabilization. But David only did what he was told."

"Who did the telling?"

"Ingrid Calloway."

LaRue grunted. "Why were they doing this? Forming an assassination crew?"

She shook her head. "I wasn't told a thing, except to be quiet."

"What does Andrea Pio have to do with this wacky cover-up?" he demanded.

Bates stiffened and again lost her focus. As we watched her she looked just like someone was yanking on her mental chain. When she came around, she said: "I don't know anything about Andrea Pio. Nothing."

I had an idea to throw her off balance. "You took some blackmail photos for Sam Arkin, didn't you?"

My question had the intended effect. "What?"

I repeated myself and she nodded slowly.

"You don't need to be in the same room with the etheric energy to take a photo," LaRue said flatly.

"You're right," she said. "I can take pictures remotely."

"How do you do that?"

She seemed to shake off the demons holding her collateral thoughts hostage. "By impressing the film frames with my psychic images. I work like a remote viewer and home in on the target."

"But your psionic talent isn't infallible," I said. "You get some sort of psychic backwash."

"Yes. Things don't always come in as clear as they should."

"I'll bet those pictures for Arkin came in crystal."

She hesitated. Then: "Yes, they did."

"Let's give this scenario the nice twist it deserves," LaRue said. "Arkin and his crew were plotting revenge against someone for the axing they got so shortly before retirement. My guess is they were hoping to make enough to disappear to a far-off island somewhere."

"Yes. They started having peeks into Ingrid Calloway's personal life. Sam asked me to help them and I did."

"Why?"

"Because he gave me a red seven in return. I needed new camera equipment. The OI doesn't supply me. If I wanted to keep my job, I had to do it."

"What was so incriminating about the photos?"

She shrugged. "Nothing. All I got were a few pictures showing her in conversation with Taggart."

"Then Arkin knew something he wasn't telling you."

"Maybe."

"Or maybe he was blowing smoke," I said. "Trying to diddle the diddler."

"Arkin went with the info he'd collected," LaRue said.

"Yes," she answered. "He had this irritating attitude of invincibility. I tried to make him take his time, since I couldn't stop him, but he wouldn't. He said there wasn't enough time. His health was failing and he might not be able to continue on for much longer. He wanted to be wealthy and comfortable in his final years."

"Did Calloway give him the money right away?" LaRue asked.

"No. He told me she threatened to turn him and his team in to the Marshal's Office on another scam."

"Selling forged paintings as the real thing," I said.

She scowled. "Yes. You know about that?"

"We know more than we'd like to," I answered. "Tell me the truth now. Do you have copies of the pictures you took for Arkin?"

It took her a moment more to wrestle with some invisible demon, but she won in the end and went to get them.

42

WHEN WE LEFT Kelly Bates's apartment, we were greeted with new warnings of the approaching hurricane. The wind cranked down the alleys, blowing trash cans and litter into the streets. Electric lines swayed under the surge and prayer flags snapped in the gusts, throwing out petitions to a thoughtless god who seemed bent upon purging the world. Ward cops herded tent dwellers along, helping them to push their grocery carts of meager belongings toward an uncertain future.

According to reports flapping in between the growing static on the array, every available space was being utilized to house the refugees, yet the forecast was grim. The District Council estimated that thousands of people would die. Humanitarian relief would be difficult to coordinate and people were already getting a step up on the looting in case there would be nothing left to steal after the storm.

I was so preoccupied that this commotion barely registered. I kept staring at the photos Bates had given us, but truth to tell, I was past seeing because my attention lurked in an uncomfortable range of paranoia. At least I wasn't alone. LaRue was right there with me. How'd I know?

Telepathy. After years of working together, we shared this six sense during times of danger. I wouldn't have admitted this phenomenon a week ago; instead, I would have called it coincidence. Now I stretched my imagination to several possibilities, one of which was wondering if our OI poltergeist had picked up my thought transmissions via the link I held with LaRue. When I finished gnawing that idea, I hesitantly crept up to the theory that my stretches were being remotely controlled. Perhaps it was the reason for my sudden, inexplicable panic attack. If true, then how long might this have been the case? Did Gibson know, or was he simply a greedy pawn?

In the end, I decided against the whole thing and let my skepticism fall around me with a resounding *thunk*. It was far easier to deny than to accept.

My partner decided we needed a little wind in our faces before proceeding and so we took a swing through our assigned sector, but like LaRue, my interest would not be held by the bug-out being led by the Hurricane Management Team.

Finally I ventured to break the silence. "What kind of secret project do you think I am, Andy?"

His scowl lifted into a thoughtful frown. "I think whatever it is, you're not alone in this. If the OI is haunting you, then they've added Gibson, Myra, me, and maybe Baba to the equation."

He settled again into a private reverie, yet I knew he wanted to add: "And there's no place to run. Fly to the moon, and the bastards can still shuffle the cards on you."

The more we had learned about the disjointed science applied by the OI, the more unsettling the knowledge became. If they were right, then all things in life were determined by our thoughts, but since our thoughts were tricky little monsters when controlled by fragmented and diseased egos, they couldn't be trusted any more than other applications of invisible magic. This suggested that as powerful as the realm of the inner mind was, it still remained a territory fraught with uncertainty.

LaRue interrupted my intense reverie with a memory dredged up from the past. "You know, my grandmother believed thoughts could heal you. Each time I had a complaint, she would say, 'Andrew, only you can change your thoughts. Think happy and you are happy.' Yep, she believed that shit right up until the day she died." He ground the gear and hit a big bump at the same time. When we came down for a landing, he said: "If the packaging of thoughts is possible, then why would you need any of the other stuff?"

"What other stuff?" I asked.

"The amino dubbing, for one thing. What would be the point? Our thoughts determine our physical actions right down to whether we have disease or health. It seems redundant when you could convince someone of his own power, real or not."

His words stimulated one of those flashes of insight that titillates the nerve endings until you feel like someone is pouring hot cream over your body. This entire group of freaks couldn't get a handle on their paranormal talents any better than I could. They gradually devolved the longer they worked with their supernatural repertoire, seemingly heading toward insanity as their predicaments grew more confusing.

With this abrupt realization, I found I couldn't feel my butt against the hard car seat; in fact, I couldn't feel my body at all, though my thoughts continued to propel in from the fifth dimension. They fed my consciousness with ideas of danger in suggesting I headed down the same road as these other captives, but where they tread, they left shoe marks. Where I walked, I left the tracks of a wolf.

We returned to the office, clocked in our efforts for the citizenry, and returned to our cubicle to pore over the photos Bates had given us. It was a short meeting, for the very first picture showed Jerome Taggart smiling as he shook Ingrid Calloway's hand. The victim wore a strained expression, as if his grip was damaging delicate fingerbones.

Comparing the photos to cryptic entries in Sam Arkin's info file, we discovered several half-baked theories we thought belonged to this particular scam. Unfortunately, they testified to Arkin's growing lunacy, and beyond that, we got a taste of the team's ineptitude.

"That so-called psychic backwash must have been rough," I said.

LaRue nodded, but didn't reply, flipping through the folder.

Arkin's notes didn't make sense until I shuffled to a photo identified as *Taggart shaking hands with Valquez*. "Andy, there's a page in that file referring to the two specialists who died. I clipped it."

He took a quick look at the photo and then maneuvered his way through the paper, stopping when he reached the entry. His expression darkened.

"What does it say?" I asked.

"'Drake has confirmed my suspicions by providing us with a clairvoyant report regarding Valquez and Emery,'" he read. "'As with Ford, he maintains they are serving as test subjects. We are trying to determine the nature of these experiments.'"

It was true, then: Hindsight was always better than foresight. Looking at the crimes from this angle, the answer was clear. Valquez and Emery were guinea pigs, brought on board to see if Jerome Taggart could actually kill with a touch.

43

THERE WASN'T MUCH we could do at the moment. Casper Conrad proved to be conveniently out-of-pocket, as was Andrea Pio. It seemed the trail had gotten cold before we expected it. After a few hours of knocking around hunches, LaRue dropped me off to visit with my shrink while he went in search of his final spray ingredient: three ounces of formaldehyde.

Myra hadn't expected me, but immediately made a few minutes in her busy, prehurricane appointment schedule. I hadn't quite settled into the chair when she hit me with the question that was on both our minds.

"Gibson told me you know the truth about our plans."

I nodded, waiting for a smooth apology, but like a true psychiatrist, she sidestepped the comment to focus on my feelings.

"Does it make you angry?"

"Myra, let's cut the psychological bullshit for once. You two are doing what everybody does."

"But you feel we owe you something. At least, more than what we're providing at the moment."

"I suppose honesty is a little much to ask for, huh?"

She smiled slightly, but there was no charm in the expression. Lowering her squeaky voice a notch, she said, "If you don't want money, then what do you want?"

I stretched against the leather upholstery. It was going to be nice to wrap someone else around my finger for a change. "Well, I can only speak for today, you understand. I want some information."

"Let me guess: The information has to do with a criminal, not with you."

"Actually, it has to do with you."

"Me?"

I nodded. "How well do you know a man named Casper Conrad?"

"I met him some years ago while I was a resident. Why?"

"Did he work for the OI then?"

"Yes, as I recall. What are you driving at, Merrick?"

"You introduced him to Gibson, didn't you?"

She squinted at me. "Yes, so?"

"Tell me, honestly, Myra. Did you know how dangerous he was when you did that?"

"I don't know what you mean."

"Yes, you do," I snapped. "No more lying. I want facts and that's it. You owe me that from now until the sun explodes, and don't forget it."

"I'm sure you won't let me, or Gibson, forget."

I smiled. "That's right. Now stop the dodging and answer my question."

Myra seemed to deflate in the chair. She readjusted herself and I knew I was going to get one of those elephant answers, the kind so loaded with unnecessary fat that I was going to have to rip the layers away before finding a pearl of truth.

"Did I know Casper was dangerous?" she began. "I knew that he was powerful politically. But dangerous? That's your assertion, not mine."

"An employee of the OI, someone who knows Conrad intimately, told me I've been made into a special, secret project." I leaned toward her and added in a sinister voice: "I want you to explain to me what that project is."

She snorted and whined. "How would I know?"

I let her have it like the recoil from a sawed-off shotgun. "Because you've been dancing the jig around both Gibson and me."

I had bounced against a nerve. She stood up and turned away to fiddle with her tape machine, but she was shaking now, and had difficulty loading the cassette. "You shouldn't be accusing when you don't know for sure."

"I haven't told Gibson, if that's what you're worried about."

She glanced at me quickly and then dropped her gaze back to the tape player. "What gave you the impression I'm dancing the jig, as you say?"

I settled into the comfortable turn of the couch. "Well, if you don't know how suspicious I am by now, you never will."

"How long have you suspected?"

"Awhile," I lied.

She returned to her chair and flopped heavily in it, but every bit of her characteristic composure had disappeared. The best she could do for herself was announce her explanation with a deep exhale. Then: "Yes. I've gotten more from the association than either you or Gibson. It's expensive to run this practice. Conrad has helped me financially over the years."

I knew I wouldn't like this answer. "In return for your independent consultations."

"More or less. He's always looking for new people with extraordinary talents."

"He goes through people like old rags, doesn't he?"

She hesitated.

I laid it on with force. "He burns out brains for fun and profit. Doesn't he, Myra? Once a person is of no more use, he casts them aside. Or he kills them."

"You don't know that for sure," she screeched.

"Oh, sure, he's such a nice man. Conservative, clean-cut, wears a paper suit so folks won't be put off by his power and wealth. He's a fire-breathing dragon in disguise, isn't he?"

A minute washed by in silence. Finally she spoke. "I don't know any of it as truth. I've heard rumors, but he's always been fair with me."

I grunted. "You cheat your friends, Dr. Fontaine. What makes you think Conrad is not giving you the dicking of your life?"

She stared at me.

"What's the matter? Did I state it too succinctly for you?"

"There's nothing I can say, Merrick. It wouldn't change your opinion of me in the least."

No, that was true, but I wasn't done getting my goods. "What do you know about the OI conversion process?"

The change in direction stymied her and she spent a moment reacting with a series of eye blinks. "What?"

"How would you make a man think he's a demon? Better than that, how would you convince him he's healthy when, in fact, he's ill?"

She answered immediately. "The conversion process is a long intensive period. First and foremost, the convertee has every aspect of his life controlled."

I thought of Andrea Pio. "They're linked with someone who tells them what to do."

"Yes. It's a dependent relationship. The convertee can't make a move unless he has permission."

"What kind of things do they do when they convert a person?"

"They use standard psychological techniques: break down a person's will and then start to build him in a new image. Hypnosis, flooding, torture, you name it."

"Amino dubbing?"

She nodded. "I did mention torture, now, didn't I?"

"What's flooding?"

"You would be a candidate for flooding, especially since you've complained of phobic panic attacks," she said. "A person who has a particular fear can be made to overcome it by flooding his perspective with the very thing that terrorizes him. Strong, emotional connections work easiest and a good converter can attack any aspect of the personality he wishes to change."

"So, is it possible to convince a person he's a demon?"

"That's probably the easiest conversion of all. Start with an impressionable, malleable personality and you can work wonders."

"A malleable personality—a person with amnesia might be just perfect."

"Yes. As for convincing someone he's well when in fact he's ill, well, that one is probably a whole lot harder."

"Why?"

"Systemic pain is a difficult thing to regulate and control. You have to be vigilant to maintain the mind-set. Unfortunately, most people can't cure the physical manifestations of disease with thought patterns, no matter how rigidly they think. Some people can do it, but not many."

"Isn't that what you and Gibson are trying to do? Make me think differently?"

She abruptly began to wring her hands. "We've been honest with you in our clinical applications. The hypnosis and biofeedback were done in your favor. Whatever you believe, we're not trying to work a conversion on you."

That remained to be seen. "Can a person break away after having been converted?"

"You mean, think for themselves again?"

"Yes?"

"No. He could be reconverted, though."

"He'd need a new control, I take it?"

"That's right. All old associations would have to be erased."

I felled her with one more trick question. "Once the conversion is completed, does a person receive regular reinforcement by remote means?"

She sighed. "Of course."

44

THE WIND PICKED up before I was done with Myra, but upon hearing it, she grew some fangs of her own and threw me out of her office. I went willingly, determined I would not be bullied into seeing her again. LaRue waited at the curb, having found and mixed his ultimate poltergeist spray. He proudly displayed the pump bottle on the front dash.

The wind rocked the Trabi as I climbed in. "Does it work on dishonest shrinks?" I said, climbing inside.

"Bad time?"

"Couldn't be worse," I answered. "Not to change the subject, but don't you think we better get this thing back to the office parking garage?"

He nodded, fiddled and jiggled the choke, worked on his hand-and-foot coordination, and finally coaxed the little commie car to life. We chugged off, but the ferocity of the wind pushed us so hard we stalled three times. Once we managed to turn with the breeze, we blasted down the street.

LaRue is a great marshal. He can shoot a gun and hit the target dead center every time. He's street-smart and so intelligent he should have been given the opportunity for a scholarship to the university. My partner has a lot going for him. The one thing he doesn't quite have is the ability to drive. In the best of weather, he is only partially in control behind the wheel. Complicate the matter with high-velocity wind, chuckholes, bumps, fleeing people, and flying debris and you have a recipe for disaster. If it hadn't been for the sudden hailstorm, we might have been killed.

Somewhere in the heavens a celestial glacier must have exploded, because the chunks of ice were the size of old-fashioned lead cannonballs. They rocket across the district, the

189

wind driving these frigid projectiles with the ferocity of a
thousand home-run hitters.

LaRue squeezed back a cry at this sudden attack. His breath
quickened and he talked to himself as he desperately steered
his beloved Trabi for the nearest cover. It was a hard ride—
sheets of newspaper and wet litter wrapped themselves around
the windshield to clog the wipers; hail slammed against the
metal roof, and one of these missiles cracked the rear-door
window. When the wind suddenly whipped the trash from our
view, we saw our salvation: an abandoned commuter parking
lot beneath a closed section of the elevated freeway.

We were not alone. Stragglers, homeless, and those with a
lousy sense of timing crowded into this shelter. LaRue and I
climbed from the car and joined them to stare in silence and
amazement at the fury of mother nature. The hail pounded the
cracked pavement suspended overhead and the noise echoed
eerily.

Someone began singing "St. Ophelia's Litany of Death," a
hymn supposedly reserved for the end of the world, but on
questionable days like this, the sheet music was brought out
just in case.

The voices broke the surrealistic spell and LaRue started
ranting about the dents in his sweet East German jewel. He was
right. It had been dinged and puckered and gashed and so, then,
had my partner's soul. Still, when I should have been showing
him compassion, my attention refused to tarry long from the
hurricane's powerful display.

My lycanthropic sight showed me the streaking tail of ice
crystals following the hailstones, and where it had piled on the
pavement, I saw the steam rising in waves edged with glitter.
It was a damned good show.

That was until my enraptured state was halted by an old
woman trapped out in the open. I only noticed her because of
the bright pink umbrella she used as a shield against the
incoming missiles. It wasn't enough fabric and wire to resist
the crumbling sky. She cowed beneath it, and with each assault
she sank closer to the sidewalk.

I don't usually wear my lycanthropic badge with honor, but
I do exploit its insistence upon being my soul mate. Using my
supernatural speed, I bolted from cover to save the lady. LaRue

glanced up from his precious car in time to see me tear away.
He screamed for me to stop. It was too late.

It was a storm the Marquis de Sade would have enjoyed. The
wind swept in with renewed vigor, bringing a torrential rain
with it. The hail nicked me, pelted me, and banged into me, and
the most I could do was shield my noggin so I wouldn't be
brained before I reached the woman.

Zipping up my speed, I finally plowed into her, tumbling
when a frozen boulder slapped me off balance. It was only a
moment before I flipped to a stand and tried to grab the lady by
her arm. There was blood, water, and sweat—hers and
mine—and it made the attempt impossible. She wailed,
clawing for a slimy hold on my utility belt. At the very moment
I pulled her to a stand, an icy bullet whacked her in the face and
knocked her unconscious. It was a shame for her, but a help to
me. I mustered every bit of lycanthropic strength I had,
snagged her dress and the roots of her hair bun, and hauled her
toward cover like the crack of my butt was on fire.

LaRue made a brave attempt to come after me. The hail
clobbered him into submission and he crumbled to his knees,
struggling to regain his balance against the assault. In my
urgency to span the distance between us, I lost my grip on the
old lady and she fell against me. Her weight may have been
slight, but it was enough to shove me backward and momentarily pin me to the ground.

Again, I had the strangest feeling time stood still. Perhaps
I'd stepped out of my normal frame of reference; I'm really not
sure. All I know is I had a moment of obscene clarity when my
internal dialogue stopped. I floated in this dead space until it
felt as though my thoughts were being fed into my mind one
string at a time, a sensation that immediately dispelled the
enlightened tone of this odd experience with suspicions of
telepathic tampering.

As I resumed regular communications with my brain I heard
a distinct popping noise. It was a sound confined to the inside
of my skull and was much louder than the din around me. My
lucidity disappeared abruptly, leaving behind only the knowledge that my attempt had been in vain. The old lady was dead.
I pushed the body from me and crawled as fast as I could to my
partner.

45

I yanked LaRue to a stand and dragged him back to the Trabi. He was bleeding from cuts on his face and head and he had a couple of big welts on his neck and collarbone. The second he staggered like a drunk, I worried he had a concussion, so I forced him into the passenger's seat and took it upon myself to drive him to the PHO hospital.

I don't have a driver's certification, and I've never tried a clutch before, but I managed as well as LaRue. The streets filled with water as the sewers became clogged with rubbish, forcing me to gun the engine, but it was becoming a slow paddle upriver. My partner wiped at the blood tracking down from his scalp, and complained in a slurred voice about not being able to see clearly.

The hailstorm abruptly ended and that was a merciful act, indeed, but we still barely treaded water. By the time I reached the cross streets of Nicolette and Canal, LaRue was garbling words and feeling faint. I had to make a decision, so I turned toward Gibson's place, hoping he had decided to cloister there during the storm.

The rain slashed in at odd angles and I almost peddled right by his building. Slamming brakes we slid for fifty feet, trapped in the fast current of the flooded streets. There wasn't much I could do but angle the Trabi toward an alley between two high-rises. I wedged the car next to a Dumpster and helped LaRue climb out. The wind sheared off shingles and slung roof gravel at us when we stepped onto the street, but my lycanthropic strength finally won and I rushed us into Gibson's apartment complex.

People crowded inside with us, vying for every bit of available shelter, some wounded and crying out. The tempest

was still young and already people suffered. The worst of it
was still on its way, and already I was forced to ignore the pleas
for help as I urged LaRue up the congested stairway. Reaching
Gibson's flat, we found him passing out bandages and blankets.
He stopped in mid-stride at the sight of us.

"We were trapped in the open," I yelled. "Andy had his bell
rung and this is as far as we could get."

He snapped a look at me, but then his scrutiny settled upon
LaRue, and he lunged toward him. LaRue tried to reassure him
the blood looked worse than it was, but his sentence sputtered
into a groan.

The people gathered in the hallway split a pathway for us
and we towed LaRue into Gibson's lab, easing him onto the
small bunk that served as the good doctor's bed. My partner
nodded a thank you, apologized for messing up the sheets, and
then took a swerve toward unconsciousness.

Gibson cursed and spoke loudly, tapping LaRue's shoulder
as he did. "Andy, stay awake. Stay with me. You can go to
sleep in a little while. Come on, now. None of that or you'll
miss the storm." He slapped his shoulder with force and LaRue
swiveled back toward daylight.

For once, my partner couldn't speak and it was my fault.
Gibson elevated LaRue's feet and wrapped him in a blanket.
"There are bandages in that box by the closet, Merrick," he
snapped. "Peroxide and iodine are in containers in the medi-
cine chest." Turning back to his patient, he barked for him to
count the number of fingers he held up.

I ran into the other room and returned with the required
supplies in time to see Gibson peeling back LaRue's eyelids.
My partner was gone to ground, having finally slipped into
unconscious oblivion. Gibson grunted, measured the pulse in
his neck, and glanced at me before popping open the bottles of
antiseptics.

"I think he'll be all right," he said. "I know he'll have a hell
of a headache when he wakes up."

"I'm sorry about this," I offered quietly.

He shrugged, dabbing gently at a large cut on LaRue's
cheek. "I'm going to have to suture this."

When the catgut came out, I sat in a hard-backed chair,
angled slightly so I didn't have to watch the surgery. He

worked in silence and I didn't interrupt him, though I waited
for him to ask how I fared through this ordeal. After sitting
there for several minutes, I told myself his lack of concern for
my welfare was either an oversight or a trust in my lycanthropic resiliency. Still, it made me wish I had a badly split lip
or something—anything to draw his care and attention.

I followed this path of weakness until it started to piss me
off. Rising from the chair, I unbuckled my shoulder holster and
tossed it on the lab table. The clatter was enough to make
Gibson look at me, but without so much as a question after my
health, he returned to stitching flesh. I walked into the living
room and stared at the storm through chinks in his plank-board
shutters.

It raged, but no more than my own thoughts did. At some
point in my relationship with Gibson, I had become the thing
I'd fought against—dependent. I was no better than Jerome
Taggart.

Gibson apparently finished up and moved to wash the blood
from his hands in the kitchen sink. By this time I'd taken a seat
on his floor and earnestly dried my hair with a pillowcase. He
stepped into the living room, but instead of fetching a towel, he
used the end of my rag.

"I'm glad you're here," he said.

"You are?" I asked. "Why?"

He shrugged. "Because it's a full moon."

Having said it, Gibson lost all interest in everything else. He
locked his apartment door and lit several fat smoking candles.
Rolling onto the couch, he watched me, able to ignore the
sounds of begging in the hallway. I remained sitting on the floor
and pretended I wasn't on medical display, but his dispassionate
expression told me otherwise.

"Why don't you just get it over with and have me pickled
and preserved?" I said. "That way you could study me any time
you want."

By the way he frowned, I'd caught him off guard. He
recovered enough to slide on a wicked smile. "I'm afraid I
wouldn't be able to find a jar big enough to accommodate the
process."

It was too much trouble to answer. I still bled from the cuts
and gashes received during my attempted rescue, and though I

saw nothing, it felt like tiny volcanoes were exploding on the surface of my skin. I ached all over, in every joint and crevice of my body. I credited this radiating pain to the hail stoning, but found myself wondering if it might not be the effects of a lowered barometric pressure. The moment I considered it, I thought of Baba. She was alone in a killer storm, probably tipping a hot vodka toddy and thumbing her nose at fate. Her philosophy was simple. If she was going to die, she should be dead drunk first.

I turned away from Gibson's caustic review, and leaning against the wall, I curled into a fetal position. It was at that moment when lightning struck, illuminating the darkening room through the chinks between the boards. I jumped at the thunder and buried my head in my arms. The tremors of fear were back, accompanied by a panting shortness of breath and a mad desire to run. I must have cried out, because Gibson was right there, making sure I wouldn't hyperventilate and spoil his sudden change of plans for the full moon. He pressed me with his body until my resistance ran out. I dropped my defenses and clung to him as the hurricane ripped around us.

Several minutes passed. Finally the cell of thunderstorms receded and I once more felt reasonably safe. I pulled from Gibson's arms and tried to compose myself, but he openly studied me with that intense gaze I knew so well.

"When were you going to ask for my help?" he demanded.

I had all I could handle and he was playing games. "Never," I growled.

"Fine," he answered. "Suffer, then." He stood up and returned to the couch.

We fumed at opposite ends of the ring for half an hour. I withdrew from him, trying to prepare myself for a full-moon boxing match. It was during this lull that the wolf took an opportunity to flex its muscles.

I experienced an odd feeling of foreboding laced through my mental twitchings. The sensation built atom by atom until I could no longer ignore it. I crawled to a stand, drawn to stare at the barricaded balcony doors. My ears recorded the bass and treble of the tempest, the pitch and rate of Gibson's breath, and even the sounds of conversations held in the next flat. There was something else, too. It took me a moment to identify the vibration: twisting metal.

The next second the balcony doors exploded inward.

It was enough of a blast to knock me onto my back. Splintered wood and shattered glass rained into the room. I flopped onto my stomach, and with every ounce of strength I had, I clawed my way out of the impact zone. Chunks of bricks and masonry breached the hole and pelted me mercilessly, dust and dirt choked the air, and when I glanced up, I saw a gargoyle fly by.

46

GIBSON GRABBED ME by the wrists and yanked me clear of the cascading rubble. We dove for the kitchenette and used the cooking counter as a flimsy barrier. The cabinets held, and after a minute the walls stopped falling in. I smelled rain as the wind sprayed it into the flat.

"Are you all right?" Gibson demanded.

I did a quick evaluation and nodded. Even though we faced real trouble, I gave myself the satisfaction of not asking if he'd come away unharmed.

We stood and peeped cautiously around the corner. Water washed in atop a hill of cracked stone and formed a pool in the middle of the living room. Gibson picked his way around this mound to reach the hole. He then poked his head quickly outside to see if further disaster loomed, and when he turned back to me, he slung rain and pebbles.

"The porch upstairs collapsed," he reported. "My balcony is gone, too." Another fast survey. "God, what a mess."

"We better get something over this opening before we're taking a bath in here," I urged.

He shook his head, stalked to a soggy box, and threw me a wool blanket. He grabbed one himself, along with two-inch-wide adhesive tape. With the skill of the surgeon, he shored up the breach, using the cracked wood and bent metal as splints for his graft.

Gibson stepped back to admire his handiwork and shook his head sorrowfully. "I was afraid something like this would happen. It's going to cost me a begging."

"A begging?" I asked.

"Yeah. I'll have to beg my mother for some financial help." He glanced at me. "In case you're wondering, my father wouldn't give me the shit out of his toilet." Anger registered in his face, but I couldn't tell if it was over his current dilemma or some old family feud.

I decided I didn't care to hear the story. My sudden concerns were over the gargoyle I'd seen. Had it been some trick of my lycanthropy or an hallucinatory mirage sent in on some telepathic transmission wave? I'm afraid my imagination click-clacked in sequence, because I started having weird thoughts that could only have come straight out of LaRue's head.

I must have had one of those silly, enraptured looks on my face. Gibson stepped to me, squeezed my upper arms with both hands, and then steered me toward the couch.

"Did you see a gargoyle fly by?" I asked.

Gibson scowled and kneaded my arms. "Were you hit on the head?"

"I don't think so." I twisted from his hold, and laying a foot against the pile of rubble, I searched for the demon. It was then I noticed a lacy metal wing. Scraping away a couple of concrete blocks, I pulled the creature free. At least I hadn't imagined it.

"It's a balcony ornament," Gibson explained. "The lady upstairs had three of them." He didn't wait for a reply; instead he stomped to the lab and opened the door to glance in on LaRue. "Your partner is still out of action," he said, "despite all the noise. Lucky him."

"Are you sure he's going to be okay?"

He shrugged, picked up a small first-aid kit, and flopped heavily onto the couch. "Merrick, I'm not St. Ophelia and I'm not psychic. If you want to know the truth, I can't be certain of anything." He paused to wet a gauze pad and dab at the scrapes and cuts on my face. When he spoke again, he returned to his self-pity. "It's going to take months of scrounging to put that wall back in."

"You said your mother might help you."

He grunted. "I don't think I can face her crap right now."

"Do you owe her money or something?"

"No. I've always paid, with interest. My mother is a ringmaster. She should be running a circus by the way she can make you jump through the burning hoops. That's one of the reasons I'd hoped for some financial success from my relationship with you."

"Why are you and your father on the outs?"

"A horrendous argument—not over money, but over my humanitarian values. It's not good to disagree with my old man."

"Still, he wouldn't want to see you suffer."

"Don't be too sure. I'm a card-carrying member of the labor movement, Merrick. That makes me a pariah in his eyes."

"That's not it," I said matter-of-factly.

He slugged a deep breath. "What do you mean that's not it? I know my father and I'm intimate with the battle lines drawn between us."

I shook my head. "The thick and short of it is your integrity is wired into the amount of money you have. Your father probably sees it and he doesn't like it. I know I don't."

Gibson glanced at me sheepishly. "You're right. I didn't think it showed this bad."

"It turns you into a sniveling shit."

"You don't have to be rude."

"Sometimes you do."

He studied me again, and in a soft voice said: "I know you think these are empty words, but I am sorry, Ty. My dishonesty shows more weakness than I care to recognize about myself."

Gibson called me by my first name, which meant his guilt had turned him into a quivering mass of shame. I hid a smile of satisfaction, enjoying this triumph by remembering Mrs. Cagney, the head of the orphanage where I grew up. Her idea of dealing with life was to manipulate personal sins. It was apparent I'd become a sharpshooter cast in her golden image.

Several silent moments passed before Gibson dropped the bloody rag and reached over to take my hand, caressing it gently. "I'm not very good at admitting things, Merrick, especially to myself. It's time I did." Again, he hesitated, but eventually the words stained his lips. "I've grown fond of you. So fond that I think I've fallen in love with you."

I went from having the upper hand in this conversation to being wiped across the mat. His admission surprised me, but more than that, it imparted a whole new battery of emotions into my already fractured psyche. As I wrestled with both hope and denial the wolf added a component of uncertainty, for when the full moon rises, the night becomes compressed in torture, the horror of which is relieved only in lapses of memory.

I desperately wanted to recall his words, but it was already too late.

47

I LAUNCHED INTO a hurricane of lycanthropic noise. My agony melded with the howling wind as the wolf rode in on lancing sheets of rain. This stretch pulled me like hot, juicy taffy, until I felt so thin in places I thought I might snap. I longed for the break to occur. One of us would finally win—human or beast, it didn't matter which.

Poor Gibson. I'm sure he was looking forward to a bottle of wine, a loaf of bread, a good book, and his battery-powered lamp to keep him company during the hurricane. Instead, he got two bruised and bleeding marshals.

He held me tightly while I fought to regain control. Mercifully, the seizure wore down in short order and I was left with a lucid moment. Gibson cooed reassuring words, but rather than love whispers, he talked about how the drop in the barometric pressure may have played on my full-moon stretch. Before I could get the gist of his explanation, the wolf roared and rushed me into a hallucination.

Gibson believes I have a form of temporal-lobe epilepsy during the full moon, because I suffer from hallucinations framed in neon colors. LaRue describes my difficulty on a karmic level, sure I'm facing the catalog of my past lives.

What, then, happened to me now? Gibson's concerned face fled from view, replaced with a kaleidoscope of superimposed scenes. They clipped into my perspective like an illustrator flipped through cartoon cells.

I saw my partner, aged and bent, his hair just as long as it was now, but turned completely white. He sat on a park bench, sipping from a vodka bottle. His right leg was missing to the knee and he kicked fiercely at a collection of begging pigeons with his remaining foot. His anguish registered in my awareness with stark intensity, and so did the reason for his hurt. When he had needed me the most, I had let him down.

Could it be a look into my future—that "someday" which was yet to come? I tried to zoom in the scene with my mind's eye, hoping to find further clues, but ever vigilant in its duties to prevent my enlightenment, the wolf bounded through my psyche to change the landscape.

I popped back into lucidity and found that I rested my head on Gibson's lap. He stroked my cheek while he checked my pulse. The world turned like a slow-motion prayer wheel and my ears picked up sound at a dragging pace. Gibson spoke to me, but his words suddenly made no sense.

"I can't understand you," I mumbled.

He took my chin firmly in his hand and said something else in this new nonsensical language. I didn't have time to admonish him for playing such a wicked game, because I spun out of control and ended up in the future once more.

It was Baba, hunched against a winter wind. She carried an empty rucksack and a sorrowful expression, and as she plowed up the crowded street I noticed a world of burned-out buildings and riot police. Baba showed her usual contempt for government authority by slinging a handful of pebbles at a law officer. The man wrenched around at the assault and hit her in the head with a nightstick. My dear friend dropped to the cracked pavement and didn't move.

At one point during the evening I surfaced to find it exquisitely quiet. Gibson still provided his lap for my head, but exhaustion had claimed him, and he dozed fitfully. We must have been suspended in that dead zone within the eye of the storm. It was a creepy sensation and it took a moment to realize that the ambient noise I usually heard had washed away. The vibrational hum of creation had lapsed into profound silence.

I panicked. Had the wolf escorted me into the time-space continuum without so much as a guidebook to show the way? Did I function in the present, or like Teresa Yarnell, was I assessing the future while trapped within the confines of a strained point of view? Gibson awoke and stared at me, but oddly, he didn't or couldn't break this strange stillness.

"Is the hurricane over?" I asked.

He frowned, but said nothing. It didn't matter, anyway,

because I was thrown clear of the moment and into disturbing scenes of flying gargoyle tulpas and robot killers fitted with electric cattle prods. For all the twitches and moans these images caused, I could resist them in my mind, knowing on some level it was a fabrication of a convulsing brain. It was not until I was forced to review a bleak scenario that I lost the fight with the full moon.

I found myself alone, staring out of a broken window at a world of uncompromising harshness; alone, eating a stale piece of bread by the dismal light of a smoking candle; alone, walking through a gray, crumbling cemetery to stop before a small headstone.

I bent to stroke away the leaves piling upon the grave. Glancing up, I saw the name delicately carved in the marble: LANE GIBSON.

Unfortunately, I couldn't read the date of death.

48

I CAME TO late the next morning. LaRue leaned against the front of the couch. He wore a sleeveless T-shirt and I saw that his arms and shoulders were knitted together with a variety of adhesive bandages and gauze. His face and neck were welts and bruises, but he was awake and talking. As long as he ran his mouth, I knew my partner was going to be okay.

Gibson lay spread-eagle on the floor near the pile of rubble, and in this position, he fielded questions from LaRue. I closed my eyes again, drifting in and out of the conversation until I realized they were discussing our current case.

"Watch what you say about thoughts," LaRue said. "Ty and I are learning there's more to them than the noise they make."

"The OI has uncovered and proven more theories on brain technology than any other organization in the world—past or present," Gibson answered. "Are you investigating just remote viewers?"

"We're investigating a group of psychopaths," LaRue said.

"I believe that, too. Altering the brain harmonics can achieve a complete change in personality."

"Brain harmonics?" LaRue asked.

"It's an application that reconfigures the orientation of the brain. In fact, it's a new subfield of neuroscience. The whole idea is less than twenty years old and is still in the experimental stages."

"How do you change the harmonics?"

"By altering the brain wave frequencies. That's done in a variety of ways, with everything from hypnosis to drugs to intense psychological applications."

"Like shock treatments?"

"Yes. It has proven value in some cases such as clinical depression."

"What about amino dubbing?"

Upon hearing the question, I squinted to see Gibson's reaction.

He frowned slightly and wiped a hand through his hair. "That was an unfortunate discovery. It's supposed to be the fastest way to change the harmonics of the brain, but inducing the correct alterations is more iffy than trying to drag the space shuttle home from Mars."

"Well, the OI killer we have was supposedly dubbed into a first rate electrical assassin."

"Killing through touch?"

LaRue was already past this personal intermission. "Do you think it's possible for someone to affect a person's biochemical and electrical patterns that way?"

"Anything is possible, Andy. We know enough about the old gray matter to be lethally dangerous to each other."

"Do you think that continually nipping into other people's energy fields might play havoc with the person's brain as well? Would it be enough to drive the instigator crazy?"

"The brain can be clearly mapped," Gibson answered. "The area that gives your assassin his power is probably affecting surrounding regions responsible for various functions and responses. Believe it or not, these sectors can be neurologically singed when this guy lets the electricity roll. The thing to understand is that once a brain cell dies, it's lost forever."

"Either way, it wouldn't be too good, huh?"

"I'd say the person wouldn't last very long. It would be taxing on the whole body."

"Maybe that's what's really troubling Noone," LaRue muttered.

"Who's that?"

"A psychic healer. He says he can affect people's L-fields. This fellow is supposedly helping people, but he's falling apart himself."

Gibson's response held no edge of surprise. "It's something called the Holistic Phenomenon," he said. "The old adage healer, heal thyself, doesn't work."

My eyes flicked open at his words and he just happened to

be looking my way. "Welcome back to the land of the dead," he greeted.

LaRue glanced around and smiled.

My throat felt like it was coated with sludge from the Black River. I sat up and experienced the familiar gelatinous sensation of my body as it settles back into its singular human form. "Can I have some water?" I croaked.

Gibson climbed to a stand and fetched me a full but dirty glass. I drank the liquid, grit and all, and begged for another tumbler before asking the burning question that was on my mind. "Is the hurricane over?"

"The worst of it," LaRue said. "Right now it's raining like it did in Noah's day."

"Hungry?" Gibson asked.

I had to think about it. "Yes. Starved."

"You're in luck, I've got canned stew." With that, he returned to the kitchenette and began whipping up a meal atop a Sterno burner. He glanced at me a couple of times while he worked, but remained silent until after we finished foraging.

I hadn't quite stuffed the last bite into my mouth when Gibson spoke. "Merrick, do you know what aphasia is?"

"No," I answered while licking the spoon.

"It's the inability to articulate and comprehend language," he said. "When you speak, it sounds perfectly logical in your head, but comes out gibberish to everybody else."

I immediately stopped being concerned about my whining stomach. "Did I have aphasia this time?"

He nodded. "It's a new manifestation of your lycanthropy. Since I've been helping you with your lunar cycles, you've never displayed these symptoms. Andy tells me he doesn't recall you ever dealing with aphasia before."

I tried to remain calm, but felt a fire begin to burn in my solar plexus. "What causes it?"

"For a long time aphasia was thought to be a mix-up in the brain's processing centers, but then scientists discovered it happens when there's an overload in the neuron pathways."

"Well, what causes the overload?"

"Essentially, a change in the amount of oxygen getting to the gray matter. We know the nerves measure atmospheric pressure and inform the brain, which balances the organism by releasing gases into the body fluids."

"So, my neuritis is the reason for the aphasia?"

He nodded. "We had a substantial drop in barometric pressure, too. With the sensitivity you exhibit during a full moon, I think you experienced a lycanthropic form of the bends. It may have affected your brain's biochemistry and caused the switching centers to send your neurons down the wrong tracks."

"You're concerned it will happen again," I whispered.

"Yes, I am," he answered. "Dramatic shifts in weather could affect you at any point during the month. You'd still be able to talk. It's just that no one would understand you, and in turn, you wouldn't be able to understand them."

49

It was about seven P.M. when we yanked back the blankets covering the hole and then gathered around with a mixed bag of trepidation and anticipation. I'll admit, I wasn't too keen on reviewing the devastation and I secretly worried that typhoid and cholera could fly through the air. So I covered my mouth and nose with my dirty hand, hoping to form a barrier against exposure, but upon seeing the view, I forgot about diseases and dropped my guard.

It was a world that Edvard Munch could have painted. The rain had stopped, the clouds had cleared, and the garish colors of a setting sun washed over ruin and despair.

Smoke from localized fires billowed toward the heavens, and the horizon, normally jagged with antennas and chimneys, was now uninterrupted by these things. The District Council Building, the largest structure in the locality, was missing part of its golden, tulip-shaped roof and there were a couple of gaps where the university should have been. It seemed that every piece of glass had been smashed in the fury. An oppressive mixture of gray and black glazed the scene.

Cautiously narrowing my perspective, I glanced across to the neighbors and saw that the three-story walk-up there was a mountain of rubble. Water rushed through the streets and strained what little stability remained. By measuring the flow against a chain-link fence, I gauged the runoff to be at least six feet deep.

Gibson craned his neck to sight along his own apartment building. The moment he did, he whipped his head back inside and gave me a look of utter dismay. LaRue and I hung on to each other as we leaned out into space.

The apartment a few doors away had imploded, but the

residents weren't so fortunate. An old woman had been trapped in the twisted metal and now her body spun slowly in midair like a gently turning wind catcher.

"Mrs. Raines," Gibson whispered.

LaRue and I pulled back from the carnage, and before we could balance ourselves, Gibson had stomped to his front door.

Afraid I knew the answer, I nevertheless asked the question. "Where are you going?"

"To haul her body inside," he answered. "Are you two coming or do I do this alone?"

"It's going to be dark soon," I said.

"So?"

"One slip and it's the high dive. She's hanging at least eighty feet over the street."

"I'm not going to discuss it, Merrick. Mrs. Raines was a good friend of mine. If she died in that situation, then her husband must be hurt or dead, too. Now, are you coming or not?"

LaRue grumbled about still having a headache, but took a step toward the good doctor. "You got gloves? I'm not touching anything or anyone without gloves."

Gibson nodded and backpedaled to a box. Rummaging through it, he came up with LaRue's prerequisite and a set of surgical masks as well.

When we were formally attired, we stepped into a dark empty hallway. We scanned the area with flashlights, but found that the refugees had fled the floor. The building creaked and the thin carpet was mushy with water that had flowed in from under the apartment doors.

In a moment we found the correct flat number, yet no one answered our pounding. Gibson pushed at the steel door. The shifting of the building had wedged it tightly within the jamb. LaRue joined him, but it wouldn't budge.

Occasionally, my full-moon stretches leave me with a form of supernatural backwash. My pure lycanthropic potential is greatly diminished, but I can still hoist the flag when extra muscle is called for. Before this storm, I'd never realized there might be external reasons for why this surge remains some months and not others. This extreme weather had electrified my reserves and much of my paranormal strength and stamina had remained.

"Let me try," I said.

They nodded, moved out of my line of fire, and patiently waited for me to batter the door in. I took a flying leap and kicked it, but ended up on my ass when it didn't give. LaRue picked me up by the underarms and I tried again, this time inserting a bit more acrobatic flexibility into the equation. I knocked it ajar by a centimeter. Gibson took over and kicked it twice more, and finally we pushed the door open just enough to squeeze into the apartment.

It looked like a bomb had gone off. The ceiling hung in tattered fragments and support beams had cracked and crashed to the floor. We found the old man crushed beneath a ton of rubble, the weight of which had driven through to the apartment below. Mrs. Raines had apparently been near the wall when the building collapsed and had been shoved into the network of metal that once supported the balcony.

We picked our way to the hole and paused to assess the situation.

"This unit isn't going to last long," LaRue said. "A good stiff wind and it's history. So are the flats downstairs."

Gibson nodded. "It doesn't look like the remains of the porch are going to support much more weight." He glanced at me. "Merrick? You're the lightest one. Will you try to get the body untangled?"

I stared at him, amazed at his concern for a dead person, but more amazed at the seeming disregard for my safety. It pissed me off, but my anger didn't stay around long when LaRue started in about service to humanity. He reminded me about my failed attempt to save the woman in the hailstorm and then it was impossible for me to deny my sense of duty.

"We'll be on tap to help out where we can, Ty," he said. "We might as well start here."

I fumed and muttered, but knew he was right. If we weren't busy with a murder investigation, then Julie would see to it we were assigned to cleanup. "Well, if you think I'm going to monkey over that gridwork without a rope, you're out of your minds. Both of you."

"Rope, I have," Gibson said. "I'll be back." With that, he climbed the matterhorn of debris and headed for the door.

LaRue and I waited for him by studying the tangle of metal, and when Gibson returned, we had figured out a route over to the body. I threaded the rope around my utility belt, and praying to a god who had gone to an obscene length to wash the planet, I gingerly stepped onto the balcony's metal skeleton.

The rock and mortar had broken the porch apart, and then buried a portion of it before the infrastructure had completely fallen away. It was, indeed, a shaky affair. As I climbed the outcropping I felt the load quiver and then I noticed how the whole deal relied upon the stability of a single cast-iron railing.

I was a damned fool for doing this. It bothered me that I didn't know why I risked injury and death for a corpse. Was it Gibson's humanitarian determination or was it my own sense of guilt at being left alive after the tempest? Glancing out over the street, I decided it was plain old stupidity.

LaRue fed me another line before I edged my way onto the metal. The structure was sharp and serrated in some places, and it took only a second before I snagged the shoulder of my cammies. The material refused to yank loose, so I stood there like a wing walker without an airplane as I discombobulated myself.

Once through this ordeal, I inched along. I felt a shiver go through me, but assured myself it was my own cowardice rather than the rock pile ready to shift. The body hung no more than two feet from my reach, but her arm and head were locked at odd angles within the grillwork. I would have to climb slightly above the corpse to extricate it. Gritting my teeth, I worked my way to my goal, where I showed my lycanthropic alacrity by tying the second line securely around Mrs. Raines, and once done, it was time to go up.

I reached out and immediately contacted with jagged aluminum. It slashed into my hand and made me yelp, but not to compromise the works, I forced myself to be still while I cursed at the pain. I bled from the wound, adding a slippery hold to an already insane challenge.

"Are you all right?" Gibson demanded.

"Yeah. Don't talk to me. I need to concentrate." What I really needed were a few lessons in rock climbing.

I carefully pushed my toe into a crevice and hoisted myself upward. A slight breeze ruffled through to dislodge pebbles, dust, and shards of glass. The metal bent like a tree branch. I hung on, waiting for the end to come. When it didn't, I took one final lunge and clamored to a spot that would allow me to untwist the corpse. I rearranged the old lady's head, and glancing back toward the building, I called to the men. "Get ready. When I move her arm, she's going to swing free."

"Okay," LaRue called. "Release her."

I did. The body dropped from the framework and crashed into the side of the building as they hauled the rope inside. I remained where I was until they'd retrieved what was left of Mrs. Raines, but by this time the sun had set and my range of vision was narrowed to the human frequency bands.

Gibson sprayed me with lantern light, but the glare from the beam only hindered my way. I fought for each and every return step, and twice I almost lost the bargain to gravity. Worse than that, my bloody hand made it hard to grip the metal, causing me to take a different route over the rocks. I followed the glow of Gibson's lamp, and certain I would reach solid ground, I breathed a sigh of relief, but my margin of safety fell out from under me when the wind roared down the street.

The structure rattled, shook, and began to tumble away. Mortar and bricks slammed me, and within the span of a second I was caught in an avalanche of rocks and concrete. I took a flying leap toward the building, but the only thing I connected with was thin air.

50

I FLEW LIKE a trapeze artist—kicking, clawing, and scrabbling for a purchase. Gibson and LaRue gave a monumental tug and hauled me in just as the works came completely down. We fell backward into the demolished apartment, huddling against the flying debris. After the dust settled, I crawled away, afraid that if I didn't, I would choke the life out of them for talking me into grabbing a body off the high wire. I stood up, made a noble effort to pat the dirt from my hair and cammies, and turned toward the door.

"Where are you going?" Gibson demanded.

"I'm going back to your apartment," I said. "If you want to play with corpses, then that's your business. I'm done for the evening." I trudged off, feeling filthy with death.

In the time it took to return to the flat, a rain squall came up. It was my chance for a bath, so I scrounged a plastic bucket from the lab and used it to catch the water by shoving it through the hole in our makeshift curtain. Rather than being delicate, I dumped the contents over my head. I was right in the middle of my toilette when Gibson and LaRue returned to see me adding more moisture to the flat.

"Thanks, Merrick," Gibson husked.

"For dousing your floor or for my daring rescue of a former person?"

"For both, I guess."

"It's going to take a couple of days for the water to recede," LaRue said, assessing the district's sorrowful situation.

"The bodies and trash are going to clog the storm drains," I noted.

He nodded. "I can hear Julie now: Every person who thinks he's going to get some sleep in the next year might as well turn

213

in his badge and swim away." He shook his head. "Oh, shit. I just remembered my car."

I stuck the bucket outside again. "East German engineering will never let you down, Andy."

"One can only hope."

"What are you worried about?" I said. "Most of the streets will be washed away. There won't be anyplace left to drive."

"Communications might be down for a while, too," Gibson said, pointing through the hole. "The relay dish on the district array is history."

I sighted along his finger, and yes, the large antenna balanced precariously off the roof of the district broadcast station, saved from crashing to the earth by the cables threaded to it. Nodding, I pulled the bucket back in and offered it to LaRue. "It's too dark to try an escape from here tonight." Then, eyeballing Gibson, I added: "We'll try to get out of your hair tomorrow morning."

We agreed to attempt our departure at dawn and spent the rest of the night eating canned fruit, hard cheese, and soggy bread as we worried about the fates of our friends and family units.

The next morning the district still looked like it sat in the middle of a river delta, but Gibson, the surprise that he is, had a solution for us. He led us to the apartment across the hall, taking a few minutes to unlock a series of dead bolts securing the door. Once inside, I realized his storage area was far larger than I first suspected.

"I had to lease this place," he explained. "It was getting so I didn't have room to turn around in my own flat." Without waiting for comment, he walked to a large object covered with green canvas, and stripping the cover back, he presented us with a small rowboat.

"I'm having a hallucination," I said. "Is that what I think it is?"

"I've been through a hurricane before." He stepped toward another object swaddled in heavy cloth and like a graverobber relieving a mummy of its wrappings, he wrestled out a battery-operated trolling motor.

By the time we manhandled everything downstairs, it was eight A.M. We pushed off into the lake formed in the building's lobby and joined other hardy souls who had planned ahead, too. We paddled and trolled for hours. Skiffs met, exchanged information, traded foodstuffs, and passed on, dragging fishing lines of dead bodies behind them.

We stopped several times to tend to injured people who'd hopped onto makeshift rafts. Gibson carried an inoculation gun with him and pumped up any children who floated toward us. It was a crowded commute, filled with the wailing moans of the dispossessed and dying.

As evening approached we dropped LaRue at his apartment building by floating to an open window on the first floor. His neighbors helped him climb inside, and in a moment my partner disappeared in the midst of several helping hands. Gibson and I drifted on to my flat.

Thankfully, that old walk-up was still there. The water had receded enough so the top step on the stoop was exposed. Helen Yubanski from Apartment 3-C stood there pushing muck out of the front hall with a broken broom. I hopped from the boat.

"Is everyone okay?" I demanded.

"Yes, yes," she assured me. "No broken bones, no broken heads, no drowners. A couple of cuts and a few bruises, but St. Ophelia was with us and we rode it through to the bitter end."

"Where's Baba?"

"Last I heard, she was cursing someone or something at the top of her lungs. You really should talk to her, Ty. My grandchildren are starting to repeat some of her more colorful words."

I breathed a sigh of relief. "I'll have a talk with her." Turning to the good doctor, I said: "Take care of yourself, Gibson."

He studied me intently, but I couldn't read the thoughts behind his expression. Finally he waved and pushed back into the current. "You, too, Merrick. You, too."

I watched him float away, and as I did I got a tickle behind my nose. Had I not dismissed it as infected sinuses, I might have realized big trouble was coming.

51

———■———

LaRue's mother believes that no disease can survive after a person swallows a bottle of her special, heat-brewed spring vinegar, and since her son decided to swing by his partner's flat on his way to work, she made sure to load him down with several bottles to trade along the way. By the time he arrived at my place, he'd gotten rid of all the vinegar and ended up with hard biscuits, lye soap, a jar of mustard, and three sacks of coffee. He shared one of the java bags with us and Baba was off at a shot to fire up the final bit of propane left in our stove.

I pointed to his face. "How's your latest scar shaping up?"

He ran his fingertip across his cheekbone and then over the delicate stitching. "It itches," he answered. "I stopped by Gibson's on the way here hoping he'd be home to snip this stuff out, but he was gone. This mess must be keeping him busy."

I nodded. "Did you find the Trabi where we left it?"

"Yeah. Wet and muddy. My cousin and I pushed her home this morning. I don't know if she'll run again or not." He pulled on a dejected face.

I patted his shoulder, ready to help him give his concerns a heave-ho, but Baba saved me the trouble by clattering the coffeepot as she ladled water into it.

"It's always those with the least to lose who suffer the most," she thundered. "The goddamned government should have been better prepared from the start." The moment she realized she'd said a curse word, she walked away from her chores and to the door, which she flung open and screamed down the hallway: "There you go, Helen! I said the *goddamned* government!"

LaRue glanced at me with a questioning look.

"She's having an old-fashioned feud with Helen Yubanski,"

I explained. "This war has been going on for three days. One minute Baba's slinging curses, the next minute Helen is slinging insults. It's been fun."

Baba didn't apologize, and to add to the bickering, she continued to bark at the top of her lungs. "She's an old hag. So goody-goody. So proper. I'd like to rip out the roof of her mouth and let the bitch taste some of that snotty attitude of hers."

I ignored this latest episode and finished making the coffee for her. LaRue opened a package of moldy sweet bread and broke large chunks from it. The food was enough to make my roommate scuttle back to our little hearth.

"It appears you came through the worst of it in good shape," LaRue said, swinging his attention around the flat.

"No broken windows and the roof held," I answered. "We were lucky."

"Luck had nothing to do with it," Baba said. "We got through because of my air fresheners."

I smiled to myself. Her tinklers had remained unruffled during the storm, but it was the sandwich of plywood and trash blankets that had kept the windows intact. As for the roof? Our building was wedged between taller structures on three sides and the wind had funneled on by without disturbing too many of the shingles in the process.

We ate our breakfast, and then Baba immediately returned to hammer Helen's morality into the ground. LaRue and I headed for the office, grateful when we turned the corner and the bellowing faded into the distance.

The subway would be closed for several weeks, and without the Trabi, we were forced to hoof it. When we finally arrived at the office, we found the usual commotion. The place was soggy and smelled musty, but the emergency generators were up and fans blew the stink around.

Julie passed us as we entered the homicide pen. She stopped and stared at LaRue's cuts and bruises and then searched my face for the telltale hint of a battle. Rather than asking how we were doing, she said: "Raymond Vinson showed up this morning."

"Why?" I asked.

"Because he was robbed and he thinks Jerome Taggart did it." She stepped into a walk again, slinging an order over her shoulder. "Check it out. Now."

52

An hour out on the street and we arrived at Raymond Vinson's fashionable address to find a couple of muddy patrol cars parked in his nice circular drive. We were met by a bored, equally muddy ward cop, who grumbled his displeasure at being treated like a security guard.

It always damages my sensibilities when I witness preferential treatment because someone is wealthy. The district was cracked into pieces; the functioning automobiles and man-power should have been directed to the cleanup. It was too bad I wasn't the head of the District Council. I'd make all these rich pricks wait.

He allowed us to enter and we found a home in perfect condition despite the passage of the storm. The house sat on an artificial tump and the water dashing through the streets hadn't risen high enough to flood the estate. His windows were lashed shut with custom-designed hurricane blinds, which held back any shattered glass, and though there was no electricity, he had plenty of candles burning.

Vinson should have been thankful at having all of his possessions spared, but as it is with the leisured class, he was blaring about the injustices in a mad world.

When we presented ourselves in his elegant parlor, he was busy giving this lecture to the police, but he stopped midway through his discourse to glare at us. "Who let you in here?" he snapped.

"We let ourselves in," LaRue answered. "Your butler doesn't seem to be on door duty."

"That's because I fired him," he growled.

I sat my dusty butt upon a beautiful red brocade divan.

218

Vinson gave me a killing look, but spoke to LaRue as my partner did his usual survey of a room.

"What are you doing here?" he asked.

"We're investigators," LaRue answered. "That, and our watch commander made us."

Vinson snorted, rose from his comfy wing-backed chair, and stalked to a black marble wet bar. He poured a drink and fumed.

"What was stolen?" I asked.

"My tulpa-card collection," he roared.

One of the ward cops interrupted. "Mr. Vinson has a valuation of two hundred thousand credits on this collection."

I couldn't even imagine that much money. "Were you here when it was supposedly stolen?"

Vinson shook his head and knocked back the drink. "I waited out the storm in another district. My former butler was here."

"I'm surprised you didn't take something so valuable with you," I said.

"It was in a safe."

Again the ward cop spoke up. "We looked it over. The safe is a Krast Model one hundred. Floor to ceiling, solid steel."

"You'd need a load of TNT to get into it," I added.

"Yes, ma'am. We couldn't find any sign of forceable entry."

"So, someone knew the combination."

Vinson choked on his whiskey before answering. "No one knew that combination."

"Not even your butler?"

"No. I trust no one. And, it seems, for good reason."

LaRue finished up his inspection tour and flopped down beside me. The more dirt, the more satisfaction I felt.

"You've accused Jerome Taggart," LaRue said. "How could he have stolen these cards?"

Vinson studied us and then turned to the ward cops. "Are you done? I'd like to speak to these marshals alone."

The blues nodded and beat a hasty retreat. When they were out the front door, Vinson explained. "How could he have stolen my cards? I'll tell you how. He's a tulpa."

I glanced at LaRue. "For a moment there, it sounded like he said Jerome Taggart is a tulpa."

"Mock if you want," Vinson flared. "Your skepticism only increases your ignorance."

I felt a ruffle of annoyance. It was not so much his insult as it was having to deal with another gullible person. "There are no such things as demons."

"Oh? You're dealing with the OI. Everyone knows they're experts at creating demons."

"You're talking figuratively."

"Am I?"

"Why didn't you tell us your suspicions when we first talked to you?"

"Because I wasn't sure."

"But now you are?"

He nodded. "That young woman with him was his tulpa master."

"How do you know?"

"Taggart deferred to her in subtle ways. She was in complete control."

"I thought you said she didn't say much?" I asked.

"She didn't. She spoke with her eyes. This woman was powerful, but not nearly powerful enough to keep a tulpa in check."

I should start a company. Rent-A-Lunatic—wackos for every occasion.

"Have you ever been bothered by a tulpa?" LaRue demanded.

Vinson nodded. "That's why I had those cards. There are demons everywhere. A person needs some protection." He slugged another drink and moaned. "Where could my collection be?"

Knowing what I did about remote viewing and the power of thought, I wondered if his cards could be right there in his safe, dazzling and beautiful, invisible to his unwitting perspective, but still beneath his very nose.

53

THE TRAIL LEADING to our killer had been washed away by the storm, so upon leaving Vinson's quaint, little mansion, we walked back to the office, stopping once to help a couple of guys from the conscription service haul away an unwilling young man. Following this interlude our muscles were heated and stretched, but unfortunately, the energizing friction of exercise did nothing to spawn the creative hunches that could have saved the day and the investigation. We both hated to give up, but we were stymied until Taggart chose to resurface. LaRue muttered and squawked, while I silently lamented not picking up Andrea Pio when I had the chance.

As we entered the homicide pen, Wilson caught up with us. "Your detainee, Clement Noone, had a bad cough and a fever. I gave him the once over and sent him to a triage unit set up on Fourth Street."

"What's wrong with him?" I asked.

He shrugged. "Pneumonia, for one thing. God knows what else."

If Noone could send out impulses through his central nervous system and change his brain's thought patterns to do it, then why couldn't he steal the energy he needed to sustain himself? Wilson had examined him. It would have been the perfect time to put the touch on an unsuspecting donor.

"His apartment building didn't survive the storm," I said. "Noone won't have any place to go once he recovers."

Wilson shook his head and gave us a sorrowful look. "He won't recover, Merrick. The PHO is limiting pharmaceutical distribution to Class As and above. There's not enough antibiotics and painkillers to go around."

"The inequities of an equitable society," LaRue spit.

"Whatever," Wilson chimed. Then, squinting at my partner, he said: "Speaking of Class-A designations—you have one. I think it's time those stitches were removed." Continuing his inspection, he added: "And I also think I'm going to give you a shot of SPS-14, just to make sure you're good and healthy."

LaRue grinned. "St. Ophelia, Frank. I just complained with elegance about the favoritism in the district."

"Yeah, yeah." Wilson turned to me. "I take it you're all right?"

"I don't need a shot, if that's what you want to know."

He burped and waved LaRue along. "To your cubicle, then, so I can yank that shit out of your face."

We followed Wilson back to our space, where he pulled out a flashlight and a portable surgical pack from his briefcase. He tossed me the lantern, ordered LaRue into the chair, and then started bitching and grumbling about having no reliable source of electricity.

I aimed the light at my partner while Wilson critiqued the fancy work. "Mighty nice stitching. I take it your Dr. Gibson sewed this?"

"Yes," LaRue said. "We were trapped in the open and his flat just happened to be around the corner."

"How fortunate for you. That mug of yours is going to stay pretty because of his medical artistry."

"Be careful, Frank," LaRue warned.

"Not to worry," Wilson said, with a smile. "I did my residency in an emergency ward. I can pop these babies with my eyes closed." He demonstrated his claim by squinting as he came at LaRue with the scissors. Clipping a string, he said: "You know, I haven't seen Gibson lately."

I sat down at my desk and shuffled papers, just so I wouldn't have to watch the brutalizing of my partner. "I'm sure Gibson's out playing the part of the Great Humanitarian."

"Well, he may be symbolizing the compassionate ideal right now, but come tax time he's going to be wishing he didn't."

"What's that supposed to mean?"

He carefully teased the cat gut from LaRue's flesh before answering. "All medical physicians are suppose to comply with assembly regulations, Merrick. Every doctor has a re-

sponse team to report to. If they don't, they get penalized on
their environmental taxes. Gibson and I are on the same RT."

"You're saying he didn't show up?" I asked.

"That's right. Three days have gone by and he hasn't
reported. We could have used him yesterday, too. Uncovered a
bunch of people down in Ward Eleven. Head traumas out the
ying. I had six people die on me from intercranial swelling. Not
that Gibson could have prevented it, mind you. The stinking
equipment the PHO donated is straight out of the Dark Ages."
He yanked on the string and LaRue winced.

"Damn, Frank," he snapped. "I'm not a piece of sausage
you're trying to untie."

Wilson grunted. "Stop being a candy ass, LaRue." Glancing
my way, he continued. "So, have you seen Gibson?"

"Not since the day after the storm," I answered.

"He hasn't been home, either," LaRue said, through clenched
teeth. "If he had been, I wouldn't be in pain at the moment."

Wilson ignored him to direct his next statement to me.
"Well, if you run across Gibson anytime soon, you let him
know the officer of the medical response team is sticking
needles in a voodoo doll that looks just like him."

54

WILSON'S QUESTIONS ABOUT Gibson caused me mild concern. Without the Trabi or public transportation, we'd blown the day just walking around the district, so since we were reduced to jamming big ideas into small spaces, we called it quitting time. LaRue went home to his dead car. I turned my feet toward Gibson's free clinic.

Since the swing of the twentieth century, the world has known one catastrophe after another—tidal waves, earthquakes, hurricanes, tornadoes. The soothsayers have added fuel to the fire by prophesying a schedule of doom that includes such cataclysms as mass volcanic eruption and a complete shift of the planet's poles. As I walked through the streets and noticed people repairing their lives, I also saw the occasional banner proclaiming the next big event: a head-on collision with a rogue planet now steaming into our solar system.

People dusted off their magic bags as well and used this time of reconstruction to force good luck through specific rituals. I passed one group who linked hands and sang mystical chants to the sky. Five minutes later I was stopped by a maniac professing to be St. Ophelia's messenger, chosen to spread the word of abundance upon the wretched souls trapped in this material wasteland. I say "messenger" to give the guy the benefit of the doubt. He slurred his words and it sounded like he said "St. Ophelia's gigolo" instead.

As I strolled through the muddy streets I noticed how many people relied upon invisible magic to save the day, but from what I'd learned during the course of this strange OI investigation, the real miracle stuff was contained in the brain. I will admit, my skepticism grew shaky when presented with the possibilities of concerted thought. If the human species could

ever join at some super-conscious level, would it be possible
to think a storm out to sea where it would do no harm?
Unfortunately, the answer I kept getting had a poop-juicy feel
to it.

I found Gibson's clinic buttoned up tight. The boards were
still securely in place over the window and doors. It was odd he
hadn't opened for business, so I decided to check his apartment
building.

Worse than a potential shift of the earth's axis was the fear
that the electricity was never going to come back on to the grid.
Up the stairs I went, nodding to the few stragglers still using
the landings for housekeeping. When I reached Gibson's flat, I
found it locked. There were several boxes sitting on his
doorstep, and flipping one open, I almost fell over from the
whiff of rotting vegetables.

"We're worried about our Dr. Gibson," the voice said from
behind me.

I swung around to face a large man with a bald head and
arms loaded with gaudy tattoos. Just to show him I was tough
even though he towered over me, I placed my hand noncha-
lantly against my holster. He saw the movement and raised his
hands in surrender.

"You don't have to worry about me, Marshal," he said. "I'm
unarmed."

"When was the last time Gibson was here?" I growled.

"A couple of days ago, I think." He jabbed a thumb over his
shoulder. "My wife brought him some fresh goat's milk,
because she knows he likes it." Tapping down the volume on
his voice, he added: "We keep two goats in our apartment. It's
against the lease, but no one enforces it. The doc came over and
gave them each a toot of antibiotics here a while back. Said if
we were going to use the products of farm animals, we should
make their consumption safe for ourselves. Well, we appreciate
his concern and that's why she wanted him to have the milk."

"Did she connect with him?"

"Oh, sure. He took two pint jars inside with him. That other
stuff there on his stoop was brought around yesterday."

"Did you see who brought it?" I demanded.

"No, Marshal. It was just there when I glanced in the
hallway."

"Have you seen or heard from Gibson since your wife's delivery?"

He shook his head and rubbed a gorilla-sized paw over his pate. "Maybe he got conscripted into a work unit or something. That's why we're not venturing out, you know. The government coyotes are everywhere. And they're such dumb fucks, too. You might be a wizard of a medic like Dr. Gibson, but they'll throw your buns into the burner by assigning you to scrubbing the floors at the District Council Building. You marshals and the ward cops are the only ones safe. It's a disgrace. Sorry, ma'am, but it is."

I followed his logic with shakes of my head, but my focus had gone beyond the possibilities of civic enlistment. The district was a carnival of carnivores and I was suddenly worried Gibson had stepped into an out-of-body experience the hard way.

"Did he say anything to you or your wife about his plans for the next day?"

"No. He did get a lot of company that evening, though. Folks who were hurt up or hungry. Along about midnight he left."

"How do you know?"

"We had our door open, trying to coax in a breeze from the busted windows at the end of the hallway," he answered. "Didn't do a damned bit of good, but my wife swears it got cooler. Anyway, I was sacked out in the living room and I saw him walk by in a hurry with another man."

His words whacked me between the eyes, and paranoia, that gooey precursor to panic, began to leak into my awareness. "What did this man look like?"

He shrugged. "It was dark. No lights. They were in a hurry, I guess. The guy was pushing Doc Gibson."

My trepidation usually makes me dangerous and this instance was no different. I moved as fast as any thought form could and grabbed the man by his beefy neck, using my residual lycanthropic strength to yank him down to my level. He struggled, but I squeezed the armlock until I had his full attention. "What did this man look like?" I snarled.

"He had black hair, I think," he sputtered. "It was hard to see, Marshal, honest. He had a beard. Yeah, that's right—he had a beard. I remember now."

I released him and turned to Gibson's front door. Taking my aim, I kicked it in. By that time my unwilling informant had fled to his own apartment.

Gibson's place looked as it did when we left it. I checked the lab to make sure he wasn't there, and finding it empty, I returned to the living room to cast around for clues. The first thing I noticed was the ornamental gargoyle. Propped atop its flexed hand was the tulpa card of the Manjinn.

55

I COULDN'T EVEN call LaRue—not via the telephone or over the dysfunctional communications array. It meant galloping to his apartment, telling him what had happened, and then dancing in circles as we tried to figure out what to do next. If a person needed to buy time, it was certainly me.

I grabbed the tulpa card from its gargoyle perch and continued to search for a ransom note of some kind. There was nothing.

During my lycanthropic cycle I can usually rely upon the endurance and speed of the wolf, but my life had been remarkably unremarkable as far as this new month had gone. I hadn't stretched into a more powerful form and had no more hurry in my shorts than a normal person. The district was slowly being piled into mounds of rubble, and having to maneuver detour after detour, it took me nearly two hours to reach LaRue's place.

As I read the sinister meaning into the tulpa card, I realized that Gibson had become my hope, my lifeline in a day-to-day existence with my lycanthropy. Understanding this, I had to admit he had come to mean more than the occasional sexual interlude. That, in itself, was enough to scare the crap out of me.

I climbed more stairs and tripped over more refugees clamoring for an encampment on the landings. It seemed like another hour before LaRue's mom answered the door.

She's a tiny, dark-haired lady who speaks her opinions and ideas openly and loudly and the ones she expresses with the most venom concern me and my lycanthropy. So before she had the chance to size me up for a confrontation, I spoke.

"I'm sorry to bother you so late, Mrs. LaRue, but I must talk to Andy. It's an emergency."

She studied me for a moment—I suppose to assess my

sanity. Stepping back, she allowed me to enter. "Andrew," she called, "Marshal Merrick is here."

When there was no immediate response from the back room, she stalked to the door and pounded on it. "Get up, Andrew. Now."

A second later LaRue charged out of bed, wearing a pair of green-and-white-checked boxer shorts and a sleepy, confused expression. "What is it?" he snapped.

"Gibson has been kidnapped," I said. "And it looks like Jerome Taggart is responsible."

My partner lost all of his sack-time befuddlement in an instant. "Are you sure?"

I produced the tulpa card. "I found this in his flat."

"Is that the card from the crime scene?"

"No." I patted down my pockets. When I found it, the card came out in pieces. "The one from the crime scene got soggy along with everything else I had. This was sitting on top of that gargoyle ornament. I spoke with a neighbor who saw a man with a beard hurrying Gibson out of the building the other night."

Mrs. LaRue sat down in an old rocker to watch me suspiciously. "Andrew, put your pants on," she ordered.

He nodded, jumped for the bedroom, and returned a moment later with his cammies in place. "Ty, we've lost the trail on this one. Where are we going to start?"

"I don't have a clue. I checked Gibson's flat for a ransom note and there wasn't one." I walked the length of a small plastic runner protecting the carpet. "Taggart's a psycho. He wouldn't necessarily be doing things by the kidnap book."

"Did you check Gibson's clinic?" LaRue asked.

"Locked up. The boards are still in place."

My partner opened his mouth to say something, but his mother's scream stalled his sentence. We both turned to stare at her. She wore a stricken look.

"What's wrong, Mom?" LaRue asked.

"The vid," she whispered. "It lit up all by itself—lit up without electricity."

We followed her stare and our chins almost collided with the floor, for appearing on the screen in bright red letters was this cryptic message: YOU HAVE TWELVE HOURS TO FIND THE GOOD DOCTOR. FAIL TO APPEAR IN THE PROPER PLACE AT THE PROPER TIME, AND HE WILL DIE.

56

SUDDENLY THIS INVESTIGATION was about us. To complicate matters, we were held hostage in a decimated world. The thing we needed most we didn't have: a car.

We spent an unusually long time staring at the vid screen. The message remained, giving Mrs. LaRue an opportunity to rouse the whole apartment. By the time her son was properly saddled up with uniform, gun, and poltergeist spray bottle, the family unit had gathered in the living room to view this paranormal electronics display.

The LaRues hail from hardy French-Canadian stock. Though ethnic lines have blurred to a smudge, this group of people has stubbornly held on to their origins, so when my partner spoke to his cousin Henri, he forgot I was in the room and fell into a bastard dialect known as Frère Jacques. They exchanged a couple of *ouis*, a few *mois*, and one outright *non* before LaRue turned to me.

"Henri is going to loan us his car," he explained.

His cousin barked at him in Barrier language. "Please, Andy, be careful. She's mint, and I just finished rebuilding the engine." Henri lapsed off into pidgin French again and there was a moment of tussling until my partner got something straight with him. After that, we got the keys and were off to a nearby garage to find an antique Volkswagen Bug.

It was hard to believe. I was thrown from my normal skepticism into a panic over some words mysteriously appearing on a dark vid screen. This entire situation had the feel of a bad magic parlor trick.

An hour later we reached the garage. We located the Bug immediately, lovingly wrapped in a car blanket. When we ripped the cover back, we found a beautiful paint job and an immaculate leather interior. Henri must have invested thousands of credits in it. We climbed in, trying hard not to scuff the soft white upholstery.

"I'll pay till I die if I wreck this thing," LaRue murmured.

"Henri doesn't trust you?"

"Henri knows how I drive."

To prove his inadequacy, he stalled the Bug four times before synchronizing his feet with the clutch. We finally chugged off, but our trip involved a lot of weaving and dodging as LaRue tried to miss the chuckholes and chunks of debris. For myself, I spent the ride to the office laboring over the same baffling question. Why would someone want to get at us through Gibson?

If it was some kind of strange OI scam, then a reasonable answer eluded me. My lycanthropy was remarkable, but was it so interesting that the government would go to a horrendous length to test my abilities? I felt like I was sliding down a slick mountain of paranoia. What if the person they were really testing was LaRue? What if I was imagining this farce and slowly oozing into schizoid madness?

"We're dealing with an unrestrained psycho, Andy," I said. "But I'm not sure it's Jerome Taggart."

"I've been thinking the same possibility," he answered. "And I don't like the funny ideas I'm getting."

"Maybe they're not your ideas at all," I said.

He chanced a moment to stare at me. "Maybe they never have been."

At least I wasn't trying to outski an avalanche of irrational distrust by myself. "It's payback time, Andy. Turn this thing toward Myra's house. She has a place in Gibson's neighborhood."

Our drive was accompanied by a stunning pink sunrise. It electrified the sky and made the shattered glass glisten on the roadbed. The light washed away the sepia tones of burned-out buildings as it gradually lifted the district from darkness. I watched this moment of sublime natural beauty and realized that Monet would have seen an essence here that William Zane could not, because humans saw in millions of different viewpoints. Constrained by these angles of perception, we are each forever locked into this private vista of reality. It was this truth that the OI attempted to distort, but for all their heinous intentions, they had not been successful in altering the varied interpretations of life that makes us unique individuals. Whether the secret existed in the biochemistry of the brain, or whether it lurked in the subtle mind of invisible thoughts, the fact still remained a mystery.

I found this consideration comforting for a moment, but then worried I'd been belted with some telepathic ray, so when we pulled to a stop in front of Myra's brownstone walk-up, I was spitting needles of frustration. We pounded for ten minutes before she answered the door. I used my own powers of interpretation and considered it blatant bad manners.

"What do you want at this hour?" she screeched as she struggled into a filmy blue robe.

We pushed into the house. "Gibson has been kidnapped and we need answers if we're going to find him before it's too late," I announced.

She stared at me suspiciously. "You're not playing some prank, are you?"

My mood slid from aggravated to infuriated. "Listen to me, Myra. Gibson could be in danger of losing his life."

"You said he could be."

"Enough!" I roared.

She backed up, and then looked like she was sizing me up for a frontal lobotomy.

"He may be in the hands of an OI-trained killer," LaRue barked.

Fontaine swept from her fantasy of scalpels and sponges to lead us to a well-appointed den. Surprisingly, she offered us fresh coffee and banana bread. As usual, my partner had his appetite with him and he shoveled in the provisions while I punched the shrink with questions.

"Tell me, Myra, why would the OI go to the trouble of converting someone into believing he's a powerful demon ruled by a human master, but then infuse the knowledge that, as this demon, it's within his power to break away from this domination?"

She slid into a fluffy chair before answering. "It's a fail-safe method, Merrick. Should something happen to the convert's control, then another person can step into the loop and take over." Using a minute to pull down a professional attitude, she continued. "For successful neurological rebuilding to occur, the experimentee is stripped of all his free will. He no longer has the power to self-actualize and is further restricted within the rigid boundaries set by the control. This dependence is taken to extreme lengths."

"Is it possible for one convert to be controlled by two people at the same time?" I asked.

Fontaine scowled. "I don't know. I would think that something like that would cause a severe personality disorder."

57

I UNDERSTOOD JEROME Taggart's dependence issue, because my own days were pocked with bitter battles involving this same foe. I've never done much poor-mouthing, never looked for sympathy, never asked for compassion, and so what happens? I find myself all tangled up with Gibson, who quietly steals my autonomy and puts me in the same precarious position as our killer.

If Conrad proved to be behind this whole mess, then he had effectively insulated himself from prying eyes and the long arm of humanitarian justice. It angered me, but there was nothing I could legally do, so I returned to our cubicle fussing and fighting with myself. If Conrad was as talented as people seemed to think he was, then he might have the ability to climb inside my brain. He could, with complete anonymity, check out the holes in my powder-blue underpanties while he listened to every word I thought. It was time to either commit myself to the loony farm or raise the lycanthropic shield.

As I mentioned, Gibson taught me to initiate a stretch without first awakening the wolf. Unfortunately, the outcome is always unpredictable. It involves a lot of work with biofeedback and hypnotic suggestion. LaRue has helped me with the process of overcoming my human disposition so that I possess supernatural speed and endurance. It looked like this might be the only way to keep our efforts out of the remote-viewing limelight, yet my problem with this idea was twofold. The stretch might not happen, and if it did happen but came with aphasia, I would be on my own, unable to communicate.

"Andy, we've got to try," I said quietly. "Remember the tapioca and the Trabi?"

"How could I forget?" he muttered. "There's no guarantee

that forcing a stretch is going to insulate your thoughts from prying eyes. We don't even know for sure you changed the telepathic receiving frequency."

"I realize that."

"Besides, what about me? If the OI poltergeist is using me as a conduit to keep a check on us, then how will your stretching keep our actions and thoughts a secret?"

"I'll have to find Gibson on my own."

LaRue stared at me and shook his head. "No. It's too dangerous."

"I know it sounds crazy, but if we really are being spied on, then the killer can stay ahead of us. Maybe that's his game."

My partner was about to make an important observation, but before he could, the wolf took an interest in our conversation and saved me the trouble by stepping out on its own.

Whether inspired by my needs or launched by an unseen perpetrator, the result was the same: I bulked up in bone and muscle, and my eyes and ears responded accordingly. Yet when the agony was done, I was aware the pain of transformation had contained a different flavor. It was as though the skin had split from my flesh, and within these raw fissures, a hunter's cunning had taken root and blossomed.

I sat in the chair following my stretch and found myself chewing over the source of this profound feeling, but following a quick review, I decided it didn't matter if I was being directed by another person or the wolf itself. The human Merrick always went along for the ride, totally helpless, without resource or whim, and this vulnerability was the glue that held it altogether.

Finally I spoke. "Andy, can you understand me?"

He smiled. "I think you missed the aphasia train this time."

Thank St. Ophelia and every demon in the underworld. "I'm going to find Gibson. Alone."

"Ty, this isn't a good idea. Our perp could be telepathically linked to the people you interview. He'll know your movements through them."

"Agreed, but if this telepathic stuff is real and I can cut him off from tuning in to me, then he'll only know half the story."

LaRue began to patiently explain the reasons he should be in attendance on this bust. He was up to the part about the metaphysical laws governing psychos and loonies when he made the mistake of glancing at his computer screen. I'd shut my attention down to his yammering, but looked at him after he stopped speaking in mid-word. He stared at his monitor, squeezed his eyes shut, and opened them again.

"Do you see a message from our poltergeist friend?" I asked quietly.

"Yes," he croaked. "Do you?"

"No."

He sighed. "Dammit."

"What does it say?"

" 'To Ty Merrick. You're cordially invited to a murder.' "

58

LaRue insisted upon provisioning me with weapons for this solo endeavor. He broke out his favorite pearl-handled derringer complete with ankle holster and bullets and made sure I had a bayonet as long as a samurai sword. Following a reminder about the efficiency of the knife's blood groove, he then ceremoniously divided the contents of his spray bottle and tossed the mister to me. I don't usually accept these bogus magical potions, but I could see it was killing LaRue to hang back, so I accepted it just to comfort him.

Ready to leave, I assured him I'd check back every few hours. With that said, I borrowed Henri's VW, put an official blue light in the dash, and tested my new driving skills while on my way to Teresa Yarnell's house.

The storm had swiped off her front stoop, shattered her windows, and ripped the screen door from its hinges. Still, she was luckier than most—the place had remained on its foundations. I climbed the makeshift plywood ramp, and I'll admit, in the bright light of day, I felt a little ridiculous wearing a spray bottle on my utility belt.

I knocked on the front door, momentarily concerned about the stability of the porch underfoot. By the time a frail young girl answered, I was worried enough to jump inside the house.

"Your stoop is collapsing," I announced, after composing myself.

The child couldn't have been older than eleven or twelve. She stared at me absently with large blue eyes.

Her blank look made me shiver, and so to give myself a moment to work through this sudden apprehension, I glanced around. The shades were drawn over useless windows and the living area was decorated with tinklers and soup-can bangers, their nickel-plated luminescence enhanced by several white candles placed strategically about the room.

The little girl continued to push the zombie routine.

"Is your mom here?" I finally asked.

She pointed down a short hallway. "In the back room. You'll have to wait. It's crowded."

To demonstrate her honesty, two old ladies dressed in black slid by us, nodded in passing, and left without further word.

"Who are they?"

She shrugged. "They came to see my mom. Her friends. You can go back now. There should be enough room."

Paranoia vibrated my knickers and I stomped off, wheeling up short when my worst fears were confirmed. Teresa Yarnell was dead. Her corpse was artfully arranged against several pillows placed in a double bed. I'd stumbled into the middle of final respects.

The familiar odor of death burned my eyes. Rather than put myself out for another decaying body, I decided to hold an impromptu interview in the other room. I snagged the first adult I saw, who happened to be an elderly gentleman engrossed in prayers. When I tapped him on the shoulder, he immediately relinquished his piety to give me a nasty look, but his expression changed upon seeing my badge. He followed me into the next room, introducing himself as Dr. Samson.

"Is there a problem with the death certificate?" he asked.

"Did you write it up?" I countered.

"Yes. I'm an old family friend."

"But are you a real doctor?"

He ruffled. "Of course I am. Or was. I'm retired, but I still have a license."

I held up my hands in an attitude of surrender. "Did Mrs. Yarnell die as a result of the hurricane?"

Samson glanced at the dead-eyed kid before answering in a low voice. "No. She passed on yesterday evening. As far as I can tell, she had a stroke. I don't have any equipment to verify that, you understand. I'm relying on years of medical experience."

"Where's her husband?"

He shrugged. "Missing in action. He was a fireman. According to the children, he was on duty for the storm, but never showed up after it was done."

"Who found Mrs. Yarnell?"

"I did," the girl said.

I turned toward her. Though I felt a spritz of compassion, my concern over Gibson's fate far outweighed my patience. "Do you know if a dark-haired man with a beard visited your mom recently?"

She frowned and shook her head. "Nobody has been here since before the hurricane. My mom got real funny about that. She wouldn't let no one in the house."

59

I'D JUST LEFT Teresa Yarnell's place when I had another stretch and almost ran the VW into the side of a building. I saved it in the end, coming away with a bent fender that I could blame on another driver with faulty depth perception and marginal skills in parallel parking.

This lycanthropic episode had left me with inside-out fur and a bad mood. Since I was close to home, I decided to stop in and fill a bag of tricks for the final showdown. I had no reservations as to its occurrence and I was damned well going to be prepared when it happened.

Taggart and I had a lot in common. We were both freaks spawned from accidents, both entangled in a bureaucracy designed to control us, and if control was impossible, then death was the only other option. Our lives were like strings full of knots, with each jumble of the rope representing a point where our awareness jutted into the supernatural plane. We were blessed with the power of unlimited thought, but ultimately our brilliance was harnessed by the limited capacity of our own brains.

How would a man who believed he was a tulpa react to a threat? I had a feeling he'd react the same way I would. In confusion and fear he would rely upon his paranormal abilities, and with the energy of this belief to back him, he would become the thing he imagined he was.

Just as I reached my apartment building the dead com-node I wore surged to life. The static ran down my ear canal and gathered behind my eyes until I was sure the pressure would pop them onto the floor. I scrabbled to turn the volume down, and just as I did I picked up the tinny voice of my partner.

"Andy, I read you, but you're breaking up," I reported.

"Partial . . . array . . . functioning . . . percent." The transmission died away in the hiss, but the attempt bolstered my confidence. We might have district communications by the evening.

Following that bright note, it was back to worrying about where Gibson might be, and my mind scraped so hard at my thoughts, I'm sure I wore the edges off them. I longed for a resolution to this horrible situation, and as though someone had listened to my unspoken wish, I found a new storm brewing at my flat.

Baba had Helen Yubanski in a neck clinch. Helen choked out an insult and Baba turned the handle on her viselike grip a bit more. It took me a moment to get clear of the stranglehold of my own problems to react. I pulled my roommate off the woman and tossed her roughly onto the couch.

"I'm not taking any more of her put-downs, Ty," Baba growled.

I turned to Helen and patted her on the arm. "Are you all right?"

"No," she husked. "That woman is crazy."

"I'll show you who's crazy." Baba started to rise with fists flying.

"Sit down!" I roared. She did as I asked, despite the fact that she was still punching the air. I steered Helen to a chair by the kitchen table and then aimed my attention toward the cantankerous old woman I lived with. I smelled whiskey. "What started this latest war?"

"Her Holiness over there," Baba spat.

"Stop calling me that."

"Why? It's true. You've elected yourself Miss Congeniality, Miss Etiquette, and let's not forget Miss Informed."

"I'm not misinformed. My granddaughter told me what you did."

"Well, the little bitch lied to her dear old prudish grammy."

"How dare you? She wouldn't do that."

"Pucker up, Helen. One day the garbage is going to smack you in the face, and when it does, I hope the crap that hits you is some of that stinking calamari you make."

The argument abruptly boiled between them again and I suddenly acquired a migraine so slick with pain, it made the wolf in me whimper. I let them rage for a minute because my thought processes were going from hot to lukewarm to cool, and it took me that long to recharge them. When I did, they escaped my brain, rode around my central nervous system, and pausing to gather air pressure, they flew from my lips on the wind of a bellow. "I'm going to pull out your tongues if you two don't shut up!"

They stopped screaming to stare at me.

"I beg your pardon?" Helen said.

"You heard me," I barked. "Both of you. Stop this sniping."

Baba started to speak, but I threw up a warning finger. "Shush!"

She scowled and grumped, finally obeying the referee.

After they'd both calmed a bit, I began quietly. "Now, one at a time—what started this fight? Helen, you talk first."

"Her granddaughter started it," Baba snapped.

"I asked Helen to talk," I snarled.

The neighbor used the opportunity by jumping in immediately. "My granddaughter didn't start anything. She saw Baba throw sewage out your back window. It landed right on my clean wash."

"Clean wash?" I mumbled. Upon hearing her explanation, my mind leapfrogged once more into my current desperate situation. The women's fight surged up to convect around me, but it proceeded through my awareness unchecked, because Helen had used the two words that might find Gibson: back and wash. Backwash.

60

No SOONER HAD I made a mental connection than the wolf asserted its strength again and I fell into a howling stretch right where I stood. My antics scared Helen so badly, she ran from the flat screaming about unholy demons collecting on the fifth floor of her apartment building. Baba laughed, sounding like an old liquored-up hyena. The situation would be funny a few hours later, but at the moment of my agony I was ready to knock the spit out of her.

Upon inspection of my vital parts, I found this seizure had shined up my lycanthropic abilities. I panicked, nonetheless, concerned over the creeping possibility of aphasia.

Sitting there in the middle of the floor, I turned to Baba and demanded her attention with a bark. "Can you understand me?"

She stopped chuckling to stare at me. "Of course I can understand you. I'm not that drunk, my dear."

I was dunked in relief, but now snorted like a truffle-hunting pig at the insane impossibility that someone had diddled with my stretches.

"You're home early," Baba said.

"I stopped by to get some artillery," I answered. I flashed her a quick look before standing. "Gibson has been kidnapped."

She sobered in an instant. "Why would anyone want to kidnap him?"

"To get to Andy and me. More likely, to get to me."

"Oh, sweet St. Ophelia," she whispered. "Who have you come up against?"

I shook my head. "Demons, Baba. Real, honest-to-goodness, hemorrhoid-giving demons." Pausing, I took a deep breath and added: "When he looks into the mirror, he sees me. When I look, I see him."

"What does that mean?"

I didn't answer, because this analogy shoved me onto a startling reevaluation of Jerome Taggart, and in that, I gained insight into my own possible future. By using the standards of society to measure normality, we've managed to coerce accepted behavior, demonstrating through reward and punishment the correct way to think, but in actuality, those dramatic shifts in awareness come down to a personal truth: How does your brain work?

It was likely Taggart and I shared similar thought processes. Our biochemicals were the same; our neurons channeled through the gray matter with the same kind of alacrity; and yet, as far as my papers proved, I still existed, however tenuously, within the endorsed limits of reasonable conduct. So, the big question had a small answer. When did Taggart cross that invisible line into madness and how long would it be before I found myself following?

I pushed this scenario away to concentrate on filling my pockets with M-80s, sulfur bombs, and extra cartridges for my sidearm. By the time I was done, Baba had returned to her loom and was whacking away at a new rug. She didn't say a word as I left the flat and, loaded for a firefight, went to see Kelly Bates.

Her apartment complex was missing much of its roof, but for the most part, it still sheltered the people who hadn't rented out the penthouse. Fortunately, Bates had remained at her residence, trying to squeeze the water out of her camera equipment.

She answered my knock, but seeing who it was, she slammed the door. Her rude reaction gave me an instant attitude, and using every bit of lycanthropic strength I had, I kicked my way in. Bates squealed and backed into the corner, and cowering there, she pleaded for her life.

"I'm not here to hurt you," I said, but rather than demonstrating my claim with gentleness, I yanked her roughly from her refuge and slammed her into a chair.

Seeing the fear in her face further compromised my assertion by leaving me with an odd satisfaction that comes from meting out brute force. I managed to push my way by my sadistic fantasies to demand answers.

"A friend of mine has been kidnapped by Jerome Taggart," I said. "You knew it would happen, didn't you?"

"Of course not," she wailed.

I grabbed her by the hair and twisted it close to the roots. She yelped, struggling helplessly against my strength. "You knew about it, didn't you?"

"Let go," she breathed. When I twirled her tresses harder, she finally gave me a level answer. "Yes, I knew it would happen. I thought it would happen."

"That's impeding an investigation and endangering the lives of innocent citizens. You could go to a labor camp for the rest of your life."

"Please, Marshal. I didn't have any choice. I would have told you if I could."

"Why didn't you have any choice?"

"Casper Conrad owns me. I have to do what he says."

So, the paper-suited peckerhead appeared again. "Why does he own you?"

She glanced at her lap, obviously embarrassed. "I borrowed money from him to pay a gambling debt. I never realized that the interest payments would be taken from my very soul."

"It usually is."

"Is that hindsight speaking?"

I shook my head. "Just plain experience." I made the circuit around her living room before sitting down on the couch. "So, Conrad is behind this thing with the remote viewers."

"It didn't start out that way."

"How did it start?"

"I'm not sure. I think he's defusing a potentially nasty situation. It involved Ingrid Calloway, but I really don't know much more than that."

"What did he tell you to do?"

"To stall. I don't know why. It was all need-to-know and I wasn't in the loop. I received bits and pieces just like everybody else." She ripped her hair from my hand by jerking her head.

"Is he in charge now? Has he fed you excuses?"

"No. I haven't seen or heard from him since before the storm."

I studied her, looking for duplicity, but my inside-out fur

wasn't itching, so I worked on the premise that she was telling the truth. "You said you can remotely view and come away with a photo to prove what you've seen."

"So?"

"I want to know where Jerome Taggart is, right this minute."

She swallowed hard before answering. "The backwash is really bad. I can't be sure if I'm getting anything I'm supposed to be getting. I'm not sure of the scope of this scam, but Casper could have telepathic and psychic walls set up everywhere. You can't trust my final product."

"It's a chance I'll have to take. I've got less than a day to find my friend."

"What's his name?"

"Lane Gibson."

She frowned and then tried to hide it, but she was too late for that.

"What?" I demanded.

Her response dragged out for a couple of breaths before she spoke. "Tall man with long hair?"

"That's him. What do you know?"

Bates stood up and walked to a cardboard storage box sitting by her vid. Flipping the top back, she pulled out several photos. "I took this series at Casper's request. These images kept appearing." She handed me the pictures and sat down beside me. "He showed up a lot."

She was right. There were ghostly images of Gibson, LaRue, Taggart, and me. Shuffling them, I was stopped by a photo showing a graveyard and headstone. Gibson's name was etched into the marble. I had seen this before, but where? "You can take photos of the future, can't you?"

She nodded. "Still, they don't make much sense taken out of context."

Gibson's burial plot seemed a looming possibility. "Help me, Kelly. I have to prevent this from happening."

"I don't think you can."

Her statement angered me and it was all I could do to maintain my calm exterior. "We have free will. I'll use mine to prevent this event the best I can. Now, show me where Jerome Taggart is."

She stared at me and sighed, but finally rose and wobbled to her camera gear. Spinning one of the contraptions my direction, she said: "I need a coordinate."

"What does that mean?" I asked.

"I need something to focus on so I can plot the route of events and at least get you closer to locating him. Since you two claim to be tied up in this mess, I'll take your picture and see what that gives us. But like I say, the backwash is bad. Whether it's genuine or fabricated somehow by Casper, it's still bad."

"Start clicking," I snapped.

She nodded, and aiming at me, she flicked away until a whole roll of film had been taken in the low light of the room. As she worked she added a new slice to the OI viewpoint.

"You realize that telepathy involves thinking on command," she said.

"What are you talking about, Kelly?"

"Very few people can summon enough concentration to exercise the mental abilities necessary to send or receive telepathically." She paused to readjust her camera lens. Then: "It doesn't involve the intensity in the thought so much as it means being able to control the biochemical reaction in the brain."

"In other words: if you can get the neurotransmitters signaling the right section in the brain, you have telepathic capability."

"Or psychic capabilities."

"Or psychokinesis."

"That, too."

"It's the basic problem the OI faces," I said, understanding. "They can't find enough people who can shut up the internal dialogue long enough to focus. I take it the OI goes through a lot of folks until they uncover competent communicators."

"That's Casper's reason for living, if you ask me," she answered.

When she was done, she opened the camera and removed the film, taking it to the combination bathroom and darkroom. She shut the door behind her and another half hour ticked by as she developed the pictures. Instead of using the time to formulate a plan of action, I spent it worrying and, consequently, felt not one nib of relief when she invited me into the toilet workshop.

Ten pictures hung from a clothesline. She had a battery-operated bulb to cast a nice glow over her product, but moving out of my way, she announced that she hadn't gotten anything useful.

At first I had to agree with her, but I let my lycanthropic sight linger over the double images and smeared colors until I picked out a face I recognized—Andrea Pio.

61

I HAULED KELLY Bates back to the office, because she wailed about being in danger now that she'd exposed Conrad's part in this insane plot. My worries were kicked up about this guy, too, but my fear for Gibson's life outweighed thoughts of my own safety.

As we charged into the homicide pen I expected my partner to be waiting for me with a million questions. Instead, Julie waylaid me before I could reach our cubicle.

"Another person connected to this OI investigation has turned up dead," she announced. "A fellow named David Bacon. I sent LaRue over to do the crime scene."

Kelly Bates reacted with horror. "Not David," she whispered.

I had bodies falling all around me. "Who called it in?"

Julie stared at the woman before finally shrugging. "Anonymous tip." Pointing to my ear, she added: "Wear your comnode, Merrick. The array is functioning—fitfully, yes, but functioning. I don't want you out of touch."

"Did Andy tell you what I'm up to?"

"Yes. Watch your ass, Marshal. And if you find Gibson and this maniac, you call in for backup. That's an order. I'll have a team of ward cops standing by."

"Don't worry," I answered. "I don't want to take any chances with the good doctor's life."

She studied me for several seconds. "Don't let your personal feelings for Gibson impair your decisions. We need Taggart alive to get the conviction."

The law was clear. To arrest someone for murder, you must catch them attempting it. I hated to admit it, but the thought of Gibson being in mortal danger made my stomach ache.

249

"Don't worry, Julie," I said. "The bastard will reach here alive, but I can't be responsible for the condition he'll be in when he gets here."

She snorted and walked off to harass another marshal. I hurried to my cubicle, dragging Bates with me. Much to my relief, I found that the office's emergency generator fueled my stand-alone computer.

The first thing I did was scan the photo and bring the image up. We then sat there for an hour trying to find something identifiable in a picture that looked like it could have been taken on the ghost plane.

Andrea Pio's grimacing expression told me that wherever she was, she was in trouble. Sitting there staring at this apparition of impossibility, I found myself clutching to the hope that for once, my skepticism would be proved wrong and this clue from the realm of invisible magic would give me a hint about Gibson's location.

I zoomed in to the photo's upper left-hand corner and my impatience flared in the nanosecond it took for the computer to respond to my finger commands. The image grew grainier each time I clicked the mouse.

"What is that thing?" Bates asked.

I enlarged it one more time.

"It's a painting hanging on the wall behind her," I said.

It was a painting all right. In fact, it was a Monet, and it looked as though it was surrounded by a protective sheet of Plexiglas.

I glanced at her and then buzzed Julie's office. After she snapped her name into the phone, I demanded to know if we'd taken the police cordon off of Sam Arkin's apartment.

"Yes," she answered. "The hurricane took precedence. We should still have access to the place, though."

"Did the building survive the storm?"

"As far as I know, it did. Do you want a ward cop to tag along?"

"No," I answered. "It's an outside chance to begin with." I slammed the handset down, and not realizing my own strength, I cracked the telephone receiver. Crap. I was still paying for the last one I broke.

Standing, I glanced at Bates. "I've got to go."

She started whining instantly. "What about me? What do I do?"

"You can take one of the bunks in the lockup," I said, heading for the door. "I'll be back when I can." With that, I headed for Henri's VW.

As I said, the memories of my full-moon stretches fade, leaving me with only snatches and strange feelings, and the flux of my current emotions told me something important had transpired during this last episode. Yet what it might be was totally lost to me.

I reached Sam Arkin's apartment building after thirty minutes of bumps and chuckholes. The power was on in this particular complex and I was grateful to find the elevator working. I fished out my keys and quietly turned the bolt on the police-lock box.

Drawing my service revolver, I paused to listen. My supernatural hearing fed me with innocuous sounds, and rather than taking more time to verify the situation, I shoved the door open. Unfortunately, I underestimated my power and what I thought was a gentle push turned out to be forceful enough to splinter the wood. Since the door was in pieces, my advantage of surprise was blown. The only thing I could do was barge in.

The apartment lights were on and shining brightly. Andrea Pio sat strapped to a chair placed near the Monet painting. Seeing it, I made a mental note to apologize to Kelly Bates should she survive this psychic onslaught. She took a damned good remote photo. This ability might be the only reason she was still alive.

Pio was battered and bruised, but fully conscious. Her mouth wasn't swaddled with a gag rag, and the moment I crashed into the flat she demanded to be released. I ignored her pleading and carefully checked out the apartment, looking under beds and behind shower curtains until I was satisfied that she was utterly alone in her misery.

"No one's here," she said. "He's gone. I've been sitting in this chair for three days."

She was too clean to have been a hostage for long. I stepped over to her, but instead of untying her, I placed the nose of my pistol against her forehead. "You're lying."

Pio stopped in mid-breath to stare at me. Her face cycled

through various expressions until she settled upon an innocent look. "I'm not," she whispered. "Taggart is on a rampage."

I made a show of cocking the gun's hammer. "If I don't get answers that make sense to me, I'm going to kill you."

This time her certainty completely abandoned her. "You wouldn't. You're a marshal."

"Being a marshal doesn't mean I won't put a bullet in your brain." I pressed the gun into her skin. "Stop stalling or they'll find your gray matter dripping off that Monet." When I was sure I had her attention, I began. "Let's start with Ingrid Calloway. She was responsible for the deaths of Valquez and Emery, wasn't she?"

She blinked at me and I pushed a little harder. A few seconds passed before she caved. "Okay. Just don't hurt me." I eased off a fraction as she answered. "Yes. They were test subjects for Taggart."

"You found out and thought you might be next?"

"Ingrid didn't like me; it was no secret. I could have been next, for all I know."

"Why was she using Taggart?"

"Why else? She wanted to go up the government ladder straight to the top."

"So she was prepared to use the assassin to pick off anyone who might get in her way."

"Yes."

"Who told you about Taggart? Conrad?"

"Casper did. I was brought on the project to serve as Taggart's control."

"But he was Ingrid's boy?"

"Yes. Ingrid wanted a layer of insulation between her and Taggart."

"Did Conrad know what Ingrid planned?"

"Probably. He seems to know everything. I'm sure he's behind the whole thing."

"That's what everybody keeps telling me," I said. "Did Taggart kill Ingrid?"

"Yes."

"Why?"

She hesitated, so I put on a mean face and threatened her again. "I'm as dangerous as your assassin, Ms. Pio, though I'm a trifle more messy."

Her words were slow to come. "I know you are. So does Casper."

"Why did Taggart kill Ingrid?" I growled, ignoring the evil insinuation.

"Because she was in my way, dammit!"

"Oh, going climbing yourself?"

"Yes, and why not? I deserve as much success and money as she did."

"But Arkin and his team of snoops figured out what was going on."

"They didn't figure out anything. And then it became their problem."

"You ordered Taggart to kill them?"

"No. They were trying to blackmail me."

"With the first payoff, you had Taggart shake hands with them."

Her reply fooled me. "I only told Taggart to deliver the money. He took it upon himself to kill Arkin and his gang."

I jammed the gun barrel against her head until her neck cranked back to an uncomfortable position. "Are you sure?"

"Yes," she husked. "Taggart was loose by then. I thought I had complete control, but I didn't. It's why I'm here. He forced me to come."

"Why?"

"I don't know. All I know is he beat me and left me here."

I got the feeling this interlude with Andrea Pio had been prepared especially for me. "You didn't get very far with your rush to the top, so that means someone is running the whole shooting match from afar. Taggart has another master. Is it Conrad?"

"Please," she begged.

"Is it Conrad?" I barked.

After a fitful moment of indecision, she answered. "Casper is the only one who can control Taggart."

So, it really did come down to the man in the paper suit. "Where did Taggart take Dr. Gibson?"

"I don't know. Honestly."

I massaged the gun trigger with my forefinger and spoke as evenly as I could. "Where do you think he took him?"

Pio swallowed hard and blinked at me. "Try the free clinic in Ward One Hundred."

62

I SPENT THE next ten minutes trying to contact LaRue to bring in the troops, but the array communications were still fitful and I never busted through the static, so I left Andrea Pio tied up and headed for the VW Bug. In my haste to save Gibson, I turned the key in the ignition too hard. It broke off in my hand and the force behind my grip actually cracked the plastic on the steering column.

Shit. How was I going to pay for this new accident caused by my lycanthropic strength? Rather than worry about it then, I launched from the VW, and pulling out all the paranormal stops, I raced down the street on foot. The stuff I carried jangled and banged with enough noise to wake the dead. People rushed out of my path, often yelling obscenities as they did. Halfway to Ward one hundred, it occurred to me that I still had my weapon drawn.

I halted, holstered it, and panted for air. The sun touched the tops of the high-rises, casting the district in shifting gray shadows. I was reminded of tulpas, and then suddenly I felt surrounded by them. Leaping into a gallop, I tried to discount the strange sensation by considering the mastermind who was truly behind Taggart and Pio.

Riding herd over one's thoughts is an exhausting process. If Conrad were running a devious scam on some paranormal level, it might be the reason he sounded so tired each time I spoke with him. He would need to open channels of telepathy, clairvoyance, and psychokinesis, as well as pinpointing the outcome in a future unfolding second by second. Mistakes are the traveling companions of weariness and that meant Conrad had to be slap-happy by now.

One hour later I ended up in Ward one hundred, suffering leg

cramps and sweating like LaRue's Uncle Carl after he's eaten
three plates of sautéed jalapeños. The electricity hadn't come
up in this neighborhood, and though the sun had not completely set, the buildings were tall and blocked much of the
light. The shadow tulpas had melded into a single, oppressive
family unit. Time was running out.

I jogged along through the growing dusk, narrowly missing
a drunk sleeping on the sidewalk. Chugging to a stop outside
the free clinic, I tried to raise LaRue once more. There was
only static to greet my pressing need. I would have to go it
alone and pray that Taggart didn't have company with him. On
the head of this supplication, I added a request for Gibson's
life.

The neighboring walk-ups had exploded during the storm
and the clinic was decorated with their rubble. I broke out my
service lantern and picked my way through a forest of charred
timbers and glassy undergrowth in an effort to reach the back
entrance in a stealthy manner. Still, my best intentions were
undone, because my foot broke into a pile and became wedged
in concrete and stringy wire. I attempted to yank loose, ended
up tearing my cammies up to the knee and exposing the
swollen hand of a bloated corpse buried in the mountain of
trash and mud.

I disentangled as quietly as I could, but another misplaced
step found me up to my ass in twisted metal. Cursing, I climbed
from this new trap to finally arrive at the back door. If Taggart
hadn't heard me coming, it would be a miracle.

The trip through this ragged urban canyon had left me
tattered, but I ignored the breeze puffing against my underwear
to study the entrance. It wasn't boarded up. In fact, when I
jiggled the knob, I found it wasn't even locked.

I attempted one last time to call for backup, but again, the
array communications refused to respond.

Relying on the night acuity of my lycanthropic vision, I
extinguished my flashlight. This left my hands free for weapons. I unzipped the pocket I'd filled with my homemade smoke
bombs, and slowly unsnapping my holster, I drew my service
revolver.

The moment I nudged open the back door I smelled the

unmistakable odor of a rotting body. It was all I could do to
suppress a gag. Worse than that, I panicked inside.

Aiming for shadows, I slunk down a narrow hallway,
checking the examining suites as I did. The last one on the left
proved to be the stinker.

My eyesight picks up the nuances of night and I can see
movement clearly in darkness. Add a glimmer of light and it's
like someone has lit up the football stadium. In this case, I saw
more than I wished. It was Dr. Quinlan, retired early, and from
the looks of her remains, the rats had been using her as the food
for the send-off party.

Grisly though it was, I felt nothing but a fast urge to get clear
of the smell. I pulled the door quietly behind me and headed for
the stairs, pausing at the first landing to listen. My supernatural
hearing picked up the small sounds—faucets dripping, window glass rattling, steam passing through the pipes below the
street—but more than that, there was no noise except for my
ragged breathing.

I quickly checked out levels two and three and was starting
to despair. Had Andrea Pio lied, and in my urgency, had I
rocketed off half-cocked, wasting time right to the bitter end?
The possibility was swiftly turning into a probability when my
search uncovered a blood-smeared bathroom. I swiped a finger
against the runnels coating the mirror. They were slimy and
fresh. It was too bad I couldn't tell whose life force splattered
the walls.

I moved on, stalling at the door to level four while casting
around for a whiffle of noise. Except for my heart beating out
a rumba rhythm, there were no unusual sounds, so I took a deep
breath, reached for the latch, and gently pushed my way in. It
was trophy time.

I spun into the hallway, hugging the shadows. When I
paused, I noticed the trickle of light seeping around the door at
the end of the corridor, and then it hit me. What better place for
an OI showdown than inside a laboratory?

For the first time in my whole life I felt fear for another. It
throttled my resolve and I had trouble taking that next step, but
once started, I became a werewolf windup toy: my feet moved
me mechanically, but my mind lagged far behind.

I halted again upon reaching the door to recall what LaRue

and I had seen during our short visit with Dr. Quinlan. As far as I could remember, there was one way in and out. All of which meant: This lunatic could have a bazooka aimed and ready for firing.

There was nothing to do but go for the glory. I took what might have been my final breath and then crashed through the door.

No bazooka, but plenty of dead time. The killer had transformed the lab into a glittering ark of beakers and stainless steel. There were candles everywhere—long, tapered jobs, fit for a mortuary. Vinson's tulpa collection had, indeed, been stolen, because the fancy cards formed a circle around a dissecting table. Safely ensconced in the center of all this was Gibson and Jerome Taggart.

The good doctor sat upon a stool and feebly yanked at handcuffs chaining him to the brass drain and waste bowl. His hair flowed about his shoulders and his head dipped toward the collection sink. At my clamor, he fought to look up, and when he did, I saw the blood, sweat, and filth, as well as the myriad razorlike cuts upon his face. He recognized me and spoke my name, but no sound escaped his lips.

Sometimes I wish my vision wasn't so sparkling or my hearing so whisper sensitive. I lifted my eyes and my gun toward his tormentor, but in an instant I knew we had a Mexican standoff. Taggart yanked Gibson by the hair and placed the tip of his index finger against his temple.

"I'll shoot," he said.

63

WE STARED AT each other, and in the vague light, I saw only a normal man. No demon lurked there. Still, I dared not risk Gibson's life with a bravado that would get him killed, so I made a show of holstering my weapon.

Gibson's head lolled forward. This action apparently angered Taggart, because he jerked him backward until he exposed Gibson's neck. Laying his thumb across his Adam's apple, the lunatic gave me a demonstration of his power. He drew a thin line of blood simply by pressing on the skin.

"No!" I barked.

He shot me a lizard look and mocked me by repeating his performance just under Gibson's left ear. The pain brought Gibson back into an agonizing awareness and he groaned, coughed, and fought for air.

"What do you want?" I demanded.

He smiled. "You, of course. You're my tulpa and I control you. It's necessary."

"Why?"

"Because my demon is out of control. I need to have sovereignty over another person and that way this horror can end."

This boy had boarded the Schizo Express. "You talk about the Manjinn as though it's not part of you."

"It's not," he answered. "It lives within me, but we don't share the same sensibilities. Do you know that it tries to kill me?"

"Really?" It was a shame its aim wasn't better. "How does it try to kill you?"

"With the hand, of course." He demonstrated by clasping Gibson's neck. "It squeezes my throat, and I can't stop it. Had

258

it not been for my master, I'd be dead and the tulpa would be gone. She talked it into submission."

"Where would it go if it escaped?"

He shrugged. "I don't know and I don't care. All I want is my autonomy again."

Gibson summoned one last bit of energy to yank from his grip and then I did my best to deflect Taggart's attention. "What you have is a neurological disorder," I said quietly. "It's called alien hand syndrome. Your brain isn't switching hemispheres like it should. Dr. Quinlan told us this."

He frowned. "Dr. Quinlan. My tulpa killed her, too. He used the life force of the Manjinn to do it."

"So, you can't make the electricity flow. It's the demon who does it."

"I'm innocent."

It rang more ridiculous by the moment. I did my best to stay with him while I studied my options. "I'm not a tulpa."

"The tulpa lives inside you. It possesses your thoughts, your deeds, and your free will."

"Did Andrea Pio make you kidnap Gibson?"

He laughed. "No."

"You wouldn't have known about me if someone hadn't told you," I countered. "Who was it? Casper Conrad?"

"That's none of your business."

I let disgust bounce across my breath. "You're not a tulpa, Taggart. You're a human being who can't remember who he is. I can help you recover your memories, but I won't do it under coercion." I inched my hand slowly toward the pocket loaded with my smoke bombs.

He noticed my movement and raised a warning finger. "I will kill him. Now that you've arrived, his usefulness is at an end."

"No!" I growled. Then, readying myself for the negotiation of this life-and-death parlay, I said: "You're right, I do live with a tulpa. It's a lycanthrope, a thought form who holds the truth of mankind." I made a show of swooping down and picking up one of the cards decorating the floor. "As a matter of fact, this is my symbol."

"It's not."

I pushed a growl into my voice. "My symbol."

He studied me and I could see his brain's gummed gears trying to turn. "What's the truth of mankind, then?"

Think quick, Merrick. "The truth? We're the watchdogs of the night. We are the ones who creep into your dreams and make you see yourself as you truly are." I took a step toward him. He flinched and threatened Gibson, so I stopped and held out the card. "My tulpa is more powerful than your Manjinn can ever hope to be, Taggart. My tulpa has learned to procreate. A lycanthrope doesn't need a human to help it."

"A thought form creating other thought forms?" he asked breathlessly.

"Without a master in sight." I feigned a dark laugh. "You honestly think you can control me?"

My theatrics threw him for a loop and he couldn't respond. I used the opportunity to claim my territory. "Let him go," I husked.

He panicked and went for Gibson's jugular again. I started to come at him, but skidded to a halt when I realized I couldn't outrace his finger. "Easy, there, partner."

"Partner?" he mused.

"Let him go and I'll give you the secrets of the lycanthrope."

It appeared he weighed his options, and while he did I scanned the room out of the corner of my eye. I logged a variety of useful weapons—everything from scalpels to rubber hoses—but nothing that would trap him faster than he could crank in the killing thought. It was then I noticed the door on the hyperbaric chamber was ajar.

I edged toward Taggart, carefully maneuvering myself between him and the steel cylinder.

I banged him with annoying accusations as I figured my next actions. "Manjinns think they can procreate by killing humans. That's false thinking." When he didn't respond, I knew I had him as confused as I had myself. "Did you kill Amarilo Valquez and Dixon Emery?"

"I had no choice." Like a fairy spell had been broken, Taggart dropped his attention back to Gibson's throat. He made tiny little slashes on the skin, timing his insidious work to the rhythm of his words. "I loved her and would have followed her into hell and back again, but then I found out she used me. There never was any desire for me."

"Who? Andrea Pio?"

"Yes. She was so beautiful, but so devious."

"She cured you of a life-threatening illness by taking you to all the healers."

He nodded. "Still, she lied. It didn't make up for her deceit."

My brain raced as I calculated the distance and speed I would need to move. "Did you murder Teresa Yarnell?"

His answer came slowly and with a note of confusion. "I don't know her, either. I don't recall killing her."

One more step placed me within arm's reach of both Taggart and the door on the chamber. He watched me, but apparently saw nothing awry.

"What about Sam Arkin and his team? Did you kill them?"

"Their greed killed them."

"Not your touch?"

"Oh, yes, my touch facilitated their demises, but they were already dead, you know. They were bound and gagged in the material plane. I released them so their thoughts could be free of the dismal shackles of their possessions."

"Per instructions from Andrea Pio?"

"No."

"Casper Conrad?"

Again, he didn't respond.

I tensed, waiting for his hold to slip a little on Gibson. I knew the risk of contact with this maniac and yet, standing there, I pushed the nagging fear back into place and made ready to free the good doctor.

Taggart grunted, rubbing a fingernail over Gibson's neck and releasing a little spring of blood.

"You have no right to harm him, Manjinn."

He glanced at me and shook his head. "You don't speak the truth, lycanthrope. I know how these things work. It was explained to me in full by Raymond Vinson." Then, like a parody of LaRue, he gave me a lecture. "You're tied to this one through emotion. Sacrifice him and the union is broken. The moment you lose yourself in his pain, I'll steal your will."

It was act now or bury Gibson the day after tomorrow, but of course, no rescue could ever come easy. During my interment with this lunatic, a summer storm had rolled up, and the moment I was ready to pounce on the bastard, thunder cracked and I was undone by a panic attack.

My neurotransmitters must have reached the frontiers of my brain, because I cowered and whined. It was not until I found my human spontaneity that I defeated this invisible monster. I swallowed that impending feeling of death, and putting some spit behind my words, I snarled: "Here's my free will. Good luck."

Summoning every bit of lycanthropic speed I had, I ripped the spray bottle from my belt and stung him in the eyes with the juice. He dropped his hold on Gibson to scrape at the burn. I punched him in the chops and blood squirted from his face like I'd opened a hole in the Black River dike. He reeled backward, roaring at the pounding I gave him.

I did miscalculate his strength, though. At one point he lunged at me and slapped my face, but his timing was off. I ducked out of the way and his forward momentum rushed him past me.

I laid a roundhouse kick to his head to knock him senseless, but he had a harder skull than I imagined and he returned my brutality by turning and punching at my midsection. His swing grazed me, and thoroughly annoyed me. I'd had enough bullshit for one day. This was one lunatic who was going down.

With no thought to my own safety, I grabbed Taggart by the arm and wrapped my free hand around his neck. I yanked him like a top and spun him toward the hyperbaric chamber. He yelled and struggled and we did a dance as he clutched my waist.

I felt the area grow hot beneath his touch until a slashing pain hurled up my side and into my head. Dizziness threatened to undo me, but I forced my recovery and twirled to stomp on his instep. It was enough to toss him off balance. I shoved him, and using my muscle, I finished off the attack by kicking him in the kidneys. Cursing, he landed face-first inside the cylinder. He scrabbled to right himself, but it was too late.

I slammed the door shut, set the lock, and flipped the unit on, watching with unparalleled satisfaction as the atmospheric pressure pushed his brain out through his nostrils.

64

As Taggart turned to a nitrogen fizz I went to Gibson. He was conscious now, and giggling insanely, splattering us both with his blood. I placed my fingers against his chin to hold his head still, cooing softly until he settled down with a moan to punctuate his fit.

His throat was a wreck from days with no water. He dipped his head toward the brass faucet to show me what he wanted. I turned on the spigot and splashed water into my hands, tenderly feeding him the liquid from this makeshift cup. He drank greedily.

When he had his fill, he gazed at me with such a look of relief, I thought he might cry, so to avoid having to deal with any emotional displays, I quickly turned my attention to releasing him from the handcuffs. Thankfully, they were standard issue and my key unlocked them. No sooner had I done that than Gibson heaved into the waste bowl.

I'm not a very good wet nurse, and illness usually wears my patience down to a millimeter of thickness, but at this moment I was glad to help him. It was during these compassionate seconds that I understood the scope of my own needs, realizing what the sages said was true: in the brevity of a single thought, there is enlightenment.

I held Gibson tightly. When he choked the last of his pain away, he enfolded me in his arms and sighed. I'll admit it; I almost started crying myself.

He let me guide him from the stool and ease him to the floor, helping him stretch limbs frozen into numbness after hours of sitting. He dipped in and out of consciousness, and while he faded I worked feverishly to contact dispatch. Miraculously,

Sylvia answered after only three tries and it was less than an hour before the mop-up crew arrived.

LaRue was the first to charge in, demanding to know the situation. Seeing Gibson alive launched him into a thousand questions, the first of which was wanting to know about Taggart.

I directed his attention to the hyperbaric chamber. He inspected the suspect, pronounced him breathing and gooey, and then demanded to know if I was all right.

"The bastard had me in his clinches for a minute."

"What happened?"

I shrugged. "I'm not sure, but to make an educated guess? I think my lycanthropy is stronger than his electricity."

Wilson walked in to interrupt our conversation. He gave Gibson the once-over, started intravenous glucose, and then bellowed at the paramedics to be careful as they lifted him onto the gurney. No sooner had they rolled him toward the meat-wagon than Casper Conrad showed up, wearing a wrinkled paper suit and a sly expression.

"So, you caught him, huh?" he said, by way of greeting.

I wasn't surprised by Conrad's appearance, though I was surprised by my reaction. The words weren't out of his mouth before I used my lycanthropic strength to drive him against the hyperbaric chamber. "I ought to throw you in there with that freak," I snarled.

He remained unruffled. "You're out of control, Marshal Merrick."

LaRue joined me with his own threatening posture. Using his knuckle, he tapped on Conrad's flesh in time with his words. "You were behind this whole mess, weren't you?"

"Release me," Conrad commanded.

I chuckled darkly and crowded him. "No. Answer his question."

He fumbled for a stall, but could find none. "All right. Unhand me and I'll tell you."

Seeing that it was a draw, we let him go, and the truth wasn't far behind.

"Yes. If you really want to know, I was the instigator of the whole thing."

"You were our poltergeist, weren't you?" LaRue demanded.

"Yes. You figured out it wasn't a goblin early on."

"We figured out a lot more than that," I rumbled. "You know, Casper, when it comes down to it, you're an accessory to murder."

"You can't prove anything," he said. "I haven't been around for days. You wouldn't be able to legally keep me at the office for more than a few hours. As you've uncovered during your investigation, you know it wouldn't be a good idea to cross me."

I glanced at LaRue, who slugged a deep breath and shook his head despondently. "Why these lethal games?" I asked.

He smoothed his jacket and straightened his lapels, pausing to take a quick look at Taggart through the chamber's window. "God, what a waste," he whispered.

"You don't seem to care about waste, Conrad," I said.

He turned toward me. "You're wrong, Marshal Merrick. It's my business to worry about waste. I'm the one in charge of saving the world by changing the way humanity thinks. I turn prisoners into model citizens, murderers into saints, thieves into honest men."

"You controlled Taggart."

"Of course. Do you honestly think Andrea Pio could have done it on her own? Besides, her climb up the government ladder was doomed from the start."

"Why?" LaRue asked.

His expression reminded me of one a parent might give to a three-year-old. "The only people who move into the highest ranks of the OI get there by the amount of psionic talent they have," he said. "It was acceptable for Ingrid Calloway to have the Manjinn, but not Andrea Pio. That was the very reason she filled a temporary position."

"She doesn't have any psionic talent?"

"None. So normal it hurts. You see, then, Marshals, it was necessary to interfere."

"You created an elaborate game of murder," I said. "Why not just fire Pio and recondition Taggart? Why go to all the trouble to move people around before you kill them?"

He shrugged. "Simple economics really. I have to review my inventory by the fiscal year." He took a step into the room and ran a hand languidly along the top of a table. "Sometimes, you discover the supplies on your shelf have reached their date of expiration."

"This logic justifies murder?" I said. "For what reason?"

"To make room for fresh stock. Of course, I really don't know what I'll need until I've had a chance to review the new against the old." He stepped to the door, placed his hand on the latch, but instead of leaving, he turned to study me. Speaking in an ominous tone, he said: "You're right, Marshal Merrick. I know about you. I've known about you for a long time."